Hello Mr Bones / Goodbye Mr Rat

'Stark, fierce, and wonderful … McCabe is a master of both the demented narrative and demented narrator. Beneath the ghosts and ghoulies, however, lies a compassionate exploration of the aftermath of psychological damage.'
— *Claire Kilroy, The Guardian*

'A rewarding experience which sees the master of the Irish gothic genre return to his best form in years.'
— *JP O'Malley, The Observer*

'Both bits of Hello and Goodbye are exuberant and witty and *Goodbye Mr Rat* deserves to rekindle his former glories.'
— *Paul Dunn, The Times*

'McCabe is especially good at conjuring up the menace of psychopaths who perpetrate acts of barbarism under the spurious guise of ideologies.'
— *John Boland, The Independent*

'[McCabe] is expert at making the darkest deeds funny, forcing us to laugh at the worst things in the world. He writes like an Irish Lenny Bruce, riffing at warp speed, swerving from one time to another and one place to another and strewing the landscape with allusion … and somehow it all makes sense … The stories McCabe tells have a terrible beauty.
— *The New York Times*

McCabe

The Butcher Boy

'The most astonishing Irish novel for many years, a master-piece'
— *Sunday Independent*

'An insidious, funny, breathtakingly horrific novel set in small-town Ireland, switching from mischief to madness as an adolescent obsession turns Dennis the Menace into Jack the Ripper.'
— *The Observer*

'Compelling, unashamedly horrible, memorable and sensitive'
— *Times Literary Supplement*

'An almost perfect novel ... A Beckett monologue with plot by Alfred Hitchcock ... Startlingly original.'
— *The Washington Post Book World*

'Stunning ... part Huck Finn, part Holden Caulfield, part Hannibal Lecter.'
—*The New York Times Book Review*

'Brilliant, unique. Patrick McCabe pushes your head through the book and you come out the other end gasping, admiring, and knowing that reading fiction will never be the same again. It's the best Irish novel I've read in years.'
— *Roddy Doyle, author of Paddy Clarke Ha Ha Ha*

'A chilling tale of a child's hell ... often screamingly funny ... the book has a compelling and terrible beauty'
—*The Boston Globe*

'Lyrical and disturbing, horrific and hilarious.'
— *The New York Times*

Breakfast on Pluto

'Dysfunctional Ireland in all its glories is here, with humour of the blackest hue, madness and violence, hopelessly randy priests, dodgy politicians, a grand gallery of misfits culminating in McCabe's hero in *Breakfast on Pluto*, Patrick 'Pussy' Braden, the transvestite prostitute from the village of Tyreelin ... Wild, hilarious, merciless and fiendishly clever'
— *Ronan Farren, Sunday Independent*

'He is the fortunate possessor of a savage and unfettered imagination; his books ... dissect life's miseries with a gleaming comedic scalpel'
— *Erica Wagner, The Times*

'It finds humour in places that other writers are afraid to look for it'
— *David Robson, Sunday Telegraph*

'This is a savagely funny and authentically tragic novel of an Ireland in unhappy transition and beneath McCabe's perfectly delivered black comedy lies an angry heart'
— *GQ Magazine*

'Without drawing breath, McCabe mixes camp comedy with brutality, making *Breakfast on Pluto* both funny and deeply shocking'

— Maxim

'Told with irresistible zest, brio and gaiety ... McCabe's brilliant, startling talent is to make enchantingly dashing narratives out of the most ghastly states of mind imaginable, and to induce compassion for lives which seem least to invite it ... He is a dark genius of incongruity and the grotesque'

— Hermione Lee, The Observer

The Dead School

'McCabe can make you howl at the darkest antics ... He never sets a foot – or syllable – wrong. His novel is death on a laugh-support machine. Stupendous.'

— Scotland on Sunday

'Raphael, the great headmaster, is a marvellous creation ... McCabe has a charm as a storyteller which is all his own'

— Sunday Telegraph

'Exhilarating. Reading the distilled gouts of consciousness which pour from the minds of these characters is like being trapped on a big dipper with articulate maniacs ... Horribly funny'

— The Times

'An appallingly funny story ... horribly memorable'

— Times Literary Supplement

Winterwood

'A true original'

— John Banville

'This is McCabe's greatest work ... A sustained achievement of often dazzling brilliance ... *Winterwood* is that rarest thing: a novel dealing with humanity at its most twisted and bleak, but one that leaves the reader feeling curiously uplifted. And that's because we realise that we've been standing in an illuminating beam whose source is, and can only be, truly great art'

— Irvine Welsh, The Guardian

'A masterpiece'

— The Observer

'He is the fortunate possessor of a savage and unfettered imagination; his books dissect life's miseries with a gleaming comedic scalpel'

— The Times

'An eerily kaleidoscopic mix that reads like a modern rendering of Poe'

— Daily Telegraph

'*Winterwood* is a masterpiece, even though the word is a little overused, especially about contemporary fiction'

— Adam Phillips, Observer Books of the Year

'*Winterwood* is as close as you could get to understanding the nature of evil, as close as you would ever want to get'

— Irish Sunday Independent

Heartland

Heartland

Patrick McCabe

NEW ISLAND

HEARTLAND
First published in 2018 by
New Island Books
16 Priory Hall Office Park
Stillorgan
County Dublin
Republic of Ireland

www.newisland.ie

Paperback ISBN: 978-1-84840-660-5
Hardback ISBN: 978-1-84840-692-6
Epub ISBN: 978-1-84840-661-2
Mobi ISBN: 978-1-84840-662-9

Typeset by JVR Creative India
Cover design by Kate Gaughran
Printed and bound by TJ International Ltd. Padstow

New Island received financial assistance from The Arts Council (An Chomhairle Ealaíon), 70 Merrion Square, Dublin 2, Ireland.

New Island Books is a member of Publishing Ireland.

This is a work of fiction. The characters in this book are fictitious and any resemblance with any real person is coincidental and unintended.

10 9 8 7 6 5 4 3 2 1

For David Monagan, with thanks.

Contents

Chapter 1

The Cockloft

Sneeze you're a stiff – couldn't have been simpler.

The story, if that's what you want to call it – 'spiritual pilgrimage' would be my own preference – took place some time ago in Ireland, deep in the midlands and a long way from the sea.

Quite exactly when don't make a whole lotta difference.

I can't say for certain how long I'd been lying there – all I remember is swinging around when I heard my name, and must have passed out after that.

When I came to finally my head was splitting.

I've really gone and screwed it now, I said.

The pub underneath had once housed hens and livestock – and, to tell the truth, it didn't look like a whole lot had changed.

The attic itself was a narrow slanting space running all the way along the length of the barn.

Through the chink in the floorboards it wasn't easy to make them out, shuffling and muttering and arguing, but there could be no mistaking the compact sinewy build of ginger-haired Red Campbell – in his late forties, with those long tapered sideburns coming down to meet a small frizzy thatch of beard, making wild, unexpected swipes at the furniture as he pulled out a match and sparked up another rollie, clearing his throat and heaving harshly into the grate.

–You know what, I've been thinking, I heard him declare softly, as he exhaled an abundant lungful of smoke, lately I been figuring that maybe, you know, autumn is a good time to die. When the brown brittle leaves are just on the point of falling – you reckon?

He tilted his head slightly and I heard him whisper my name.

–I'm afraid that he's been an unobliging feller, Ringo Wade. Now why'd he have to go and do such a thing? Why, I wouldn't be surprised if that sonofabitch ain't so very far away at all, with them rattler eyes o' his all bright and fixed. Same as always, no-good fuck …

He swung sharply on his heel, inhaling a series of rapid-fire drags.

As the stoop-shouldered figure of Sonny Hackett stepped from the shadows, his chain-smoker's face lined like a biscuit – so tall and thin he'd have had to stand in two places to make a shadow.

With his gleaming, jet-black hair slicked back as he thrust his brooding aquiline countenance forward and sat down in silence, straddling a grey plastic chair.

Continuing to say nothing.

But you knew at any time that he was capable of flaring up.

Which, as a matter of fact, was what he did now.

With absolutely no hint of warning, shooting unexpectedly to his feet, his clenched fist smartly thumping the hollow of his hand.

–What the fuck's keeping them? he spat sourly. What in the hell can be keeping them till now? Those lousy unreliable fu— !

He didn't bother finishing the sentence.

But just stood there, almost ill-looking, clenching and unclenching his fists.

Red Campbell was pissing out defiantly into the night.

—Man, that's good! he groaned with immense pleasure. Bates fucking Banagher, that does.

I followed its trajectory as he swayed beneath the moon, slamming the door with a deft flick of his heel.

A wisp of straw was tormenting my right nostril as I stiffened.

—Two in the head is what the sumbitch deserves, grunted Red Campbell – to no one in particular, it seemed.

—And that is what he is going to get, he added.

A gutful of jungle juice rose sharply to my throat – as I watched the back door open and the two McHales coming tumbling in, in their grey trackies and white high-back trainers – a pair of sad baby-faced blue-eyed farmboys whose father had left them way too early and whose mother was in a state of long-time depression.

For just a split second, I could have sworn I'd seen them both lift their heads as well.

But it was nothing, just another predictable episode of paranoia.

As a shower of balls came crashing down the pool table, and both McHales stood arrogantly along its side, chuckling provocatively as they wielded their cues.

With their identical faces displaying traces of hastily wiped machine oil.

—Move over, bro, said Shorty, short and chunky with a malnourished podgy face, swaggering past, absently chewing on a hoodie toggle.

As his twin did his best to steady the cue-rest, laying sprawled across the wide expanse of baize.

—These two fellers are made of strong stuff, growled Sonny, just like their father before them, eh boys?

—That's right Mr Hackett, The Runt McHale called over, brazenly gratified, our old man was a hero back in the troubled days. We heard all the stories. He was a top man, right Mr Hackett?

—You had better believe it, boys. When things got rough and the cause needed men, your old pop was always there. That's something that can never be taken away. And I can see by the cut of you, that you two bucks are made from the very same stuff. Cut from the same cloth, you boys are. I can tell. We all can.

—When this is all over, when we get this job done, me and this brother o' mine here — we are heading straight over to the States. We're going to see our Uncle Wylie. You wanna know about him, Mr Hackett? Well then I'll tell you. He's a road warrior, that's what he is. Man you had better believe it — motherfucking speed king, woah boy, no prisoners … !

He swung around to see if anyone might happen to be prepared to disagree, raking his fingers through his highlighted quiff, windmilling the cue-stick as he breathlessly continued:

—You see that Uncle Sam? You wanna know about him, Mr Hackett? Way back up in them hills they got themselves snake handlers, coon dogs, and all the sumbitch moonshine you can drink. And if'n you wanna know how we come to know that — then just call up our father's brother on the phone. Yep, you go right ahead — just call up Uncle Wylie.

—That's right, agreed his brother, they got themselves wind in the pines out there, and all the liquor a feller can drink. Now get that ass right on out of here and let me in there in front of you, bro, for I want to pot that sweet there waiting blue …

—Aye, our fella, you strike that ho' and make sure and sink her down …

—Ah shore as hell will, brother o' mine, this very second I'll drop her plumb …

And that exactly was what young Shorty McHale proceeded to do.

−Yep, when all o' this is over, friends, The Runt resumed,
the two of us are gonna go to Amerikay − over to see that
crack-cat Uncle Wylie, and along with him tear up the dirt at
every goddamn stock car meet in the place. Right, our boy?

−You got it, fella − you got it in one, affirmed Shorty,
beaming.

As another ball ker-plunked, sinking into the depths of the
north-eastern pocket.

−Good call, hollered The Runt, giving his twin a hearty
clap on the back.

As everyone else present looked on in silence, seeming
content to remain that way for what might be left of the
game.

As, high up among the brooding rafters, I hauled in
another hesitant, tremulous breath − stiff as a board on the
straw-strewn floor − and never once taking my eyes off the
door.

−How much you reckon Uncle Wylie is going to pay us?
I heard Shorty inquire.

But never got to hear what his brother's answer might be.

Because just at that precise moment the pub door swung
open and the stout, bearish figure of Big Barney Grue came
barrelling in, dressed in a heavy coat and muffler.

Dragging something, with great ceremony, after him −
tossing it in front of him like a wet sack of grain.

−Evening ladies, Big Barney beamed, tipping down his
baseball cap just so.

As the only friend I've ever really had in the world did the
best he could to escape − groaning for a bit, and after that not
making a sound.

Yes, Jody Kane − my soul-brother comrade, for years down
the line.

And this was how I'd shown my appreciation.

—Breed gon' die! Sonny Hackett sneered, loudly clacking his tongue against his teeth.

—Adios, Jody boy! It sure has been nice knowing you, fucker ... !

Chapter 2

The New Arrival

Hughie Munley was short, a little baby-faced banty of a man in his fifties, friendly as tap water – with a head bald as a duck egg and a habit of showing the point of his tongue through prominent teeth whenever he smiled.

A medallion gleamed underneath his open shirt.

El Paso, read the lettering woven in the shape of a bridle.

'Wee Hughie', as they called him, was generally regarded as funny – with the only problem being that, soon as he got going, he would talk the legs off a stove.

But a straight arrow, nonetheless.

Always ambling and angling, and hoisting up his britches, fixing to get into the company whatever way he could, with that trademark brawny handshake and distinctive *aw-shucks* grin.

–Man could I use me a shot of your best jungle, he hollered, as up rose swiftly a bottle of colourless liquid, with Mervyn, behind the counter, grinning from ear to ear.

–'Bout time you'd arrive, Mr Munley, if you don't mind me saying so, because some of your companions they were starting to just get that little bit worried – ain't that the case?

7

Wouldn't you say that's true? Wouldn't you say, fellers, that that, perhaps, might be the situation?

The nerves in my stomach were all but shot to pieces, watching Hackett as he stood in the centre of the room.

'Sunny' Sonny, in his worn black Wranglers and Cuban-heeled boots had to have been close on six-foot-four – and with them spindle shanks, he might have been a scorpion walking.

He looked like hadn't shaved for days.

–Yep, he nodded, I really must say that I got to admit that I, for one, am in agreement with that there statement. No, in my mind ain't no dispute about that at all. So thank you for that, good brother Mervyn.

The barman smiled as he stood back a little, folding his arms.

As Sonny Hackett raised his glass and sighed.

'Sunny' Sonny – no description could ever have been more inappropriate.

–Cheers, you fucks, Sonny growled as he emptied another shot, man does that bug-juice taste sweet or what ...

Then he suggested it was time to inspect the new arrival.

As Red Campbell stood looming over Jody, temporarily removing his greasy camo cap and running tobacco-stained fingers through a rug of tight, greasy copper curls, gravely stroking a spry thatch of chin beard as he flicked a ball of saliva past the new arrival's ear.

–So, he snorted, seems like we got ourselves a brand-new guest. You reckon that I maybe got that right?

–Correct, replied Sonny.

–Abso-one-hundred-per-cent-lutely, nodded Hughie.

With the two palefaced twins just standing there louchely in their loose-fitting tracksuits, holding a cue apiece, on either side of the pool table.

–Not that it ain't like we been waiting long enough, hollered Campbell as he wrenched a brace of fantails from the tyre-circled dartboard.

It was all I could do not to throw up whenever I saw Jody's face – bruised beyond all recognition.

–Jesus fuck! I heard him plead. Is there anyone out there please who can help me?

–You know what I think I hate more than anything? announced Campbell. Folks as get above their raising. I mean, look at this specimen right here, fellers. Born a gypsy in the open air under canvas and somehow still can't learn how to know his place. It's a disappointment, that's what it is.

–Help me, Jody repeated, please for the love of God!

No one said anything.

As, behind the counter, Mervyn Walker, the proprietor, gave a little weary sigh, absentmindedly humming a soft little tune.

Chapter 3

The American Eagle

There was no excuse sufficient – every last thing was down to me – no debate or equivocation.

The hell with you, Ray Wade, I spat, only for you this nightmare would never have taken place.

Might never even have begun.

I had arranged our rendezvous for the One Tree Crossroads – with the New York tickets bought and paid for, long since.

But by going back to the attic, still so roasted I couldn't remember where I'd left the bonds, I'd gone and fucked whatever chance we might have had.

Yep, Brother Wade, you've gone and done it now, I said.

Now I was history.

Dead meat as soon as Tony Begley arrived.

With the thing about Begley being – he actually liked it, what it was he was known for.

Ending people's pain, as he described it.

Especially whenever he felt justified in his actions.

Which he certainly would now.

I found myself on the point of weeping as I heard a sudden noise below and the tiniest of cries escaped my lips.

That's it then, I said, I'm finished now for sure.

But nothing happened.

Maybe if I hadn't known what it was they were capable of.

But that was the problem, because I very much did.

Oh yes. Knew only too well.

Because, once upon a time, we had all worked in the factory together.

Back in the 'old times' when the troubles were at their height, and bodies turning up in a condition similar to that of Jody's would have been a routine occurrence.

Yes, way back when – when we'd all been employed on the killing floor of Glasson Meats, apart from the twins who had the good fortune not to, as yet, have managed to get themselves born.

Me and Jody would have been fifteen at the time.

I shivered a bit as I looked down at Mervyn – standing behind the counter, tall and erect – seeming inscrutable as he stared at something far away. With those long arms folded, impassive, as always, with the bearing of an American eagle.

He was odd, all the same, that old Mervyn Walker.

There was just something about him that …

Then I heard Red Campbell guffawing.

–Thought you had it all figured out, didn't you Jody? You and Wade – thought you could just up and leave the sinking ship. But we've been ahead of the pair of you all along. You see, we been watching old Ringo – and you too, Jody. We followed you all the way, right out as far as the One Tree Crossroads. And we got you fair and square – with the only pity being that we didn't lay our hands on that other backsliding no-good. But don't worry, we'll get him. We'll get him all right. All it is is a matter of time. That's all it is, gypsy boy – just a sweet little matter o' time.

The clock ticked and the fire burnt low.

The bar was the same as many another mountain establishment.

With a couple of high stools scattered here and there – and, in the corner, a massive oaken table.

Sawdust covered the greasy black and white tiles.

A couple of pictures hung sideways upon the wall.

A football team.

A butcher's calendar depicting a blocky heifer turning incuriously towards the camera.

And a dusty Woolworth's portrait of a little toddler holding a bear – sitting on a potty with a silver-blue tear in his eye.

–It's bye bye, I'm afraid, Jody Kane, I heard Red Campbell whisper softly, releasing an extended plume of smoke. By the time Mr Begley gets through with you, I'm afraid you ain't gonna be around no more. Ain't that the case, wouldn't you say, Mr Grue?

Big Barney came lumbering over, hitching up his trousers over his built-for-diesel girth, his three hundred pound bulk bursting out of a red and black lumberjack shirt, eyes blazing above that rusty foot-long straggly beard.

Standing directly above Jody Kane, wheezing as he tugged nervously at his whiskers, speaking in a voice close to falsetto.

As he grabbed Jody roughly and yanked back his head, sweeping his fingers through his mop of bloodied black curls.

–I guess, said Barney, yep I guess I got to say that you're right. That you are exactly one hundred per cent right there, ol' Red, and I reckon too that that old Tony he ain't gonna be long. No sir, not long at all.

–Never mind all that, barked Hackett, losing patience, for it seems to me that you fellers are starting to fall in love with the sound of your own voice. Way too much speechifying already. So take that sumbitch out to the shed – and leave him there – because I'm just about through having to look at him!

–Fourth pocket, shouted Shorty.

Ker-plunk went the yellow.

As they made their way towards the outhouse with their quarry, from deep within its bowels, I heard the most abject howl.

One which filled me full of self-loathing – how could it not?

As a matter of fact, even now, all these years later, as I sit here alone in the dim light of a single bulb penning these words on a rickety old wooden table, even yet I can feel my face burning. With the shame spreading out, right across my neck and shoulders, I swear.

Still clinging to the hope – that, maybe in the long run Jody Kane *did* forgive me.

Because I'd do almost anything if that could possibly happen. And which is why, no matter where I go, or in what condition I find myself – I always make sure to carry this bundle of letters with me.

I've got a couple of them here in front of me right now as I write.

This particular one dates from the very late nineties. I happened to be going through it earlier on – just to refresh my memory and help me with all of my recollections – as I do my best to get them down on paper.

I don't know how many times I've read it, to tell the truth.

I just can't describe how good it makes me feel. So hopeful, you know?

213 Cypress Grove
Sweetwater, Georgia 15309
USA
March 18 1998

Dear Ray,

I guess when you open this and realise that it's me that you're gonna be surprised after all this time.

And, to be honest, I got to admit that the truth is, Ray, that you're far from being the only one.

For after I left Glasson County, in the aftermath of what happened to us both that terrible night, every time I thought of it I found myself getting all tore up inside, the way any reasonable human being ought to when they cast their mind back to that hellhole and what was done.

And by nobody more than you yourself, Ray, I'm sorry to have to say – and which is the reason all these years why I've carried so much bitterness in my heart.

But things change, don't they, and I'm proud to tell you that since coming out here to Sweetwater, fortune has smiled on me and I'm now, in spite of any past transgressions, welcomed in a manner you would expect to be exclusively reserved for close kindred.

With the sweetest wife you could ever dream of looking after me – and who keeps on insisting she loves me, although sure as hell I can't for the life of me figure that.

For, after shipping for the last time out of Glasson County, I didn't feel like I'd ever come back to myself again and that, when all was said and done, I was worth less than nothing.

To tell you the truth, what had happened was I'd become what you could only call a drifter, rambling in a daze from one drinkwater town to another.

Before finally landing here in Georgia – in what can only be described as God's own private kingdom, where they still got themselves a claim on their own souls and where the talk, I guess you'd say, is kind of slow and syrupy, like molasses in the wintertime. They like their sour mash and football here, let me tell you, and they got no objection to chasing after the odd judy maybe. The town we're living in is a good way off the beaten track – with a body shop, a pool hall, a honkytonk and a livestock sale barn. Most folks work either on the land or in the textile mill, which has been there, they tell me, since Old God's time.

And which I know you'd love – and maybe, at least I'm hoping, after you receive this letter there might be some way we could patch up all our old differences. Yeah, once and for all lay to rest them ghosts, all the memories of that dreadful night. There really are some great people, Ray, and whose company I know you would enjoy and get to love. Hell, in that old Courthouse Square, whenever they get started, I swear to God, it's all the old times and the code of the hills just like we ourselves have lived by and know. In a country where history runs so deep you could almost cut it up with a chainsaw. In the Courthouse Square, you can still hear some of the old timers wail at the destruction reaped by Sherman's March to the Sea. Maybe with one small difference, though, and that is that these people, Ray, more than anything what they hold dear is family and you ain't gonna find so many Sweetwater fellers cutting loose so much and howling at the moon over a grievance or some battle long ago, chaining themselves to the jug and the Mason jar. But that ain't to say that they don't know how to enjoy themselves, for that they sure can do. With their country dinners at noon and evening suppers of chicken fried steak, milk gravy and black-eyed peas. And when the sun goes down there'll be a little drinking and conversing but after they've sipped their share and are kinda tired, it's then that the bandstand will become a pulpit, and the pages of the most important thing to them all are turned – and that's the Good Book, Ringo Wade. Yes, they gladly turn em, one by one. Just like I do myself these days, because if I've learned anything since coming here – yup, if I've picked up anything during my time with all o' these decent here people – it's that we're all sorry bastards but that God above loves us, each and every one, Ray Wade.

What you got to remember, too, and maybe most of all, is that these Sweetwater folks have got their pride and don't take too kindly to folks as maybe got a tendency to maybe undervalue 'em. What they'll always tell you is that the Yankee just don't get it – even yet, with too much reason still binding his head and allowing him little space to record and recognize the value of southern intuition. Because here we prize the imagination and the dream, they'll tell you – here in Sweetwater, God and romance will always be in the ascendant.

And if anyone figures that ain't the case then they ought to come down some Saturday to the Courthouse Square and seat themselves on the bench beside that old bronze Confederate general. And watch how, out of nowhere, if even the slightest slur is cast, how right out of nowhere a Cain-raising fury can erupt like a thunderstorm. So you got to be on your guard just in case things like that happen. But then, we got some experience of that, don't we Ray? And how a perceived injustice can set alight a ring of the most furious fire.

I don't mind telling you that my partner Greta Mae, the love of my life, is a genuine, high-toned Christian woman – can you believe that she goes to church every Sunday, and that I go along with her and her father Otis, whose folks originally come from

Africa. Otis will often tell me that, for him, stepping back into the past is like a dream world that once was real and now is gone. Where you find yourself remembering the old people you used to talk to and you wish you could talk to them again, he'll often say. People don't seem to sit on the courthouse benches the way they used to, he said to me only yesterday. That's because all the old men who used to sit there and talk are probably dead. People are too busy these days. Life tends to move faster now. With it being a long way from the slumbering little village he was born and raised in – where life was lived out in the soft light of a tree-shaded street on a summer afternoon, to the soft clip–clop of horses, the drone of bees and cicadas, the clink of ice in the lemonade pitcher, the creak of the porch swing. And, further out in the country, you can find the farms and the cows and the vegetable gardens, boats in the racks of pickups, watermelon stands in summer, coonhounds in pens.

A time of pause and prosperity, he calls it, Ray. When even Old Glory was contemplated in a more relaxed way, with time devoted to lying beneath a shade tree, watching the cottony clouds drift in the hot blue sky. 'But though a lot of things are gone,' he says, 'and you can see this every morning of the Sabbath, if you've a mind to go along to our little White Church in the valley – one thing around here remains stubbornly firm and solid, Jody my new friend – and that is the ideal of family as identity. Because that's the unshakeable country belief – that, simply by being born into the family, love and self-esteem are simply and unequivocally conferred upon you. And, by extension, one's home town is a community to which one belongs by birth. Simply by your very presence, you belong – thereby having something larger than yourself to which to cling. You try to tell the younger folks about your own childhood but it's like another planet to them.

So you can see where it might come from, Ray Wade my friend, what you might call my 'new persuasion'. Or 'conversion', if you got yourself a mind to go that far ha ha. And which is something that I know you and me would have laughed at in the past. But when you been running all over hell's half-acre like we have in our time, maybe eventually you get to see – you come around to a different way of viewing things. You and me we got lots to talk about regarding that subject, Ray. And that is what we are gonna do just as soon as you get yourself on that plane and make your way out here to see us. Because everyone here would, really and truly, love to meet you. I've told them everything, Ray, you know? About the orphanage and our time there. You just wouldn't believe how much she understands – that's why I want you to meet her so much. Because she, and the people around here, they get it, you know? Especially about folks like us, Ray – you and me.

Especially that it's all about forgiveness in the end.

And if we don't have that, we have nothing.

I hope you don't find this too forthright or intrusive, old buddy, but I been in touch with one or two people, and they been tell me that you been hitting the hooch mighty hard in recent times – is that, in fact, the case?

Anyhow, I know you'll tell me in your own good time – that's if you decide that it's any of my business, Ray. But what definitely is my primary concern is seeing that things get fixed up between you and me. And if we can somehow do that, return you and me to the days when we was true, gentle partners – fellers who would do most anything for each other – before the shadow of misfortune fell.

Because I won't lie – I still get the sweats and the horrors when I think about what they did to me.

But that's all history now and there ain't no point in going over much more of that old ground.

It's beautiful here, Ray, it truly is a sweet and bonny land. You can see the blood orange sun going down behind the hills as I sit here composing these few words on the front porch.

I'll be maybe writing to you again after this – that's if I hear from you, which I really hope I do.

Because I still got some problems with my nerves, I guess you might call it, and can often find that setting my thoughts and emotions down on paper like this, that it kind of helps me in a way I can't really say.

Like the old songs, maybe, that we all used to listen to before it all turned into an early-morning vision of hell. You know the kinda tunes I'm talking about, Ray – Merle Haggard, maybe – but that ol' Hank most of all, at least as far as I'm concerned. Because, the way I see it, there ain't nobody who's come as close to mapping out that territory of pain and desperation. Showing you to a place where it's OK to say: I'm broke, and I don't mean money. A place of emotional release is what I mean, a spiritual pilgrimage. Where you can just let it go and give it permission to pour right out of you – in a torrent, know what I mean?

I knew what he meant, all right – and still do.

Anyhow, Ray, the letter continued, I hope when you get this that all is coming together in your life and that you don't mind me saying this couple of things. It's just that we've a lot to talk about, you and me – and I don't, like a lot of people, want to do the fool thing and leave it too late.

So long then, partner – I'll be in touch with you again real soon.

I hope you don't mind me writing to you out of the blue.

But it's been a long time, Ray, ol' pardner.

So that was it. That was what that old Jody had to say. That was the first of his many welcome letters. I got them all tied up together, for safe keeping.

And, like I was telling you, no matter where I went or in what dire circumstances I might happen to find myself,

I always made sure to have those envelopes close to my heart.

If that sounds strange, like something you'd expect from lovers or something, then that's OK – but that's not how it was between me and Jody.

And if you happened to see me weeping when I was reading them, then the reason for that is because I was ashamed – of failing him.

Not just him, in fact, but everyone.

Which is what I've been feeling for most of my life, at least until recently.

When things started improving dramatically, I somehow found the courage to look directly into my soul and get it all down among these pages – like Fr Conway says, warts and all.

Talking about my drinking, it's like staring down the lens of a telescope and viewing this wild, unkempt creature – coming stumbling past, waving his arms like some deranged Willie Nelson in a long duster coat, talking to himself, just like I used to, slugging from a bottle, stumbling onward, day to day, in an inebriated haze of abdicated responsibility.

All of which, thank God, has changed.

But I couldn't have done it on my own.

No way – not a chance.

Without the assistance and support of a couple of very special people, I'd never have had a chance of making it through.

And it's thanks to them, I think it's fair to say, that I'm capable of saying these things at all – and am not in some long-stay institution or other.

Or worse.

Because, for the best part of the late nineties and early noughties, it really and truly was very bad.

I did have a sort-of relationship with a woman. But no matter how we tried, me and that old Angie Brody, we just couldn't make it work.

You're not thinking about me, I remember her saying, out of the blue, one night.

And again – many times.

You're thinking about her, aren't you Ray, you're thinking about the singer. She's still there inside your head.

You don't have to lie.

I heard you calling her name in your sleep. Dawn, you said.

Even though she played you, just like she did everyone in that dumb fucking valley that you come from – even in spite of all that, I swear to God you're still thinking about her. I can't believe it. After all this fucking time, it's still true.

No, I protested.

After all this time, and everything we've been through, she's still there inside you – working your mind. Playing you, Ray. Because she was good at that, wasn't she? she said bitterly.

No, I insisted, you've got it way wrong. Because that just isn't the way it is, Angie.

She hadn't even bothered to answer.

She'd also begun warning me too – about my drinking, I mean.

But as soon as she found out about the affair I'd been having – just a brief fling with someone whose name I can scarcely remember – after that, there could be no going back.

She announced I had given her no choice and showed me the door.

I've still got her picture – convinced that one day, out of nowhere, she'll arrive back.

Ray, she'll say.

And I'll say: Angie.

But that's not actually going to happen, is it?

And deep down I know it.

For nothing, as we know, cuts deeper than betrayal.

I've never met anyone with such an open and generous nature – the exact opposite of me, more or less.

The problem with you, Ray, is that you got a good face but a bad heart, she always used to say.

And I got to admit that she used to look so lovely, my Angie, in her red bandeau and figure-hugging denims.

But not anymore.

Not since I'd given myself away in my sleep.

Into that velvet dawn we'll ride, I'd moaned, apparently.

Speak her name, Angie had bitterly demanded the following day, go on – say it to me here, right here and now. In the cold light of day, declare her name like you did last night. Say: Dawn.

But of course I couldn't.

And just stood there, looking dumb and hangdog-stupid.

It's just a pity it wasn't me you were talking about, were her last words to me before I left. Because for a while I did sincerely think we had something that just might be worth salvaging, Ray.

But not now, she said.

Not now, Ray Wade. So go – and don't look back. Don't even fucking think about it, looking back.

And it wasn't so very long after that that my life slipped completely off the rails and I found myself surrendering to the hooch, full time.

Straying through the bars and anonymous dives of every distant small town, lying sprawled across the counter as I raved and rambled to myself, hurling it down as fast as I could.

But it doesn't work, does it?

Because it just sits there, waiting, doesn't it – your heart-break.

Knowing that, inevitably, you'll always come stumbling home.

One of the first things I wrote in the pages of this 'spiritual pilgrimage' – which, as I say, is how I prefer to describe it – somehow it turned into the strangest kind of ... I don't know, odd dark fairy tale or something.

And which, whenever I showed its contents to my faithful supporter Fr Conway he observed that – incoherent though it might be in places – in its own crude way it exposed certain things. And which was why I ought to keep on going.

A kind of 'emotional espionage' is how he likes to describe it.

Anyway, this weird kind of fairy tale I was telling you about – it was kind of based on the memory I had of everyone who was there that night in Mervyn's Bar.

Only it was a long time before any of that had happened, when they were gathered together for an occasion of great celebration – way back when the very first ballroom opened in Glasson County. *Heartland*, it was called.

Where they were all awaiting the arrival of its owner, the legendary William Walter Monroe.

The one and only WW.

With them all as excited as kids, and now again keeping their eyes on the door. Only this time, as I say, in anticipation of an evening of tremendous pride and happiness. For they, more than most, had reason to be grateful to WW for all he'd done. Having given them all employment when the meat factory eventually had closed. Red Campbell's job was tending bar, Wee Hughie was now the full-time booking agent for Monroeville Promotions, with Sonny and Big Barney his proud appointed 'chucker-outers'.

He sure did figure on himself having a good team, WW had always been fond of saying.

–Hometown boys, just the same as myself! he would declare, fingers drumming exuberantly on his lapels.

And it was true.

For, he too, in his youth, had hustled pool and shot the breeze and, indeed, raced cars whenever he got the chance.

Yep, a whoopin' and hollerin' upcountry feller like themselves – someone no one could ever have credited with meeting his end, like he did many years later, in a shocking and unexpected manner, at the end of a rope under a sourapple tree.

Not in their wildest fevers could any of them have imagined that ever happening.

But there it was – with the corpse of WW Monroe attired, as always in his Stetson and bootlace tie, only now with eyes bulging and his tongue protruding vilely, with his hand-tooled boots suspended six inches from the ground.

To make matters worse, it was his wife Connie who had made the appalling discovery.

It was also rumoured that his right-hand man Tony Begley had been next on the scene, having by chance been visiting at the time – standing enjoying a smoke as he gazed out across the splendour of Kentuckyland, when he heard the scream.

No one could have foreseen such an unwarranted and lamentable end.

Because it just wasn't the sort of thing a person the like of WW ever did, irrespective of any downturn there might have been in his fortunes.

As a matter of fact, it wasn't the sort of thing *anyone* did – not when they'd only just left their wife sitting there contentedly in the drawing room approximately one half-hour before.

No matter what they might try to say, me and Jody knocking over his precious treasury bonds, dumb though it had been, it had nothing to do with WW's financial and emotional collapse – or very little.

But someone had to take the blame.

So the brutal, savage drinking had begun almost immediately after WW's funeral.

As they all sat, stunned, underneath the motionless, unlit glitterball, facing each other and staring dazedly at the mural of Old Glory, with Elvis in his leathers jacknifing on the wall opposite.

Sonny Hackett was staggering around like a blind dog in a meathouse, just about managing to speak and no more.

–I know there's them that didn't like WW, he thundered, and that they resented his swagger and the habit he had of lording it some. That's because some folks they just can't handle how well the man has done ever since leaving these watery hills and hollers. But he's come back to live amongst us, ain't he – and I got to say that, to me, he ain't ever been nothing only courteous and attentive. You hear?

–Polite, that'd be him, Wee Hughie Munley agreed, that'd be Mr Monroe OK, and there ain't a soul around here can disagree.

Sonny Hackett, simmering, leaned against the bar counter and snarled:

–Anyone hereabouts as ever says a word against him, I'll drop them. Drop the bitches right where they stand. You think I wouldn't? For Heartland and the upcountry code … yeah.

Once upon a time there was a tumbledown shack just lying there by the roadside – until a certain WW had transformed it into what could only be called some kind of magnificent temple. But not remaining content with that – he had been possessed of the impertinence to mount an enormous confectionery-pink fibreglass heart, hoisted on metal supports on top of the roof, with magnificent effrontery shedding its romantic glow all across the wooded slopes and shallow lakes and little mountains of Glasson County.

Because lighting was important, WW had always insisted, especially for half-blind bitches such as us as has spent way too long, maybe centuries, in the dark.

From now on, he announced one night, us'n's ladies is a-gonna be in the pink.

An idea which, he'd gone on to explain, derived from the entertainment world of the nineteen-thirties, when pink lighting had been used in clubs and glamour spots to give skin tones a healthy and attractive glow.

Who would ever have believed it possible?

In a 'nowhere place' the likes of Glasson County?

As the elaborately animated sign surmounting the entrance – The Heartland Ballroom – seductively flicked its lights on and off.

With the giant rooftop heart revolving in its radiant blush-pink glory.

Just as it had been doing that same night long ago, in the early seventies, when they had all been sitting there waiting in the back bar of Heartland, excited by the prospect of their new boss's appearance, for the purpose of congratulating them for having made the first night of Heartland such a success.

Big Barney Grue – eyes blazing, whiskers flaring – saw no option but right there and then to stand out on the floor and, rotating his fists, threaten there and then to take on all comers.

–Any man-fucking-jack, that is, who is dumb enough to have the nerve to run down any of us what comes from Glasson County.

As they cheered him on, and he stomped the floorboards, fists still flying.

—Because we all know what them city boys they say about us. A gang of thieves and outlaws defying the laws of their country – that's all they ever had to say about us. That was before Mr Monroe come home. Yes, that was before the first block of Heartland ever was laid. But now things are different. Me and you, we gonna show 'em, Big Barney, Mr Monroe says. And we will. We – goddamn it! – we sure as hell will!

But all of that now was history – all of twenty years ago, and more.

And now Mr Monroe, that old WW, he was dead.

Well, of course he was. For they'd all just watched his coffin being lowered, right up there on the hillside in that garden of stone lying in the shadow of Glasson Mountain.

And which was why it was proving so hard for any of them to be there, there in that same back bar, the site of so many possibilities long ago.

Having arrived there immediately after the ceremony – like all of them had been drawn there in some inexplicable trance, just sitting there in a kind of daze.

Red Campbell had looked up as though he were ashamed.

As Wee Hughie came over and generously replenished his glass.

—Someone has got to pay for this, said Sonny, for I'm not sure I can bear this pain.

—Someone, vowed Red, has got to make this cruel day right …

Big Barney Grue's lips were moving all right, but he couldn't have told you what they were saying.

Or even if they'd said anything.

—Someone, repeated Sonny, you believe me, someone is gonna have to pay this check.

And, just at that moment, he lifted a bottle and drained its entire contents by the neck, momentarily experiencing a dramatic vision of the recently deceased WW Monroe – having, astonishingly, without any form of warning at all, suddenly appeared there in the ballroom's back bar.

Quite alive, oh yes. More alive than ever, in fact.

No mistake about that.

Striding, or so it seemed, right through those swinging double doors, laughing and hollering in the company of his loyal and trusted lieutenant, Tony Begley.

Before swinging right across to 'talk turkey' to his 'favourite barman', the one and only Red Campbell, as he gave Wee Hughie his great big broad twinkling smile.

–Hell, Hughie, whooped the businessman, if you don't look like that old bluebird of happiness has this very second arrived at your front door.

Before standing in front of them, with his fingers drumming on his lapels as usual, and suddenly appearing almost twenty foot in height. Or, at least, that was how it had seemed to Sonny Hackett – with a kind of peace and contentment about him.

Of achievement, maybe.

Or satisfaction, Sonny thought to himself.

Now that his life's dream of Heartland had been realised, with many more equally magnificent ballrooms to come, he had assured them.

–With a spectacular restaurant service, three or four weddings on weekends, and live music several nights a week. So, hold your head up here, sweet little Glasson County, for you just fell in the shithole and come right up with the gold watch and chain – right Tony?

Tony Begley stepped forward into the light, smartly dressed for the opening in country-club casual, dark-coloured slacks with an untucked sports shirt smoothed out over a ballooning stomach, and high-sided elasticated brown boots.

—They're done laughing at the country boys, he continued with some insouciance, they've done their share of patronising us fellers.

—Damn right, agreed Sonny, you sure have got that one right, Tony Begley. Good on ya, buddy!

—They think they can tell us mountainers what to do, Begley continued, but that, you see, is where they are wrong. Because that only works when folks are poor. Or crushed, maybe – when they get to figurin' themselves boxed in by rules all got up to suit someone else – lawyers, bankers and corporate hustlers. Yeah, the dirt-poor's soul feels trapped and smothered and what's it gonna do only seek freedom in sweetness and wildness. So when you see someone like, say, Teddy 'Buckfast' Carson on a spree – or even that old rascal Red Campbell over there – when you see them getting a little drunk and cutting loose on the world, what you got to understand that what is happening is that their souls is trying to fight free. And that there ain't all that much bitterness, nor attitude neither, when you get to looking deep into what they will tell you is the country hill boy's cold cold heart. And which is why – now that the first of WW's mighty arenas have been built – there are gonna be some serious changes around here. Because now that we have found our voices, we are gonna sing them high and strong right from the roof of this here Heartland Bar. For, sure as a goose he ain't got no shoes, we have got them big wheels rolling – and right from here on in, Glasson County gonna be smokin' with the hammer down thanks to a feller name o' Monroe who made it all happen. Right, fellers? So if he wanna ride the high horse around Glasson County, then let him, I say! Because I, for one, got no objection.

As WW himself nodded in approval, and then swept, flamboyantly, without further ado, in behind the counter and announced, with a flourish that it would be his privilege to stand all of his tried and trusted 'loyal hombres' a drink.

−A double, he cried, a double brandy for every man−jack right now in this place …

It really had been a beautiful moment, all those many many long years ago now.

There simply couldn't be any doubt about it.

And a long way, for sure, from the black and miserable evening of the funeral they'd just attended − as a consequence of which they now all found themselves literally struck dumb and on edge.

Why wouldn't they be, when the truth was that they were heartbroken?

And left feeling abandoned.

But − all the same, Sonny Hackett had suddenly stood up and snapped abruptly that there was no reason for Red to keep on making that fucking grinding noise with his teeth.

−How many times have I told you to stop it? he spat again.

No one said anything.

Through the window leading to the foyer you could see the elaborate, ornate fountain − some kind of marble goddess imported from Italy, surrounded by plants.

At the start, Sonny remembered, they had all been embarrassed, just by the fact of her being naked.

But, after a while, nobody had minded.

Because Mr Monroe liked that kind of thing. And whatever was good enough for him, well then that suited every else just fine. Because WW knew what was good, if not better, than any know−all from the city.

Red Campbell sounded like he was choking.

−That dumb fucking statue, they heard him curse, rising up to his full height in the chair, I'm going to break it so I am. I'll bust it!

Still nobody said anything.

−I'll break it into a thousand pieces so I will − you see if I don't! he wailed.

Working himself into such a state that Wee Hughie Munley was obliged to go across and restrain him.

−Easy now, Red, Wee Hughie urged, easy now friend. It's gonna be OK. We'll always have our Heartland memories, whatever else happens, WW will always be there. In here where it matters …

−And where's that? spat Red Campbell. Where the fuck is that, may I ask? Where is it?

−In our hearts, explained Wee Hughie, in here like I say.

As he watched Red Campbell rest his forehead on the table before releasing a mournful and protracted howl.

And it wouldn't have been very long after that that they decided to go on the hunt for me and Jody.

Which didn't take them very long.

For there he was − yes, that old amigo − hopping from foot to foot beneath the sycamore as he scanned the road up ahead, looking for me.

Before Big Barney Grue crept up behind him and knocked him senseless with a single blow of the heavy metal wheelbrace.

Chapter 4

Snow In July

Jody Kane, in his heydey, had been the county bareknuckle champion.

—And look at him now, hissed Red Campbell, moving from the table over towards the fire. Well hell yeah, just look at the big-time slugger now, he spat again fiercely, as I watched from the rafters.

Wee Hughie Munley cracked his knuckles and showed his prominent teeth, talking trip-hammer fast as his little round head began nodding furiously.

—That's the thanks Mr Monroe received, he complained, the kind of gratitude he was shown by the people he looked after – the people who'd have been nothing without him.

—It was the biggest funeral ever in Glasson County. The largest, I think, I've ever seen, Big Barney observed regretfully, lowering his eyes.

—There'll be nobody missed more than Mr Monroe hereabouts, said Sonny, for as long as we live there'll never ever be another WW.

—Never, agreed Red.

—I loved him, said Sonny.

–We all did, said Red.

–When I get my hands on that snake Wade, I'm going to do it, and do it fucking bad – stiff him, vowed Barney, eyes blazing wilder than ever.

–You want to know the truth? began Sonny Hackett as he flicked back his forelock, well then here it is. From the start I can't say I ever liked him – never took to Ringo Wade.

–Neither did I, said Red Campbell, couldn't stand the sight of him, to tell you the God's honest truth.

–I'm going to do it, and don't think I won't, Big Barney repeated, and the reason that I'm going to is because – right from the start, from the very first days when he was a kid in those stables, I'd always had him figured for being a lowbelly fuck.

–King Slimeball Snake, Red Campbell growled, that's what he is. Ray Wade the Diamondback King.

–That's right, agreed Barney, seeming somewhat dazed, that's right. I agree.

Then, looking like it took all he had to contain the abundance of repressed fury inside of him, Big Barney heaved and sat down, with his chin sinking deep into the enormous rampart of his chest.

–With them shifty eyes of his, continued Red, and that smile of his that'd make you throw up – I hate it. I'm going to waste him. Sure, stiff the sumbitch right where he stands – even though I know in truth he ain't worth the shot.

–Because one thing, interrupted Sonny, one thing that you never ought to do is turn around and bite the hand that feeds you. Let your own people down – it's a crime. Especially not them as has gone out of their way to show you assistance. Right Barney?

–Correct and right, agreed Big Barney Grue, one hundred per cent for sure, no question. Right there, Hughie?

Wee Hughie raised an approving thumb.

—Because, he agreed, because that is one thing you just ought not ever to do – big-time transgression in my book, Barney.

—In anybody's book, Sonny Hackett seethed.

Nobody said anything for a long time after that. Before Red Campbell smiled and, with a distant look in his eye, observed softly:

—Do any of youse remember the night I won the Dance-Off Competition?

Before anyone could respond, they heard him continue:

—I was only just thinking about it the other night – when me and the missus won the big dancing prize. Did youse know this as well? That that was the night I finally picked up the courage to ask her to marry me. O man. What a night. She'd gone to the trouble of getting a costume run up for me real special. She said I looked like Elvis in it – she really did, I'm not kidding. Maybe youse remember. It was a kind of red little bolero jacket. Even yet I can't believe she talked me into wearing it. But the thing is, we won. We won the competition, fellers – the Heartland Trophy. Me and the Kid. Bingo. *Hola!*

As everyone nodded, before privately returning to the magical, never-to-be-repeated events of that avowedly unforgettable night.

When Mr Monroe himself, as a matter of fact, had arrived up onstage for the purpose of presenting Red Campbell with that very award.

Just the slightest remembrance had the effect of making Red Campbell impossibly bitter.

—I still can't believe that the two of them could be so dumb, he spat, to jack over the one man who had ever shown them kindess. But they did it. They did it all right.

Big Barney got up and struck his chair a vicious blow.

—Don't worry, folks – we don't got to worry about that. For Tony Begley is the man who will soon sort it. Yep, Tony will skin that snake for sure, and skin him but good.

Soon as I heard that, the perspiration came lashing off me like cold, bitter, stinging rain – as the McHale twins started an argument about America.

–California isn't anywhere near Idaho. You're a doofus, that's what you are, our fellow. You're making a dick of yourself, coming out with the like of that. Do you hear me, our boy – so for once in your life maybe try shutting your mouth and giving your arse a chance.

Talking about America, I suppose on account of Jody's letters, I almost feel like I know it inside out. Even though I've never been there.

To be understood by such great people, he wrote, why it's almost as if I've reached what we used to call our 'promised land', Ray.

That was how he had here described it, in the letter I have in front of me. And it made me simultaneously sorrowful and sad. Just thinking about the way that he used to speak those very words – standing there, staring, looking out across the fields.

Or maybe the two of us would be standing on the top floor of that grim fastness, looking out the window of that grey, forbidding Victorian building.

Now, however, with my whole body still stinging, I hadn't so much as the strength to blink my eyes.

Beneath the flyblown Venetian blind hung a lopsided sign for Coors.

On the back of the door, a peeling decal for Gold Flake Satisfy.

As the little boy clutched his little teddy on the wall, with that same silver tear forever frozen in his eye.

Out across the valley, the tall stately pines rose up to meet the sky.

–Talk of snow, said Hughie Munley suddenly, forsaking his post by the window before returning to the table.

And breaking the seal on a pack of cards.

—Snow in July, murmured Red Campbell, to no particular individual that I could see.

As Sonny Hackett fixed him with an unflinching dark stare. Before lifting an eyebrow and inquiring, matter-of-factly:

—That song that's playing on the jukebox — does anyone know what it might happen to be called? Like it's name or something ...

Big Barney Grue lifted his head and stretched, with a yawn.

—Not me anyway, they heard him say.

—Nor me either, Red Campbell muttered.

Wee Hughie Munley said that no he didn't either.

As Sonny Hackett heaved a lengthy sigh.

Before leaning forward and repeating the question.

—Look. That song that's playing right now on the jukebox, would anyone present happen to know what it might be called? And maybe do me the courtesy of ...

Nobody at all replied.

As Sonny frowned, gnawing his underlip.

—Merle Haggard — maybe that's who it is, he suggested drily.

—Nope, demurred Hughie, no it isn't. Merle Haggard, I mean, Sonny.

Red Campbell flung his chair back and began laughing loudly.

—What I would like to know — yes, what I would like to know, Sonny Hackett — is how in the name of cursagod Christ it could be Merle Haggard, when he never recorded no record by that name ...

—By what name? replied Sonny. What name you referring to here?

Red Campbell was patiently picking his teeth.

—'Snow in July', he replied with a smile, you would be a long time going through his songs, I reckon, before you came on one called that.

−You're an authority, then − is that what you're saying? That Red Campbell knows it all about Merle Haggard? That Red Campbell runs the Country Music Authority. Is that what you're saying? Because if it is, I think it's pretty funny.

Red Campbell sighed and ran his tobacco-stained fingers slowly through his moistened curls without once taking his eyes off Sonny.

−It wasn't my intention to suggest that I was an authority on anything, he went on, and to tell you the God's honest truth, Sonny Hackett sir, I ain't got the faintest idea how you might have gotten that into your head.

−You don't, huh?

−I don't, huh.

Sonny Hackett drummed rapidly on the table, clicking his heels.

−I see. Well. How about this?

−How about what? Red Campbell said.

−How about the Country Music Authority goes over and takes off that fucking thing that's playing and shoves it − and put on one, maybe, say, by Charley Pride.

−Charley Pride?

−That's what I said. But, seeing as you are such an esteemed authority on the subject I am gonna leave the selection down to you.

−That's good, smiled Red, that is generous and mighty generous of you to do that, Mr Hackett sir. Except for the fact that it doesn't make a great deal of difference to Red Campbell what it is you might decide to do regarding your choice of music or anything fucking else. Because right at this moment I intend to enjoy this sweet little shotta jungle juice I got me here. And which is why I ain't got the slightest intention of getting myself up out of this chair for anybody. Not even you, Mr 'Happy Days' Hackett sir.

Sonny said that that had made him laugh.

—It amuses me, he sourly declared.

Before shoving the table back with a screech as he stood, bolt-upright, in front of the disinterested Red Campbell. Sweeping back his hair, before slamming his fist down hard on the table.

—I don't want no 'Snow in July'. You hearing me, Campbell? Because what I want is *Charley* — and it's Charley Pride I'm going to fucking get! You listening to me, shit-for-brains? You listening to me? You listening to what I'm saying to you right here?

But Red Campbell remained implacable, making an elegantly dismissive little gesture with his fingers, as a furious rush of blood shot right to Sonny's face.

—You know what, Red? You ain't worth it, he decided.

Before sloping over to the Rock-Ola and dawdling there, with his hands tentatively hovering above the selection panel, intermittently delivering vitriolic glances in the direction of Red Campbell.

With the latter returning them, tenfold — clearly having resolved not to speak a word.

Chapter 5

Uncle Wylie's Wrecking Yard

I watched closely as The Runt, very slowly, began rising to his feet, with his pupils dilated as he took up position at the head of the table, looking huntedly all around him.

Before suddenly lurching forward and heaving violently, but nothing came up.

Beside him, his brother made sympathetic noises.

–You know, began The Runt, his freckled podgy face obscured by a dangling quiff, I didn't really want to say this. But the truth is, and I hope our Shorty doesn't hate me for saying it – but, if I had the choice, I'd rather not be here at all. To be honest, the way that I'm feeling right this minute I just wish that the whole thing was over. So that me and bro here could just walk out that door – yes, turn around and get a plane to America.

His brother now seemed equally agitated – stopping and starting as he circled the pool table.

–That's right, he snapped sharply, agitatedly upending the cue, once and for all get away from here and forget that any of this has happened. Because if you want to know the truth, I hate Glasson County. I know it's what my father might have given his life for and all, but it isn't any good for the likes of you and me, is it bro?

—Zackly, stammered The Runt, wiping his mouth, now you are talking a bunch of real good sense, our boy …

Both McHales were apprentice mechanics, until recently employed by WW, working out at Kentuckyland. We all knew that they'd been happy there – but now that the banks and the money men had taken over, what was left? Where would they go?

That was the question on everyone's lips.

—Where can he be? What's keeping Begley? Where can he have got to? The Runt snapped sharply all of a sudden. Oh Jesus, I don't feel so good …

—It's OK, Runty, he'll come – don't worry, Shorty reassured him. Sooner or later Tony Begley will walk in. That door will open and he'll come strolling in.

He sparked two smokes and handed one to his brother.

—Ker-plunk! went the balls and:

—Clink clink clink.

As another minute went by on the clock.

Red Campbell had lifted his boots onto the table, his fingers beating time on his flat stomach along with the music.

Smiling over at Big Barney, as his lumbering colleague grinned right back.

—So how have you been this past while, big feller? What 'n hell you been up to, you great big hunka beef. Ha ha!

Barney Grue parted his legs and began to rhythmically pat his thighs.

—Matter of fact, I've been doing real good, he replied, that is to say I got no complaints.

He laughed in that familiar, high-pitched, uncertain manner.

—That's real good to hear, Big Barney, smiled Red Campbell, yes that is real damn good to know.

Then he turned his attention to the barman.

Who, as always, was just standing there, lithe and silent behind the counter, gazing off.

At something so very far away, it seemed.

−And you there, Mr Walker, Red continued, would you say that's also the case with you? That you're doing good, I mean to say?

The barman relaxed as he smiled from ear to ear, spreading his hands in that predictable, avuncular fashion.

He seemed so happy as he blithely responded:

−Not only that, Red old friend, indeed as a matter of fact, I would have to say that I'm doing *real* good. Yes − I would definitely say that. Yep. For sure.

Red Campbell looked down and thought for a second or two, turning over a couple of crumbs of sawdust and then looked up with the sunniest of sunny grins, which was directed, or so it seemed, almost exclusively towards Sonny Hackett.

Who was still preoccupied, examining the cards spread out in front of him.

The history of tension between the two men was well known. It had always been there, going right back to their time in the factory.

You could tell Sonny Hackett didn't take to being scrutinised.

Any more than he liked the noise that Red was making with his teeth.

And, being uncomfortable enough already among those crossbeams, I wasn't taking very much to it myself.

You could tell by Sonny's expression, which he didn't do much to conceal, that, more than anything, what he wanted to do was cry:

−Cut it out, will you? Stop making that fucking sound.

But decided, in the end, against it.

As Red, with an extended toe, fashioned another zigzag shape in the sawdust.

–You been watching the games? he inquired out of the blue, staring right at Hackett.

Sonny bridled.

–What're you talking about, Campbell – games? Watching what games?

–You know, just the sports. You been watching them much, in recent times?

Sonny Hackett leaned across the table, resting his long unshaven jaw on his palm, as he gazed unflinchingly into Red Campbell's drawn face.

–So he wants to talk about sports, is it now? That's what it's come to now – you all got that? We've been waiting for over two hours for Begley – and all he wants to do is talk about sports. I'm sorry, Mr Campbell, but somehow I don't get it.

–Just making conversation is all, explained Red, with an exaggerated nod, just a conversation about sports and games. Games and sports. That's all, Mr Hackett. But if you are of a mind that you don't want to talk about that particular subject, then that is perfectly fine by me.

A fragile silence began to descend.

Before Wee Hughie Munley, seeming almost jubilant, stuck his rosy face in between them and ejaculated:

–Look, fellers, listen up now lend me your bunnies for a second. For this, right now, is all I got to say. That, whatever differences there might have between certain of us individuals in the past, at the end of the day there is only one thing that all of us here got to remember. And that is – that, very shortly now, this whole unfortunate darned thing is a-gonna be over. Why, swear to God, it'll almost be like it never happened at all. So I've said my piece. Now if you gents don't mind I think His Majesty Hughie Munley, he is going to help himself to another little drink …

As his banty frame and little baby face went turtle-nodding towards the bar and immediately caught the barman's attention – with Mervyn unfolding his arms as he twinkled accomodatingly and leaned across the counter.

–Do you know who our barman reminds me of fellers? I heard Red Campbell call out across the room, seeing as I am something of an authority on country music according to Mr Hackett, I would have to say that he reminds me of nobody so much as Charlie Rich, that good old silver-haired Southern gentleman singer. Man, when you look at him sideways, he sure does resemble that old American eagle …

As Mervyn 'Charlie Rich' tapped his thumbs and smiled down at Hughie.

–Mr Munley, sir, your wish is my command. So what's this drink of yours gonna be, if I may be so bold as to inquire?

–Another shotta jungle would be my pleasure, said Hughie, nodding enthusiastically, slapping his small pot belly, that would make me sure as hell happy. You want anything over there, Red?

–Nope, don't think so.

–'Bout you fellers – what about the twins?

As The Runt belched vigorously, piercing the air with the uplifted cue, rifting loudly as he swayed from side to side, before finding support on his brother's proffered shoulder. With those bloodless podgy faces, the pair of them looked like they hadn't eaten in weeks.

–Our father Trampas McHale died in the old times, fighting for Glasson, The Runt continued, quite out of nowhere, and that's OK. But me and Shorty, we're a different generation. And now after what happened to Mr Monroe there ain't nothing left anymore for us in Glasson. So, listen up and hear this, for this is for certain sure. That when all this is over, me and him we're going to America – heading Stateside to see our Uncle Wylie …

Looking all around him, staggering clumsily.

—Breaker 1-9, Breaker 1-9, this here's a Rubber Duck. Are you receiving me, over?

—10-4, we got you loud and clear, Rubber Duck, c'mon back!

—Tell them where he lives, our fella. Go ahead — tell them. OK?

—Saginaw, Michigan, that's where our father's brother the famous Uncle Wylie lives. And where he got the best and biggest wrecking yard in that there county. To which they come from all over.

—Yes, Saginaw, Michigan — it's class, real class, Shorty squealed. Nearly as good as Kalamazoo …

—Kal-a-ma-fucking-zoo, yelled The Runt, all them places that they got out there. Glasson, hah? It ain't nothing …

—For sure as hell not now it ain't. Not now that Kentuckyland and WW are gone.

—Look out, Uncle Wylie's wrecking yard and all of America too — for here we come. And with them diesel brakes squealing and our smokestacks blasting, we are gonna be Kings of the Road.

With the pair of them launching into a crazy, intoxicated, arm-flailing buck-dance before eventually landing in the middle of the table.

—I don't mean to spoil the party, interjected Mervyn, but in the circumstances I don't think, maybe, that that kinda behaviour's appropriate …

—We're sorry, called The Runt as he windmilled his arms and dusted himself down, I'm real sorry Mervyn and so is my brother …

—That's OK. It ain't no problem, Mervyn replied, returning to his business behind the counter.

As Sonny Hackett warned both brothers to go easy.

—It's just that we don't want no cops coming snooping around.

Then both boys sat back down, clearly well on the way to being hopelessly out of their heads, staring in silence straight ahead of them, like orphans.

As Sonny went wandering over in the direction of the Rock-Ola.

−I'll put me on another little record, I reckon. That, you reckon, meet with your approval, barman?

−That is absolutely one hundred per cent, nodded Mervyn, because I know you ain't gonna be playing it loud. On account of I've had it set on low right from the get-go, from before you all came in. Just in case ha ha. You know what I mean? Just in case of the law − yeah you got to be careful and keep it right down.

−Well, hell if you ain't the canny old customer, laughed Sonny, sometimes I think you're way ahead of us all, old Mervyn. You reckon, when it comes it, that maybe that's in fact the case? Charlie Rich, you good old boy?

−Maybe, smiled Mervyn, I guess maybe.

Then he cracked his hands together.

−Hey, Sonny cried, here's a thought. Would anyone maybe care for a little tune by Elvis? Yep, anybody fancy a few bars of the King?

Nobody replied.

As Sonny just stood there, with his elbow angled on top of the machine, whose neon pastels flowed across his swarthy face.

Not making a sound as he stood there, rapt in thought.

Before, all of a sudden, seeming to change his mind, his expression twisting grotesquely as he sat back down at the table.

He couldn't think of anything he fancied, he announced.

−I thought you said you were going to put on Elvis, Red Campbell said.

Sonny glowered.

−What? he said. What was that you said just there?

—I thought you said you were going to put on Elvis. I thought you said you were going to put on the King.

—Is that what you thought? replied Sonny Hackett, bringing his two thumbs together as he thought for a moment, gazing hawkishly in Red's direction.

—Is that what you thought? Well, it just so happens that I'm not, you see. And that is where you went and got it wrong. Because, like I say, I changed my mind.

Then he hit the table another severe blow.

—Where in the name of fuck is he gone – where has Tony Begley got to? Because he swore to me that as soon as he was finished all his work he'd be down– and now look …

And he might have been an aged version of the early King himself, as he went over and stood by the window once more, with the collar of his black leather jacket pulled up, and the oily wing of his forelock hanging down.

—You know, began Hackett, you know as sure as I'm standing here I could never – not really – ever figure him out. Tony Begley, I mean. Even when it looked like things were going good for him, you still couldn't be sure. One night in particular, I'll never forget it. All of us were drinking in the bar with WW and he kept on saying to me: you think there's something wrong with me? Tell me honestly, straight up, Sonny – look in my eyes and tell me. Do you think, maybe, there's something amiss? Because if you want to know the truth, all of my life there have been pressures on me, Sonny. Pressures that I do not need. I don't mind you knowing this. I don't mind telling you because the way that I figure it, you and me is Glasson kindred. Then what does he do, right out of the blue, starts singing with his eyes shut tight and I swear to God I've never seen in the world seen anyone look happier. As he kept on talking about the most wonderful lady he'd ever known in his life. She's the foundation I lean on, he told me. Without her love and affection, all my life'd have been nothing, he said.

Even from the rafters you could see the blue of the veins in Hackett's forehead.

As he swung around and gasped, clenching and unclenching his fists.

−You're a lucky man, Tony, I said − you really are. Because that's all any man ever could have want in a woman − one to whom he is going to be wed, at any rate.

He looked pasty and unwell as he passed directly underneath me, resting his forehead against the wall.

−And I swear to God I thought he was going to hit me − I really did, fellers. Standing there staring at me, patting his hair like he was trying to calm himself down. You want to know what he said? Who said anything about being wed, he says.

Hackett shivered a little and then just stood there, saying nothing.

−WHO SAID ANYTHING ABOUT BEING WED? he said.

He looked at the floor.

−I'll never forget it as long as I live, he said.

After which Sonny Hackett sat down, not uttering a word, as he reached across, stonily, to get at the bottle of jungle.

Chapter 6

Kentucky Fry

–That pair of imbeciles should never have been brought near the place at all, do you hear me, not at all, Wee Hughie complained. What in the name of God are they doing here anyway – who's idea was it? That's what I'd like to know.

–Spike your scrake, for who are you to go around mouthing about imbeciles anyway? So maybe save your breath for one of your famous jokes. Because their father was the hero of Glasson County once upon a time and they'll be cut from the same cloth, you'll see. So the idea is that they're gonna be bled. That's the thinking, pure and simple – we're gonna break 'em in, same as happened to us in our time. Yep, in the exact same way as, in the old times, each and every one of us had to learn how it's done. Because, now that WW is gone, what we are gonna need more than ever is them as has the gall to, once more, fight the tiger. These hills need fresh meat and plenty of it. Hardened up, that's what they gotta be – for there's way too many daisyboys dodging about.

Sonny Hackett left down his drink and folded his arms, choke-holding the chastened Hughie Munley. Before turning to scrutinise the sickly looking twins.

Just a single look would have been more than enough to tell you how far gone both McHales actually were – for like everyone else they had been drinking most of the day to anaesthetise themselves for what they knew was coming.

Shorty's eyes rolled as he repeated, once again:

–Tell them everything there is to know about Uncle Wylie, our Runty. Do it.

–I sure as hell will, hollered the Runt, I sure goddang will do that, bro. Because Uncle Wylie says that over there they got canyons and timberwolves. Now that's a mountain country. And us suckers, what we got over here? Hills that got no right to even think about going by that name. See, Uncle Wylie lives in the proper upcountry – with white lightning and blood-red suns. Coyotes, fuck.

His eyes went swimming back in his head.

–That's the truth, ain't it, Barney Grue? Huh? You tell them that what I'm saying here is fact.

But Big Barney Grue wasn't listening to a word he said. Completely ignoring him as he paced up and down, kicking out wildly at the sawdust as he bit his knuckle.

Before returning, preoccupied, once more to the window – pushing down the slats and leaning over to peer out into the night.

–Any sign yet? queried Hughie. Any indication of you-know-who?

–Nope, replied Barney, nothing so far.

–Hey, shouted the Runt, hey there, listen up. Because way back in the fifties or some of them times, that old Uncle Wylie he worked awhile in the Mississippi State Prison. Ain't that right, Shorty? Tell them what they call the electric chair down yonder.

Shorty McHale blankly shook his head.

–I don't know what you're talking about, he said, I don't know nothing about chairs.

−Sure you remember it, our feller. So come on!

−The electric chair? Is that what you're saying? That the one you're talking about?

−Yeah. Like I said. So tell them − tell them what they call it in Mississippi, USA.

His brother shrugged.

−The chair, maybe. Maybe just 'the chair', he suggested.

−Well that is where you are wrong, our feller. Because what they been calling it this past fifty years or maybe more is − yep, Old Sparky.

−Old what?

−Old Sparky, that's the name they got on it, our feller − and you know it. Sure, the name that they got on that chair. Sparks. Sure as a jackass likes his briars, that is the name it goes by. And would you like to know something else about that chair? Why, they'll tell you that the very second that lever's pulled, you can smell your own flesh beginning to fucking roast!

Red Campbell flicked a cigarette butt which struck Shorty smack on the ear. Then he leaned over and glared directly at them.

−Now you listen to me, both of you − if you don't wise up, the both of you, and quit this dumb fool talk, then I swear by Christ … !

But he didn't say what it was he might do.

−Running off at the mouth, he growled sullenly.

−Way too much, Big Barney agreed.

Nobody spoke for another two or three minutes.

−I seen this movie, said Shorty, are you listening, our boy? This film − I seen it.

−You seen a film. A film, what about?

−There's this fellow screaming out there in the prison − going *wah wah wah*. All the time, yeah, *wah wah wah*.

—*Wah wah wah*?

—The whole fucking time. That's what he kept on doing, over and over. Screaming. Screaming half the night and him stuck there inside the cell.

—What was he doing that for? What 'n the fuck was he hollering about? Tell me, our boy — what was this fellow screaming ab—

—*Wah wah wah* — all he kept saying, yep. All night. That, and: *Mommy Mommy, where's my Mommy …*

—Mommy. Mommy! Where's my Mommy?

—That was all. No more. Just that.

—Saying all he wanted was his mother?

—Asking them please to go and get her for him. *Mommy Mommy*, over and over. You want to see the face of him, bro.

—I'd let the fucker fry so I would. Let him sit there, I swear to God — I wouldn't care. I'd let him sizzle like Kentucky Fry. Then I'd spice him up, like Colonel Sanders' recipe.

—Colonel Sanders?

—The fellow with the suit and the white moustache. You can see him in Dundalk — laughing in the window, with his stick and white hat.

—Good call. That's what I'd do too, agreed his brother, stumbling awkwardly and banging his head against the mantelpiece.

Still seeming unfazed as he cupped his hand and called out to the barman:

—You listen up here, Mervyn Walker my man. Because I got a question I would like to ask you!

—Go right ahead, replied the owner, rhythmically polishing a glass.

—OK then. You are a man that I know has been around. So tell me this — which would you say is the best place in the whole USA?

As, without a moment's hesitation, the tall barman cursorily wiped his hands with a cloth and replied:

–Paragoul.

Staring off at the leaves brushing softly against the glass. The willow.

While Shorty frowned and slugged down another shotta jungle.

–Is that near Mississippi? he wondered.

–Couldn't say, replied the barman drily. Can't say that I remember, to be honest.

–Thanks anyway. Thanks, Mervyn. I appreciate you telling me that.

Shorty paused for a moment, deep in thought as he savoured the word.

–Paragoul, he murmured, shaking his head, Paragoul. Hmm.

As the Runt struck a pool ball and shouted across to his brother:

–I wonder would that be anywhere near our Uncle Wylie? Would you say that's near our uncle's place, our boy? Huh? Come on – I gotta know.

By now the rest of them reckoned they had endured enough – as a chair came screeching right across the floor.

And Sonny roughly grabbed a hold of Shorty. looking out from under his dark eyebrows and warning:

–You had better listen to me. You too, brother.

Shorty and the Runt said nothing, scowling resentfully as they slouched back across the floor.

And Sonny Hackett rose to his feet, striding towards the window as he hit the venetian blind.

–Where can he have got to, the greasy fucking freak? Why doesn't he come when he says he's going to? Does he think that any of this is easy for us?

Then a heartbreaking howl tore the air apart – spiralling from the depths of the outhouse next door.

Jody.

Chapter 7

Some Velvet Morning

Everything he'd been experiencing in the darkness of that tumbledown shack had been as bad as the days back in Whiterock, he'd written.

Lying there, broken and slumped in the gloom, plagued by the constant, steady buzzing in his ears.

And, if that wasn't bad enough, at one point looking up to discover Red Campbell standing in front of him, smirking as he blew a cloud of smoke into his face.

The finest bareknuckle boxer in a generation – and this was what it had come to, in the end.

We'll always be there for one another, he used to say, no matter what happens we'll always be sure of that. The one way we might overcome what has happened to us – in the prison they called the Whiterock Orphanage.

Where no one had ever bothered taking the time to tell us anything about our backgrounds.

With everything we knew contained in the few bits and pieces that we ourselves owned – scraps of letters, a couple of grainy black and white photos – or 'likenesses', as they always used to call them in Glasson.

In the one I had of my mother, she looked not unlike a youthful Patsy Cline – full-figured, big-boned, and holding a straw hat, like she was all dressed up for the day, but in the only fancy dress she owned.

For his part, my father looked mortified – having to be photographed at all, I mean. As he stood before the sun, in the centre of a field dressed in his work overalls, doing his best to avert his eyes from the camera, covering his face with a shapeless hat.

He had always been a kind man, Marty Wade, or so they said. Had been solid and dependable, devoted to his wife. It had been such a sad thing to happen, the accident – but at least, if nothing else, they had died together. In one another's arms, close by the sycamore at the One Tree Crossroads.

Jody was the only real friend I'd ever made there – not that there was anything wrong with anyone else – just that, with him, it was somehow easy. Because you didn't have to try with Jody. Like he'd said in his letters, there are just some people who instinctively understand. And that was the way it had always been with us.

For as long as we'd been there, prospective parents came and went – checking out the quality of the merchandise, I guess you might say.

Searching for a vulnerable little orphan on whom they might shower all the love they reckoned they had to give, affection that had nowhere else to go.

However, I'm sad to say – certainly during those first couple of years when the death of my parents was still very vivid and alive in my mind – the degree of hooded, withdrawn sullenness which they tended to find themselves encountering in my case proved more than enough to dissuade them from making any kind of offer.

And as for Jody Kane – who wants to take home an itinerant orphan?

At least that's what you think.

That's what you become convinced of, in the end.

And then it happens – right out of the blue, you find yourself completely upended.

When we looked out the great bay window facing onto the terrace and who do we see there, laughing away in his hat, only that good old Mr Monroe, leaning across the hood of his convertible.

What could he want, we asked ourselves.

But didn't even dare to hope.

Because how could we ever – how, in God's name, could we ever expect to be bailed out by the likes of him?

By the likes of WW Monroe?

No chance.

But that, whether we knew it or not, was exactly what was already in the process of happening. Apparently we were the first to be selected as the subjects of some enlightened scheme or other.

That, at least, was the public story. But, given WW's well-known interest in gambling, and the fight game in particular, his motives may well have been a lot less altruistic than had been acknowledged at the time.

But, either way, he ended up liberating us and giving us both jobs in Kentuckyland racetrack and breeding farm as his apprentice grooms.

How could we, possibly, have believed our luck?

–I've decided to look after you on account of I knew your, father, young Kane, he declared as he drove us both away, and seen him fight once or twice, as a youngster myself. The Hero Chester, man what a slugger, a true-to-the-end-of-the-world goddamn pugilist. And, as for you, Wade Junior, when I first started out as a farmboy, I used to work in the fields with your old pop Marty. And your mother, son, I knew her too. One hell of a gentle creature was Tessie, before they were both tragically

taken from us in that heartbreaker of all fucking accidents –
pardon my language – out at the One Tree Crossroads.

After that, he had taken us under his wing permanently –
in Kentuckyland, as I say.

Which was the very first of its kind in the country.

Whose grounds were marked by pebbled plazas and walk-
ways, numbered horses idling in the shade of stately oaks as
its dark grandstands and towers of granite rose majestically
over the blanket bogs and forest plantations, their reflections
shimmering in the meandering waters of Ireland's central
lowlands of flat rolling plains dissected by bogs, loughs, rivers
and surrounded by low hills and mountains.

–Talk about the promised land, I remember Jody saying
as he threw his arm around me. We are one pair of sweet
motherfucking fortunate orphans – huh, amigo?

But not now.

With him lying there, half dead, in the darkness of a
miserable outhouse, a long way now from any promised
land.

With Red Campbell still standing there, snorting and
heaving above him, shadowboxing as he kicked up the dirt.

–So this is what it has come to, Red Campbell snarled,
the eye of his cigarette glowing away, the so-called greatest
bareknuckler in the county.

Campbell began muttering incoherently to himself, almost
as if Jody Kane wasn't present.

And then walked around, obsessively tugging at his little
thatch of beard.

–Who, in the glorious days of the early seventies, Red
Campbell continued, could ever have dreamed – who, in their
wildest imaginings, could have predicted such an outcome for
me, Red Campbell! Yes, for me – the one and only fucking Red!

He cleared his throat and aimed a wild, furious swipe at
nothing.

Then, quite unexpectedly, Red Campbell seemed surprisingly sad as he gripped the captive by the chin and yanked his head right back on his shoulders.

−You made a lotta mistakes in your life, Jody boy. But this is just about the worst thing you ever could have done. Because you really should not have tried to jack Mr Monroe over. No, that was a bad thing you and Wade had to do. Why did you have to listen to that snakeyed diamondback rattler, huh? And after everything WW did for you − all the kindness that he showed you, Mr Monroe … So now you gotta pay your dues, gypsy boy. You hearing me, Breed?

He riffled Jody's bloodsoaked hair, Red's single gold incisor glinting momentarily in the moonlight as he grinned:

−But I guess you're happy that it ain't gonna be very much longer now. And that soon, on this approaching velvet morning you, very shortly, will be breathing your last. Did you expect it to come so soon, old friend? Come on, little feller − you can tell your old Red. Because he's your tried and trusted friend. Tell him what it is that you dream about in the night − of a golden world, bright and shining in the purple morning …

−You been reading too many fucking books, spat Jody, maybe too many fucking books been coming your way. But which I have to admit comes as kind of a surprise, because I hadn't actually figured on you being able to do that. Read, I mean.

The moon stood impassive in the porthole window high above his head as Red Campbell groaned and began to grind his teeth, seeming pained.

−O you are a very unwise little fellow, Jody. O yes but you are the impudent smoke-and-horses little tinker boy. And which is why − even more than Wade − yes, even more than that diamondback fuck, you have got it coming mighty bad. Because it won't be very long now before Mr Begley comes walking right in, without a care, in through that door. And then we'll see what you're made of, deep inside. Yes, then we'll see just how much of a champion you are. Because I've seen, you see, what he can do, Tony Begley. I've seen him make harder nuts than you weep like sweet little girls. And tonight, my friend, that's gonna be you.

–It's not over yet, not by a fucking long shot, Campbell. So don't go making that fatal mistake. No, don't go counting chickens, Red, because that just might be the most serious fucking miscalculation ...

Red Campbell laughed and blew his nose before breaking into a broad, indulgent grin.

–You know something, Jody? You know something, smoke-and-horses? Somehow I don't happen to reckon you're right about that ...

He snorted again before turning on his heel and skipping lightly back up the concrete steps.

–No, somehow I fucking don't think so, champion, he shouted back.

Slamming the connecting door with his heel.

I managed to put up some kind of a show for him, Ray, Jody had written, but the harsh, bitter truth is that never in my life have I experienced anguish like it, but it wasn't just the pain of my body, you know? Such loneliness as came over me in there – with all the time I had to go back to places that I really didn't want to visit – where I found hurt I thought had been safely buried for a very long time. Forever, maybe.

I can clearly recall the return of Red Campbell back into the bar on that occasion – seeming troubled and resentful as he stumbled through the doorway, out of breath, looking combatively all around him.

Then I started imagining things again – that he was lifting his head towards the ceiling, where I lay curled up, with my knees tucked into my chest, the cold chills racing across my back and up the length of my spine.

As I observed him standing there, directly underneath me, just sitting there folding and unfolding his arms, with the folds of his eyes creasing up as he rocked, evenly, back and forth in the chair.

But finding himself, ultimately, unable to settle as he once more rose to his feet and, with his teeth still grinding, leaning against the heavy iron mantelpiece, staring into the embers of the fire.

Before softly remarking, to no one special:

–Maybe some velvet morning it might happen. And it'll all be golden in the purple morning. Some velvet morning when we wake, fellers. Yeah?

Repeating, obliviously, the words of the record.

–Some velvet morning when we ride, he whimpered, some velvet morning in that purple and golden dawn.

Retracing his steps once more – and, eventually, sitting down.

Chapter 8

Good Times

How can it happen, Ray, Jody had wondered, a heart turn around and break itself in pieces, the way it sometimes does, like Hank or Cline or any of them will tell you.

I don't know for certain, but this much I do.

Know, I mean.

That the hooch, the jungle, call it whatever you like – in the end it's going to ruin you.

Sure, for a while it might help, even banish your pain for a while.

But make no mistake, that day you've been dreading all along will come eventually.

I'm still terrified of it, to tell the honest truth.

All the same, I reckon that it's going to be OK. And there can be no doubt but that just keeping this journal, this 'spiritual' account – it really has been of the most enormous assistance. Maybe even, like Fr Conway says, the best, most important thing I've ever done.

The heart stripped bare, he calls it, the open wound.

—It's hard, father, I told him, it really can be difficult sometimes.

—No one said it was going to be easy, he told me, when did anyone ever say that?

—So keep on writing, Raymond, he advised me, and don't flinch from confronting whatever you find inside. Just remember that it couldn't have been easy for Hank Williams either, reaching down into his soul and coming up with the truth.

Back in Mervyn's Mountain Bar, well over an hour had elapsed since Red Campbell's return from the outhouse – and, thanks to the jungle juice, most likely, he had been laughing steadily for close on ten minutes. Yes, smiling and chuckling to himself as he stared, with a twinkle, right into the centre of the smouldering ashes before turning to look at each of his companions in turn.

—Yeah, Tony'll finish him all right, he suggested breezily. Tony'll finish him good and proper.

He looked down and examined his nails.

—Ain't that so, Mervyn?

—Uh-huh, replied the barman.

As Red smiled again, moving into a slanting shaft of moonlight.

—Hughie? he resumed.

—Yup, the small man nodded, producing a hankie. He began mopping his high gleaming forehead.

—Sonny? He'll finish him.

—Yes, if you say so. For sure, responded Hackett.

Big Barney's reaction Red appeared to take for granted.

Before, eventually, returning to Sonny.

—Because one thing for certain is – if Begley is anything he's a professional. Ain't that so, Sonny, wouldn't you say?

—Well sure, replied Sonny, I mean if you say it, Mr Campbell, then that must be the case. After all, you are the big authority. You are the main authority on everything. Ain't that so, Hughie?

—Ah now, gentlemen, here, pleaded Hughie. I mean we don't want any difference of opinion. Not tonight of all nights ...

—There ain't no difference of opinion, Sonny reassured him. None.

Red elected to pass no comment.

As Wee Hughie Munley grinned from ear to ear, seeming relieved by this response, as he folded the hankie and replaced it in his breast pocket.

—Aw shucks, he said, with his teeth showing and his shoulders rising and falling. Aw shucks.

—Aw shucks, he repeated again, with both eyes twinkling and his shoulders still shaking, laughing like it was just about the greatest joke in the world.

Except for the fact that no one else present was aware – of any joke, I mean.

But then, of course, that was Hughie.

Wee Hughie Munley, the flower of the flock.

Who, at his best, like everyone knew, could really and truly have you in stitches.

Something which he used to do all the time – way back in the old days at the factory, anyhow.

Yep, back in them old meat-packing days, in their late teens and early twenties, when they'd all been employed by Glasson County Meats – working together, as brothers, on the killing floor, close on thirty years ago now.

Back in the day when the Hombres, as they called themselves, back when they'd all been the closest of friends.

'Los Pistoleros' – ha ha, they used to laugh.

In those good times of the prosperous early seventies when everything had seemed so sweet and filled with promise.

Unlike now.

But then, that's the way.

Because things happen, don't they?

They change over time.

That's the way it just has to be …

It's always been like that.

That the water must, inevitably, flow on underneath the bridge.

But some folks they ain't so happy with it being like that – and Wee Hughie Munley, he was among them. Perhaps on account of the others, back then, they had always treated him kind of like the way you might a kid brother. And, what with him coming from a big family where he hadn't been paid a whole lotta attention, he appreciated that a great deal.

And so liked to be able to repay them with jokes.

–Aw shucks, he said again, looking around him with his big, circular, hopeful eyes.

As Red Campbell hauled a wallet of shag tobacco from his pocket.

–There won't be so much lip out of Mr Kane then, he promised, no not so much impudence out of the world champion boxer then, I reckon that is fair to say. Just as soon as Mr Tony comes around.

–He'll fix him, said Sonny, good and proper Tony Begley will fix him …

Red said nothing, inhaling a long luxurious drag of his rollup.

–He'll be quiet then, won't he? nodded Hughie, what do you say Barney?

Barney sighed and said yes he will.

As Sonny slapped his thigh and barked:

–That is, of course, whenever Begley at last does decide to honour us with his presence.

–I'm going to play a number on the juke, said Barney, so does any one of you good folks maybe have a request?

Nobody did.

Then the McHales announced they were all set for another game of pool.

As the balls came racketting into the well.

—Cookin', said Shorty, as a red sphere went skimming.

—Cookin', replied the Runt, looking along the length of his cue.

Click–clack–click, was all you could hear.

For quite a considerable period of time.

Before the barman coughed and they all looked over to hear Mervyn say:

—I think, if you don't mind, that you all ought to have one on the house ...

—One on the house? replied Sonny with a smile.

As the twins, although barely able to stand, began fencing boisterously with their sticks.

—Shotsa jungle all a-fucking round, they hollered. Yes please, barman, if you don't mind! Abso-fucking-freaking-mo-lutley!

As Big Barney, over at the jukebox, decided to make an announcement – standing there, huge, with the neon spangles decorating his face.

—I've decided what it is that I'm going to put on, he declared, pressing the buttons.

—Little green apples, sang Roger Miller.

Wondering, almost morbidly, whether or not, in Indianapolis, it rained.

—In the summertime, moaned Red Campbell softly, hiding his face in case anyone would see him.

And, after that, that was about as much as anyone could hear – what with the continuing racket the McHale brothers were making.

—Good times, they bellowed – and then went and shouted it out all over again:

—Good times ... yeah!

Before Sonny Hackett silenced them, by lifting a playful, mildly threatening fist.

As then all went quiet – just as before.

Chapter 9

Secrets, Songs and Shadows

In the drifting cloud of smoke that hovered three or four inches over the massive table, music was again the subject under discussion – who liked what and why and how much.

–Love songs, Barney Grue said, more than anything I reckon the best kind of love song is the one that tells a good story, you know? What I mean by that is the kinda tune that tells you things you didn't know – even about what's going on inside your own mind, that you find it hard to admit to, maybe. A troubled mind and confusion and all that kinda thing. The things that sometimes go wrong in your life and that you don't have no control over, you know?

–That's right, called Mervyn from his post behind the counter, I think that maybe you got it right there, Big B. The type of tunes that you're talking about there being the kind that go out of their way to try and teach you something. Ones that are, maybe, closer to our experience.

–That's exactly what I was trying to say, Mervyn – I wish I had the words.

Sonny now had almost turned genuinely sunny – as he swooshed back his forelock and raised his glass up on high.

—Hell if that compadre — if he didn't go and get it in one ...

There could be no mistaking Mervyn's gratification whenever he heard Sonny Hackett saying that — as that old barman stood proud and seeming even more statuesque than ever, impressively rangy in his striped blue collarless shirt and black waistcoat, and that silver mane of hair reaching all the way down his back.

Sonny, emboldened, was once more up on his feet, clicking away with his Cuban-heeled boots as he tugged up his collar and curled his lip, Elvis Presley style.

—So then, he declared, I take it then, gentle barman sir, that you wouldn't have any particular objection if I took the liberty of choosing me another little disc that might belong to the category we just been talking about? Even though I'm aware of the circumstances and that, strictly speaking, we oughtn't to be doing anything like this at all ...

The barman folded his cloth and sighed as he sympathetically shook his weary head.

—That's all right, Mr Hackett sir — be assured that I understand the situation perfectly. And also that I ain't got no objection whatsoever to you playing music as a kind of balm to settle your jangling nerves, which, given the circumstances, I guess they gotta be. Jangling, I mean.

Nobody quite knew what to say to that, least of all Hackett.

As the pool balls went: ker-plunk!

And: thlack!

—I'm fed up with this game! Shorty McHale announced, flushing deeply. Do you know what I think, our fellow? That maybe you and me should think about heading home.

He looked at his brother, but his brother said nothing.

—This jungle's raw — I think it's making me feel sick ... complained Shorty again.

—Well then, don't drink it. C'mon and we'll finish the game.

Ker-plunk ...

Thwack ...

The balls were going nowhere, missing their target every time. The Runt obstreperously flung down his cue and sat for a minute on a beer keg, trembling.

–What's the matter? he heard Shorty ask. What's the fucking problem now?

The atmosphere around the table was subdued and quiet. Then Big Barney looked up and announced:

–Porter Wagoner.

–What about fucking Porter Wagoner? demanded Red.

–Yeah – Porter Wagoner. What about him? shouted Sonny Hackett.

Big Barney looked a little embarrassed as he turned away with burning cheeks.

–No, urged Sonny, we'd like to hear. What is it you want to say?

–Yeah, come on Barney – tell us about Porter Wagoner, Red Campbell agreed. Get on back here, friend …

–Yep, amigo, interjected Wee Hughie, turtle-nodding again as he rubbed his hands vigorously, you can take it from Hughie that that is a fact.

Very slowly, Big Barney began to turn around, averting his eyes. Before, still wary, explaining:

–There's this song that he sings – it goes by the name of 'The Carroll County Accident'.

–It goes by the name of – what? asked Hughie.

–It goes by the name of 'The Carroll County Accident', hollered Mervyn from the bar, it's one heckofa mighty famous tune, I got to tell you.

–Well, I never heard of it, Sonny Hackett protested.

–Neither did I, said Red, shaking his head.

As they all began arguing over the song, the hooch having pretty much taken them over.

With Mervyn coming over, laughing as he emptied the overstuffed ashtray, telling them that they'd argue over the skinning of a flea.

—And then dispute over the hide and tallow, he chortled good-naturedly.

And then – unusually for him – lit up a rollie of his own and sat down to join them.

—I've just got me an idea, he began, although it might be one that you boys find a little unusual and hard to accept. However, why don't we just try it? Yep, just for once, why don't you boys try listening to one another? Because I think that might be a very welcome and interesting departure.

—Now you are talking sense, Mr Walker, Big Barney Grue beamed, licking some beads of jungle off his moustache and hoisting his britches up over his enormous girth before hauling himself away from the table across the floor, as the record machine leaped into life.

It was Porter Wagoner.

—Who sure does paint a mighty unusual picture, mused the barman, with that old head of his, swear to God, thinner than a peanut and that great big duck's ass sweep of hair thrown back off of his head, stiff as a stilt in that glittering red rhinestone suit o' his.

—Yeah, now I remember where I seen him, Hughie Munley exclaimed. It was on *The Grand Old Opry*, on the telly one Saturday night.

—Very well then. So I suggest, for once, that you all just bend your ear and listen, suggested Mervyn.

And which, surprisingly, they did.

—Porter Wagoner, Wee Hughie Munley nodded approvingly, Porter Wagoner.

As the clean steel guitar clipped jauntily along, as though impatient to get down to the business of delivering its important message.

—That sure is one mighty fine kicker of a tune all right, observed Red. I definitely got to hand it to you there, Mr

Walker, you were right — because them's good words. Although I got to admit that I ain't altogether sure what they mean.

The older man gravely shook his head.

—Very well then, I'll tell you, he said, I'll tell you, Red, because I think it addresses a very important and pertinent subject — that of the secrets that small little out-of-the-way places can hold. Places where — so often, as I'm sure you know — no one has really figured just what exactly's going on. O sure, they got a kind of an idea. And they got their suspicions. But they know in their hearts that they ain't got it pegged. Not *really*, if you know what I mean?

All of a sudden, Red Campbell appeared once more quite agitated as he looked all about him, this way and that.

—How exactly, Red began hoarsely, what precisely do you mean by that, Mervyn — because, to be honest with you, I don't think I really understand.

Mervyn nodded and leaned across the table.

—The narrative in question, he began to explain, it essentially told the story of a road accident which had taken place just outside the county line, in a small town in the middle of America. Where decent people lead God-fearing lives.

—Leastways they were supposed to be, he added morosely.

Then he gathered his thoughts.

—You see, Mervyn continued, what we are talking about in this song here, regrettably, is adultery, Red. Yep, that reliable steady old perennial when folks, to their shame, they been playing back door bogus. And here, of all places, roundabout Carroll County, which is just about as law-abiding and God-fearing as you can get. And no place to be slipping outta the trades if you got yourself a morsel o' sense. But then that's a commodity that us vulnerable human beings don't, in the end, seem to possess a whole lot of. Which is why, when it come to it, these two folks they paid the same price as everyone does for transgression and lying and cheating – they lost their lives in what seemed to be an accident. But then we got no guarantee about that, do we?

He smiled and narrowed those kind, baggy eyes as he spread his aged hands on the table.

Sighing regretfully, long and hard, as he proceeded.

–Because I guess that's always gotta be the way in the wind-up, ain't it fellers? Whether we care to admit it or not. That in places such as that old unfortunate Carroll County – and which ain't a whole lot different to hereabouts, let's face it – what we got ourselves is a whole mess of dangerous secrets and murky shadows. O boy, the secrets that we keep.

Sonny grabbed the bottle and decided all that was horseshit.

–I don't know what you're talking about, he said.

As Mervyn smiled and gripped him by the arm, applying just a little bit of pressure as he faced him.

–That's surprising. Yes, that surprises me, Mr Hackett. Because it's not all that complicated, really. I mean it's not like I'm trying to make some real big statement or something here. All I'm saying is that, all of us, we got our quiet, unspoken-of corners.

Then he turned around and smiled at Red.

–Do you like it, Mr Campbell – do you like that song? he said to him. That tune we just played – do you like it, Red?

–No, Red retorted, sullenly avoiding Mervyn's penetrating gaze, as a matter of fact I don't. Because I don't have the foggiest what it's supposed to be about.

–A little matchbox circled with a rubber band, the barman explained, that was what they found underneath the dashboard. And right there inside of it, a golden wedding band. Now what was that doing in there, do you think?

–I don't know, Red Campbell replied, I don't know anything about rings or dashboards. And I don't care much, to tell you the God's honest truth. Anyway, it's only a song.

—Was there matches in the box as well, or just the ring? quizzed Wee Hughie Munley anxiously, feeling unbelievably dumb just as soon as he'd opened his mouth.

Everyone looked at him, and he wished the sawdust and the floor would swallow him up completely.

Sometimes that happened – he said the first thing that came into his mind.

Impossibly calm, Mervyn had decided to finish the story.

—So that was it – a dark sin had been committed and everyone in the county knew that that was the case. But the truth was destined never to come out. Because that's what happens in songs that have secrets. Do you know what I'm saying?

—So nobody was ever the wiser, were they not Mervyn? Wee Hughie choked, doing his best to get back in the game.

—That's right. And life went on just as it had before.

—Just as if nothing had ever happened, nodded Hughie, visibly relaxing.

Big Barney Grue seemed tired, tugging agitatedly at the matted strands of his beard.

—And no one ever got to know the truth, concluded Mervyn.

Then the barman did the strangest thing – rose up to his full height and began laughing uncontrollably.

And I can remember at that point coming almost close to capitulating and giving the game away – betraying my presence upstairs, I mean – because I just didn't think I could bear the tension.

As I watched the barman, in silence, just standing there with his two arms folded and his aged eyes wrinkling as he smiled and said – to himself, it seemed:

—Do you see that willow?

Its leaves were brushing, ever so gently, against the glass.

Red Campbell lifted his eyebrow as he half-turned towards the window and replied:

—So it's a willow — what about it? he said irksomely. It's there every night …

—I'll often find myself wondering about it — but not just that. Plants in general …

—What do you mean, complained Red, plants in general?

Then he got up and strolled over to the counter.

—So what if it's a willow? So what about plants? Huh?

Mervyn Walker remained implacable, electing to remain silent for quite a considerable period of time. Before, eventually, continuing:

—There was this book I read and it said in there — it said in that book: that, just like us, plants have their secrets.

Sonny Hackett firmly rapped the table.

—Ah here now — quit. Stop it, you hear, this dumb talk …

—Hur hur, chuckled Hughie, did youse hear the one about the talking plant?

But Mervyn Walker wasn't smiling.

If anything now, he looked extremely grave.

—I was just wondering, he continued, I was just wondering, Red — or any of you, as a matter of fact — might have any views on that particular subject?

Red had had about enough, he announced.

—Listen here, he began, as far as I'm concerned this conversation is going nowhere. First it was songs that mean nothing and now it's plants. And I'm sorry if it happens to bother you, Mr Walker, but I really have to tell you that right now I don't figure that I appreciate a great deal of what we been talking about in the last twenty or so minutes. Especially not now — not tonight. Not in a situation like the one we got ourselves into here.

His fingers were trembling as he reached for his wallet of shag, clearly in anticipation of the barman's response.

Only to find himself surprised – if not, in fact, amazed – to look up from his pouch of tobacco to see the barman grinning fiercely right into his face.

–For heaven's sake, man, can't you tell that I'm only joking. Or what is wrong with you? laughed Mervyn Walker.

–There's nothing wrong with him. He's just on edge, like the rest of us, waiting for you-know-who to come. If he had stuck to his word and come at the time he said he was coming, then everything would have been fine. And nobody'd be going on like Campbell, grinding those stupid choppers!

–So what if I happen to do things with my teeth? What business is that of yours, Hackett?

–Gets on my nerves so it does, and you've always been doing it. You always used to do in the factory so you did …

Wee Hughie got between them, pale and clearly alarmed, as he called out to the barman:

–Do you hear the two lads? God but things don't change very much, do they Mervyn? They were always bickering on the floor, God help them …

–Only when he started that hateful fucking grinding! spat Sonny, that accursed, cunting noise …!

–What noise? I don't hear anyone else complaining about noise …

To avoid any further disagreement, Hughie began searching in his pockets for coins – with which he sometimes performed diverting tricks.

But, right then, he couldn't seem to locate any.

Finding himself taken aback as he was roughly pushed to one side by Sonny Hackett, who was in the middle of glaring at Red Campbell as he passed.

–One of these days, I swear to you, Campbell …

–I was wondering, choked Hughie, did I ever tell youse the joke about the three wells?

—No you didn't, Sonny replied, and please don't bother for none of us want to hear it.

—*Well well well*, squealed Wee Hughie, with such a degree of fervour that his small round face was beginning to turn a dangerous-looking blue.

Chapter 10

The Story of Mickey
Wrong Moon

This bad feeling between you and me, Jody wrote, it can't go on forever and I know, same as me, that you understand that, Ray – and that's why I want you to know absolutely everything that I went through that night, both in the outhouse and the bar later on, just so as you and me can be honest and straight and direct with one another. In a way that we haven't been able to do for years.

Because one thing is for sure, Ray, he went on, there ain't gonna be anyone else on this earth who is gonna be able to understand what we been through and all the trouble the two of us has seen together.

But you go through life, don't you Ray, old friend, and you deal with things the best that you can, hopefully coming around in the end to see that if things are gonna work out at all, then what you got to do is be true to yourself. I've come to see that now, I guess, and I'm happy about it. I think it's important, though, at this point, to be straight – and to let you know that it was my special partner, my irreplaceable soulmate Greta Mae who suggested that I sit down and write this letter to you. And I pray that, in spite of whatever recent hardship you've undergone, that you'll understand what her reasons might be. Because there ain't nobody, man or woman, who hasn't had it difficult one way or another.

Most of all, I really and truly do genuinely hope that you don't mind too much me going into all of this explicit detail about what went through my mind in that stinking hellhole tumbledown shack where they dumped me – and don't get it into your head that any of what I say is intended as any form of accusation or score-settling, for believe you me, whatever it might be, it most expressly is not that.

All I am trying to do is, once and for all, my best to get things straight in my head – and, hopefully, after all these years, leave all the bitter memories of Glasson County far behind us both.

I would also like to say to you, Ringo, that if you do manage to get it together and decide in the end to take up my invitation and come over here to visit us, that what you'll find waiting for your inspection right here in Sweetwater is a garden and golden country, the most wondrous and magical estate as you could ever in your wildest dreams imagine.

And to give you some idea, as I sit here penning these coupla words on my knee, the light all around me – it's just about as pure and clear as gin, old amigo. Everywhere you can smell the scent of something perfumed coming up, such as jasmine or maybe the fragrance of the noble magnolia itself in full bloom. Somehow, friend, this here county it gets right down into your blood. Over time it bathes you.

When you do eventually get around to figuring that the time has arrived for you to get on board that plane, and you've finally laid all the troubles of your past to rest, then get on up there and haul that body o' yours right on over here to Georgia state. My love, be assured, has already heard all about you. And is more than aware that whatever might have happened in the bygone days of yore, that you and me we once were two loyal vaqueros, best compadres – and nothing anyone can do or say will ever change that. OK then, having said all that, I reckon it's time for me to get up and go. So stay in touch, my friend, and let me know whatever's going on.

Even now, after all this time, I can see him vividly, crouched in the stultifying gloom of that tumbledown wreck – shivering, a hideous patchwork of bruises, his hands bound with cable ties behind his back.

Rising to his feet and stumbling as best he can around that damp, weed-covered earthen floor – in among the truck tyres and beer crates stinking of stale ale, in the swelling shadow of the bulky propane gas tank. As the generator hummed and droned steadily on, over and over, almost taunting him, drilling right into his head.

With Jody doing his very damnedest to try and stay wake, and his stomach turning itself inside out like a glove.

High in the corner of that suffocating prison, in a tiny porthole window, he would watch as the moon took stock of the brooding Glasson hills.

Flooding the boxer's sturdy, muscular frame with light, and illuminating his square rugged jaw.

The hideous swelling was still visible above his left eye; he reckoned he had lost at least three teeth.

–I'm going to end up at the bottom of Lake Wynter, he told himself, that's where they're going to ditch me. Because there's no other way it can possibly end.

Shuddering violently as he overheard a sudden, unexpected surge in the conversation in the bar, beyond the wall – underpinned by a soaring crescendo of a church organ and piano, tambourine and background choir ascending from the jukebox as Elvis Presley lamented the sorrows of the South.

—*Look away, look way ...*

Then, all of a sudden the music stopped abruptly and he heard the sound of Red Campbell's piercing laughter.

—Yeah, that old Elvis – you really got to hand it to him, he hollered. For beside him no one got that slapback rhythm, not even Jerry Lee Lewis, yup ...

—What would you know about Jerry Lee Lewis? Sonny Hackett challenged. Now all of a sudden Campbell's an authority on The Killer as well ...

—Ah here now, Wee Hughie Munley interrupted, we've been through all of that already. Surely there's room for every opinion – so, as Barney says, come on ladies, try and ease up!

—That is right and correct, called out Mervyn, and on account of you making that wise observation, I'm gonna be extra generous and fill up your glasses one more time for nothing. Absolutely no charge, gents.

—Shotsa jungle all around, shouted Hughie, ecstatic.

As Big Barney Grue suddenly erupted into life, having spent the past half an hour snoring.

I could see him perfectly in the light – trying not to make a sound as I shifted my position.

In that high-pitched voice, slapping his thighs and heaving his mighty bulk forward, hearing him declare:

—Now you are talking my language, Mervyn Walker. Let's get one last shot down before that old Begley comes.

—Sure, agreed the barman, looking at his watch, then cocking an eyebrow before addressing himself directly to Barney:

—What time exactly did he say he was coming?

Big Barney looked blank and stared across the table at Sonny.

Who, in his turn, inclined his gaze towards Hughie.

−Whenever he was finished his work is all I know, said Hughie, with his observation followed by a protracted silence.

As the barman delivered the promised free drinks, setting them down on the table with a flourish.

−Shots for all, one two three and four is Sonny's, he said.

−Gracias, said Hackett, performing a spontaneous little jig with his Cubans as the light of the moon leaped nimble against the rim of each standing glass.

Sonny produced a comb and ran it thoughtfully through his brilliant, jet-black hair.

−This much I know for sure, he began, he definitely said that he'd make it before dawn.

−And what time is it now? broke in the Runt. Because I feel lousy. I want to go home. Do you feel like going home, our boy?

−Just one more game and then we'll hightail it for sure, his brother agreed, because I know how you're feeling. I know you're feeling bad, our boy.

−You're not going anywhere, warned Sonny, nowhere at all − that's where you're going. Do you want your old man to be ashamed? You want to tarnish your father's memory?

−It'll only be another hour at the most, promised Red, so just let's get this game under way and then go.

−Like fuck, growled Hackett, you pay attention to what I'm saying now.

As one two three four five cards wildly fluttered.

And the barman went back to staring at his willow, just watching as it brushed this way and that.

Folding his arms, and thinking about something only he would ever be aware of.

Someplace far away.

That no one in Glasson County was ever gonna know about.

All the things that wise old-stager had seen, down the years.

And which, you could tell were still on his mind as he came down to the table to gather up the ashtrays.

Before returning again to his station behind the bar.

—Hey, called Sonny, what you looking at?

Then he laughed.

—I say — what you staring at up there, Mervyn?

—You know, murmured Mervyn, barely audible under his breath, whether us simple folks are aware of it or not — or choose not to be — it is inevitable that soon there must come a time when each of us must face his mortal due.

—What'n the hell's he blathering about now? complained Sonny.

—Did I ever tell youse the one about Mickey Wrong Moon? Hughie interrupted. I was wondering did I ever tell you that story?

—Mickey who? said Red.

—O it's a right while ago now, I have to admit. I was doing roadie for all the bands, do you see, at the time — The Freshmen, The Plattermen, Gregory and the Cadets — all them ones. Anyhow, we were playing the marquee this summer's night in Longford and what's he supposed to be singing only an old-time set, a waltz by Frank Sinatra. 'Blue Moon', it was called — I wonder did any of youse ever happen to hear of it. Anyway, just as soon as the music starts up what's he doing there holding the microphone and squawking away — as God is my judge, you never heard the like of it — only making matters worse by it not being the proper song at all. Because, do you see, what the fool has gone and started up singing is not 'Blue Moon', but a completely different tune entirely. I mean, can you believe it? Yes, as God as my judge, if the complete and utter imbecile he hasn't gone and started into a completely different tune — aye, 'Moon River'! Singing about the completely wrong fucking moon. I mean, honest to God lads, did you ever hear the like?

But no one was listening, giving all of their attention to the cards.

As Hughie slunk over, in silence, to the window, and found himself privately regretting ever coming near Mervyn's Mountain Bar – or to have even bothered trying to amuse them by telling a joke either.

Maybe he wasn't all that funny, he thought. That was what they used to tell him at school, anyway. We're sick of all your dumb funny stories, Patches Munley, so why don't you just go over there to the corner of the yard and tell them to the wall, for nobody around here is interested.

Go on, Munley – get on back up to Hickory Holler where you live with your mom and all them easy sisters o' yours.

Patches, that was what they had used to call him, because he always used to wear these dumb flapping britches. Which used to have so many squares sewn into them by his mother they would almost remind you of the baggy pants that a circus clown might find himself decked out in.

–But I can't even be that, croaked Hughie, wringing his hands, craning his neck as he peered out the window.

No, I can't even be a clown in the Big Top, he thought.

As he shuddered and confided silently that he regretted the day he had ever met them, especially on account of what they had gotten him involved in all those years ago, in the seventies.

That night when the moon had turned to blood over Glasson.

And now, as far as Wee Hughie was concerned, when all of this at last was over, and the famous Tony Begley had been and gone, he hoped he never saw any of them again.

Chapter 11

The Glasson County Accident

Where a murder most foul had once been perpetrated – a long time ago, in the dark heart of the mid 1970s – a deed of dark and damning atrocity. With everyone present around the heavy oaken table having slyly convinced themselves that what had taken place on that 'unfortunate occasion' had been a completely unanticipated calamity – a quite dreadful and shameful, bitterly regretted accident.

But an accident nonetheless.

That night on the farm belonging to Wilson Gillis, a loyal, God-fearing Protestant farmer, in a time when such things tended to happen, during the time of the trouble and strife.

They had only gone out there for one reason, they told themselves – to get their hands on the moolah he'd got stashed there.

That was all they'd wanted, they said.

But Wilson Gillis insisted on putting up a fight.

Quoting the bible and roaring it back at them, and acting generally like a man possessed and doing the best he could to wrestle the gun from Red Campbell's grasp, as he vowed that retribution for this act would one day be paid.

—For the evil that men do lives after them, he had cried, and that what they reap in this house or any other they shall surely have to sow.

And it was at that point the double-barrelled shotgun had been accidentally discharged.

And, before they could even gather themselves to find out what was happening, they were running after one another through the farmyard and down the lane past the howling sheepdog, in a state of hopeless disarray and panic.

All of them.

Hughie

Barney

Sonny Hackett

&

Red.

Leaving Wilson Gillis bleeding to death on the cold stone flags of his kitchen floor, crying out hoarsely through the wide-open door:

—Believe you me but there will one day come a time when this night will return to visit you in your inglorious dreams. Aye, and haunt you, each and every one of you that has come to this Saviour-pledged abode. For the evil that men do lives on after them, and let none of you that has done this begin to think otherwise …

That was happened on the night of the Glasson County Murder.

Or the Glasson County Accident.

Depending on your point of view.

Chapter 12

The Wonderful World
of Jim Reeves

Red, in his worn-down boots and scruffy army cap, was drumming steadily on the top of the juke-machine, thinking to himself out loud.

−I love that one, they heard him softly acknowledge to himself − to their surprise, it was 'Peace in the Valley' − before adding that the King, he could move him so much that, at times, he could actually draw tears from his eyes.

−I'll shed them, on occasion, like petals from a rose, they heard him murmur, rubbing the small thatch of his chin beard, absentmindedly, with his fist.

−Did you ever hear of a dog being a ghost? asked Hughie, out of nowhere − with his teeth, not unexpectedly, prominently displayed − and a strange fearfulness evident in his eyes.

Sonny Hackett winced and looked over at him, scoffing impatiently.

−You been at all o' this already, Patches − and I told you, give it a rest. You start anymore of that dumb foolish talk, and I swear to God, I'm gonna go over there and knock you down. Because, if you ask me – if you wanna know something, Hughie – I don't reckon that you're able for this jungle. It's gettin' to ya. So come on and ease up. Ease up, I'm telling you now. And quit any more of that crazy thinking.

Hughie's eyes were like mis-cued pool balls and his speech was now profoundly slurred.

He refused to be deterred, however.

–Well that may be your opinion, Sonny, he countered, yes that might be your opinion for sure, and that's OK. But you want to know what I think? Yes, would you like to know what my opinion is? Then here it is – Sonny, I think you're wrong. At least, that is, if the famous crooner Jim Reeves is to be believed.

–Jim Reeves? snapped Sonny. What have you got to start talking about him for? What has an old-time crooner that everybody has long since forgotten about, what could he have to do with anything? I don't get it, Munley.

–Gentleman Jim to you, bristled Hughie, who just happened to be one of the finest country singers ever. Yes, a velvet-voiced chanter of that good old down-home style. A proper gentleman – that's what he was. We used to have this picture of him over the fire. I can still see it now, so I can, when I think about it. With that kind face smiling like he's everybody's friend. As he looks down and says: I've built us a world where we can all be happy. Would you like to come in?

–That sounds good, Hughie, yep sure does – where everyone can be happy. That's good. But it's also a lot of loco bull. And, as I said before, if you don't stop running off at the mouth with all this sideways baloney, then I'll … I'm warning you now, Patches – I'll …

But he never got around to saying what it was he was going to do. For, right at that moment, Red Campbell had got up and was starting to grind his teeth again.

Sonny lifted his elbow and shot Red Campbell the filthiest of looks, swallowing the remaining contents of his glass in a single gulp.

But Red's gaze, in its uncompromising ferocity, impressively matched his.

With Wee Hughie just sitting there, describing the world in which Kimberely Jim, as he called him, lived.

−*The Wonderful World of Jim Reeves*. We used to have that record, Red. 'Peace in the Valley' was on it, as a matter of fact, and if you'd like to know he sang it even better than Elvis. With that voice of his like velvet.

−The tune that he sang about the dogs was on it, recalled Red, I remember it well.

−What fucking dogs? Big Barney sharply demanded, as he shot up in his chair. What song is this about dogs? What dogs?

−The one where the faithful terrier gets killed but comes back, explained Wee Hughie, Old Tige was his name. There's a story that they tell about Jim when he was driving − down in Texas where he comes from − one where he nearly runs over the fellow dressed all in white.

−Maybe it was Colonel Sanders, shouted Shorty, ask him to give us a snackbox ha ha.

−I never heard tell of any of that, said Big Barney, are you sure?

−Yes, all in white he was, Wee Hughie continued, and what happens is Jim slams on the brakes and nearly runs him over. He jumps out of the car and started looking all around, but can't find anyone. He thought that maybe the person had gone ahead on down the road, so he started driving very slowly looking for him, figuring that he must surely have been injured. Then he came upon a bridge that had been washed out by a raging river. And realised that, and for the rest of his life continued to believe it, that who he had been saved by was his guardian angel.

Then the twins returned, slamming the pub door loudly behind them. They had gone outside briefly, searching in vain for Begley.

–He isn't there, they shouted angrily. There isn't a fucking sign of him no-place!

Red, unconsciously, was still making the noise with his teeth.

Sonny repeated that he couldn't take it.

–One of these days, they heard him hiss, one of these accursed days, Mr Campbell …

–Anyway, that was the story behind Old Tige, concluded Hughie, the story behind the faithful dog who was a ghost.

Sonny broke and lifted a bottle, levelling it threateningly at Hughie.

–One final time, do you hear me Munley? One last time I'll tell you, you hear? That, faithful or not, dogs don't have fucking ghosts. Say that after me. Say it, damn you!

–Dogs, obliged Hughie, dogs don't have ghosts.

–That's right. Dogs don't have no fucking ghosts, Sonny. Say it directly into my face. Say it, I told you!

–Dogs don't have no fucking ghosts, Sonny Hackett.

–That's more like it, said Sonny, setting the bottle down, relieved.

As Wee Hughie Munley covered his eyes with his trembling right hand, not able to admit it, but feeling utterly, quite ashamed.

Chapter 13

The Indian in the Caravan

With five or six empty jungle glasses in front of him, Sonny Hackett shot forward abruptly and let out a shriek, knocking over a tray of bottles in the process.

—Would you like to know who's to blame for it all? It's the Indian's fault – it's him that I fucking blame!

As over came Mervyn armed with a dustpan.

—Because there ain't no one else to answer for it only him, Sonny Hackett continued, his dark eyes flitting wildly. That's the long and the short of it.

—What's that? Hughie stuttered. What was that you were saying about Indians, Sonny?

Wee Hughie was sitting up, ramrod-stiff.

—What? Who? Which? Why, Sonny? he repeated. What was that you were talking about just there … ?

Sonny Hackett was inhaling very heavily, his dark, narrow face now patterned with an assortment of roseate blotches.

—The Indian, I told you, that's who I was talking about – you fucking deaf, Patches?

Big Barney shifted his buttocks and pulled in his chair, resting his chin on his hand as he squinted.

—Which Indian would this be? he wondered, folding his enormous arms. Because I don't really know who it is you're talking about, Sonny.

Then the colour began draining very slowly out of Sonny Hackett's face as he extended his hand to pick up a card.

Which he turned over once, then again, twice. Before, yet again, scrutinising it acutely.

Or, at least, appearing too.

But, in actual fact, paying very little real attention at all.

Then it was Hughie's turn to speak.

—If you don't mind me asking, the small man began hesitantly, what exactly are you doing with that card, Sonny? Because, if you ask me, it seems to me like you don't know exactly.

—Ha ha, the funny man is getting all lippy, laughed Sonny, he's getting all lippy, the funny man is.

As he left down the card in question.

—You sure have got to hand it to Hughie, laughed Shorty McHale uncertainly, for if there is anyone around here who can laugh and make a joke, it's him. Ain't it, our boy?

—Yes, agreed the Runt, that's it for sure — jokes. Yeah, Hughie.

—Did you hear him just now? Sure is a good Hughie-style joke. What are you doing with that card there, Sonny, for it seems to me that you don't know what exactly you're supposed to be doing with it. Haw, Hughie, you sure are some comedian. Right, our fella?

—He's the funniest man in Glasson. And that's for certain sure, Shorty — yeah, Hughie.

Wee Hughie Munley got up and stared at both of them.

—Think you're all the hard men, is that what you think? Think you can come around here and laugh at me as you please? Laugh at me, and call me Patches, huh?

—It's only a joke, said the Runt, staggering awkwardly.

—Aye. That's all it is, agreed Shorty, slurring his words, not antin' else.

Sonny Hackett wasn't listening to a word they were saying, being much too preoccupied giving his attention to …

Well, as a matter of fact, listening to himself.

In an extremely private and distant place that was a very long way from Mervyn's Mountain Bar. And, indeed, from everyone in it.

—It's to do with the trouble that the two of us had in the early days of our marriage, Sonny murmured, after she gave birth to our very first child.

As he persisted with that strange, glazed look, picking away at a beermat.

—Some of the women who used to come and visit, they started telling her not to mind the priests, what the priests had to say. That they don't belong in the world anymore. Because all they'll do is fill you full of out-of-date talk. So what you got to do, Mrs Hackett, yes what you want to do now is go out and visit the Indian in the caravan. Because he knows it all. He has bells and sits on a mat for hours.

—A mat? Big Barney interjected abruptly. Is that what he said?

As he leaned forward, with every muscle in those enormous arms contracting.

And stared right at Sonny.

—Now you listen and you listen to me good. You pay attention to me here, Sonny Hackett. You listen to me, Sonny, and I'll give him mats and bells. What are they giving Indians permission to come around here for anyway? Tell me this, my friend – when zackly did all this start?

But it was more than evident that Sonny wasn't listening to Big Barney.

Being too preoccupied trying to find expression for his thoughts.

Sonny proceeded.

−It's on account of the Indian that she gave our son that stupid fucking name, Cosmo. Cosmo − that's what he's known as now, I'm afraid − I mean, can you believe it, Barney? I'm worried about him, fellers, I really and truly am. I genuinely am now, I won't tell youse a word of a lie. O God. O Christ. Is there any sign of Begley out there?

The beermat he'd been holding was now shredded into pieces.

−You know what he did only the other week, he resumed, as he wiped his forehead, when we brought him off to the seaside? He sat in the car and refused to come out. This lovely little child with the sweetest smile as pale as death now with his little blond pudding-bowl haircut. No Daddy, he kept on repeating − no, Daddy, I'm not coming out. And I'm definitely not going down there to the shore because the sea is filled with dead men, he kept on saying. Of course my wife said nothing − she thought it was great. Same as the Indian in the caravan when she told him about it, banging his tambourine and saying that our son was special.

He lowered his head and for a long time said nothing.

Before lifting it again and picking at his teeth with the point of one of the tiny cardboard pieces.

−Then what happened. She started saying that it was me who was to blame. And that I had a reputation, same as all of our family. O aye, the Hacketts, she used to say − och sure everyone knows about them. Yes, the Hacketts. And I admit that some of what she said was true. I mean, I won't even pretend that they didn't used to say certain things about me at school. When I was in fourth or fifth class, when I used to like to hang around on my own. And when the teacher started saying that it could be that perhaps I was in some sort of category all of my own. And that, like one or two others in the Hacketts, maybe I was what they called 'special'. It was after that then that they said they were going to have me examined. Yes, Master Hackett, we're going to have you tested, they kept on saying.

He fumbled for a cigarette and lit it as best he could.

His sleeve was completely covered in ash.

—I had to write it all down on this great big yellow pad with lines, all the things that came into my mind, including everything about the shirts.

—Shirts? What shirts? asked Big Barney. Which shirts now would this be?

—I was duty bound to tell them the whole truth, they warned me, and I wasn't to hold anything back. But then when you do, they use it against you. I should never have told them anything about it.

—What did you tell them? asked Barney. Take your time Sonny.

—About how they used to come and strangle me in the night.

—Strangle you, said Barney, but how?

—They'd come out of the wardrobe just before I fell asleep.

He looked directly at Barney.

—It isn't any use. It's a total waste of time. Because I can tell by the way you're looking that you're thinking the very same as them. And there's no point in trying to tell me different because it's there, I can see it. I can see it, Big Barney – right there in your eyes.

—I'm afraid that I think you're mistaken, Barney protested, because there isn't anything to see in my eyes.

—Yes there is, insisted Sonny Hackett. You may not know but yes, there is. The very same as them, back then.

He tapped his cigarette repeatedly into the tray.

—That's what makes her say it, I suppose. The fact that she knows all this stuff about our family, all our history and the things that happened to us years ago. Yes, that's probably what makes her come out with all these hurtful things, always insisting that it's our family is responsible for what's been happening to Cosmo. She says that the Hacketts were always odd. Queer from the very day they're born, she says. But it's not true, Barney, and it isn't fair. Not when it comes from a woman who goes running around the country, baring her soul to Indians in caravans. What are you looking at, Campbell – why are you laughing?

He clenched both fists and glared across at Red, who suddenly began once more to grind his teeth. Ducking sideways in anticipation of a blow from Sonny's clenched fist.

But that didn't happen.

As Sonny Hackett sighed and tugged up the collar of his black leather jacket, like he was doing his best to hide in behind it. Now he was whispering again, trying his best not to twitch as he continued:

–I just don't care what anyone says – because I know in my heart that it just isn't fair. You ask anyone, Barney, go on – and anyone else that is sitting here around this table. You ask any person that's got a mind to be fair, and I guarantee that they'll tell you this – that although the Hacketts didn't have much by way of riches or property in this world, they were well known to be intelligent and brainy. My great-grandfather was a genius at languages, in case you didn't know. In a big university in Dublin. It's true – you can verify it if you want.

His eyes blazed with an unnatural fire.

–Because if youse don't believe me, then all you got to do is take a look at what I got here in my hands. Here – go on, take a look. Don't be afraid, it's not going to bite.

He began awkwardly unfolding a crumpled scrap of a blue-lined exercise-book paper he pressed first on Barney and which they then began to, gradually, pass around.

–Our little Cosmo wrote all of that – everything in it came right out of his own little head. The teacher says that he never seen anything like it.

Giving the note just a cursory glance, Red Campbell impatiently pushed it on, already in the process of doing his best to erase its memory – that of the crude and childishly pencilled representation of a group of weary-looking men bent over double, lashed to the perimeter of a grey stone grinding wheel, enduring their punishment under brooding, remorseless skies.

–Here, he snapped, and handed it over to Hughie.

Wee Hughie turned pale and said that it meant absolutely nothing.

–It means squat to me, he vexedly proclaimed, once again dismissing it with a contemptuous flap of his fingers.

–Give it over here to me, Barney Grue insisted.

Snatching it gruffly as he began to read aloud, in his trademark falsetto, with each word being dragged like a fish-hook along his gut.

The small piece of paper was trembling in his enormous hairy fingers, at times to such an extent that he had no choice but to recruit both hands in order for it to remain still.

The handwriting underneath the drawing was crude.

But nonetheless eminently legible.

As Big Barney Grue, ever so tentatively, began reading the contents aloud:

> *Here saw I people, more than elsewhere, many,*
> *On one side and the other, with great howls*
> *Rolling weights forward by main force of chest.*

> *They clashed together, and then at that point*
> *Each one turned backward, rolling retrograde,*
> *Crying: 'What do you think it is that you're doing?'*

> *And then, upon the next return:*
> *'What do you think you are doing – you murderer!'*

Thus they returned along the lurid circle
On either hand unto the opposite point
Shouting their shameful metre evermore.

−I don't like this, complained Big Barney Grue, placing the paper on the table in front of him. I'm afraid I have to say I don't like it one bit, no matter how good it is.

−Ah, to hell with this. Somebody tell us a joke, demanded Hughie, wailing as he buried his face in his hands.

−He must have got it in the library, decided the Runt. No child could know the like of that. Or maybe the teacher could've wrote it out for him. Could he?

−Yes − that's what happened. The teacher wrote it out, agreed his brother, barely aware of what he was saying, seeming almost terrified as he looked all around him.

−No. No library, Sonny explained, because he wrote it right there with a pencil in the school. It's a fact, I'm afraid. There ain't no library involved. I'm sorry to have to tell you all that. I'd rather, to be honest, not to have to say it at all. But that's the situation, men. No library. Nope − none at all. And that's something that, like it or not, we're just going to have to accept.

−Ah look here, snapped Red Campbell, it's clear as day that what happened with this is that Mr Hackett over here − that for some reason best known to himself, he goes off and writes down all this cockamamie crap. And which, on another occasion, might all be fine and dandy. But not tonight − and not when we just lost Mr goddamn Monroe, do you hear? I said − do youse hear?

−You quit grinding your accursed teeth, demanded Sonny, that'd be the best thing for you, Red Campbell, to do. Because I warned you once, and I ain't sure I'm going to do it again.

Sonny Hackett flung back his chair, and drawing himself up to his full six-foot-four height, momentarily blinded by his oily, flopping forelock, stabbed the air with a forefinger and seethed:

–No-I-ain't so goddamn sure anymore.

–Ah here, pleaded Hughie, you two fellers just take it easy. Everybody just ride easy down, you hear me now?

–That's right, agreed Barney, please if you don't mind …

Before stumbling awkwardly and falling against the side of the table, covering his eyes with the heels of his hands, saying:

–I don't know why you were giving me that paper. Because I wasn't even in the house that night.

–It's all his fault, Red Campbell bridled, it's Hackett's to blame for that, don't ask me why. It's him's to blame for everything anyway, because he always had it in for poor old Wilson Gillis. Every single protestant he'd ever met, he'd no time for. That's what he said. Those were his words.

–I've met rotten liars, Sonny Hackett retorted, but you, Campbell, you're the worst.

–Is this little soldier dead? wondered Mervyn Walker as he approached the table, shutting one eye and elevating a single empty bottle.

With a capacious silence now slowly descending, as the barman returned, whistling softly, behind the counter.

Like the great big magisterial eagle that he was, examining his watch. Before returning his gaze to the sweeping, brushing willow.

–Is there anything out there? inquired Hughie, optimistically.

–No sign, the barman murmured, no sign as yet. None, gentlemen. No, none at all.

As the piece of paper was returned to Sonny Hackett's possession.

His complexion seemed deathly.

–The other day, he recommenced uncertainly, the other day he turned to me, Cosmo, and without even flinching, looked me in the eye. Daddy, he said, do you think the evil men do lives after them?

Wee Hughie kicked his chair and irascibly announced that he was going to the bathroom. That is, if you could call it that – that ancient lavatory with its wooden seat and deafening flush.

–And would you like to know why? he called across as he departed. Because I'm fed up listening to this no-account jabbering.

The others completely ignored him.

–She never talks to me now, continued Sonny hoarsely, she says she thinks that I've turned against the boy. But that isn't true. Because I haven't. I'm just afraid of what might happen, that's all. To him, to us all. You know?

Then he lowered his head, so hoarse when he spoke he could scarcely be heard.

–Although I sometimes think that maybe she's right? That there is something wrong with us – the Hacketts? Do you think so, Barney – what do you think?

Big Barney looked embarrassed, gazing down into his lap as he searched frantically for an appropriate response.

–How do I know, Sonny? I mean, I'm not qualified, I'm not a doctor. In fact, to tell you the truth, it gives me the twitches even to have to listen to talk like that. Because, between you and me, I often have wee little private troubles of my own. Troubles that I never told anyone about, and that have nothing at all to do with what we done on Wilson Gillis.

He shot to his feet, eyes flaring, looking all about him.

–Because that was an accident, wasn't it, Sonny? Everyone knows that.

As he swayed in space, still clutching the empty bottle, looking like all the sorrow of the world was packed right into three hundred pounds of meat, with eyes that looked like they'd have given almost anything to be accorded the permission to burst into tears.

Sonny seemed to be on the verge of asphyxiation.

—I hate Indians, he screeched, slapping the table. I didn't used to but now I do.

—Hello there guys! laughed Hughie hysterically. Welcome to the Wee Hughie Munley Comedy Show, where every Saturday night our aim is to put that sad right back in the bottle where it belongs! Comprende?

—I want to get out of here, said the Runt.

—Me too, said Shorty McHale, because that there jungle, I think it's off. I reckon it's bad.

—You ain't gonna be permitted to sully the memory of your father, Red Campbell warned. You agreed to come here so now you gotta stay. You got that? Now be a pair of good cubs and douse the glimmer for Red. Have yourselves another shotta bug-juice there.

As they all looked up and stared at the clock, waiting for the wavering strands of grey smoke to clear, which they did.

And saw that it was coming very close to dawn.

Chapter 14

The Wildwood Flower

The last thing I would ever want to do, wrote Jody, is to cause any unnecessary misunderstandings between us, Ray – for, God knows, there have been enough of those already. I don't want to lay it on you, Ray, not in any way, because of all bloody things, it's not my intention here to give you grief. And if there's any specific reason for what might be described as the directness of some of my words, it's that the trouble between you and me, it has gone on way too long.

And nobody knows better than me how a grievance nurtured can so cruelly devour.

So anything you got to say to me, Ray, I'll listen and I'll hear it, he had promised.

And all the pain, rancour and disappointment that has existed between us can be history.

That was what my old friend had written to me, more than once.

And, as I sit here scribbling my story on an old rickety table underneath a dim bulb, all I can think is: if only a few of those who had been present that night in Mervyn's Mountain Bar had, at some time in their lives, been privy to such heartfelt sentiments.

All I can say is, such a declaration, in its honesty and sincerity, it might have helped them in some small way.

It's just faintly possible that something like that might have been what been what a person like Wee Hughie Munley needed – because, right now, you could tell that something bad was getting to him. He hadn't been the same after coming back from the lavatory.

As he swung a poorly aimed swipe at a chair, and plunged the remains of a cigarette into the the tray, and then announced that, as far as he was concerned, already he'd had way too much upset and 'consternation', as he called it.

–There's been way too much grief here in Glasson and on this mountain, he declared.

Warning, uncharacteristically, that it had better stop.

–Because I don't want to hear any of it anymore! he shouted. All of this slander – all these names!

As he pawed away at the sawdust, like a pony.

–Because I didn't happen to be christened Patches, in case you didn't know, he spat out bitterly, in case you might think that that's my name. But it's not, you see, it's not. And, for your information, there ain't nothing wrong with any of my beautiful sisters. You think I don't know what you say about them? O we know what goes on in Hickory Holler, you say, and that there's a scarlet lamp burning there, above the door, every weekend. You want liver for your pup, gravel for your goose – then it's them Munley girls that you got to go up and talk to. That's what you say – that's what all of them say – and I know everything about it. But I also know this – that all of it is lies. Because, all of us, we're a God-fearing family. And there ain't no shame in having once been poor.

Fourteen children was a lot to have to have, he whooped, so what if his mother had had to wash their clothes in the river.

—Because if the truth be told, he went on, there were a lot of people in Glasson County who'd had to do the same. Yes, and had tramped to school wearing hand-me-down rags, looking no different to any of the Munleys. And, just the very same as them, had had to wash their clothes in throwaway plastic buckets filled with water from a drainpipe.

He forcefully struck another chair.

—So what? Wee Hughie rasped. What in the fuck about it, yeah? Just do me the courtesy of calling a halt to your gossip – and calling me 'Patches' whenever I'm not around.

—Nobody's calling you Patches, Big Barney protested, no one at all. You've just got it into your head. Everyone knows you're a great comedian, that there's no one in Glasson who can makes us laugh like you.

—I've had enough of this already! barked Sonny. Do you hear me now? More than enough – so give it a fucking rest.

Then the Runt stepped forward and announced that this time, for certain, he was going to be sick. Yes, this time for sure.

—And bad, he gulped, I know – I can tell. I know. I've got the shivers, you see, them shakes that sometimes come on me. Then I know it's coming. My stomach, you see, it gets all tore up.

—His stomach, from time to time, it gets all tore up, explained his brother.

—These feelings, when I get them, it's sort of like I'm not gonna make it. Like someone is trying to tell me – you're not going to make it this time, Runt. Because that's the way. That's the way it's been decided it must be.

—Don't piss down my back and tell me it's fucking raining, sneered Red Campbell, because the truth fucking is that neither of you ought to have ever been brought near the place. Whoever's fucking idea it was.

—Take him out, Sonny Hackett ordered, take him away on out to fuck and get the daisyboy some fresh air. Get him some fresh air, I said. For all the addition that he is around here.

—OK, replied Shorty, somewhat cowedly, leading his brother towards the door, indeed retching himself.

With the whole bar shuddering as the door closed loudly behind them.

It would have to have been around the time that Jody Kane found himself waking in his cell – having passed out already a number of times.

I want to tell you everything, Ray, he had written in one of his most special letters, just like I did my wildflower rose.

Greta Mae.

My partner, my love.

There's nothing that she doesn't know about the two of us, Ray – even what happened with that lousy motherfucking dog Johnny Redlegs. You'll find in the end it's the only thing to do, look into the mirror and be honest with yourself, no matter what you might see reflected there. Because, all our lives, we been caged birds, Ray. And now, at long last, it's time to spread our wings and learn to fly. That's what I told her.

So who cares what happened to the two of us back in Whiterock? If, at the end of the day, you can find yourself fortunate enough to come across a sweet and beautiful angel who not only is happy to be in your company, but who understands you and is content to have you place a golden wedding ring upon her finger. Just like I have been more than proud to do, in a little church that her family have worshipped in for generations, the White Chapel. Not that I'm pretending to be in any way religious – not to the same degree as her, at any rate.

But she's working on me, and I got to say I ain't complaining, knowing how blessed I have been for both our paths to cross in this world. For us ever to have managed to meet in the first place.

My wildwood flower and me – did I tell you we've put a holding payment down on a place of our own already?

Because we have, old friend, on a little cabin in the woods up here in the mountains.

I know it's nothing fancy, but what you got to understand, and I think I know that you will, Ray, is that it's home.

And which is something I learned early on from that sweet little flower that I am privileged to call my own – to comprehend the value of such an unexpected blessing, do you know what I'm saying? Because ever since meeting her all of my anger seems to have fallen away. Sometimes I can't believe my luck. Because when the two of us first met, I still was that old bitter, resentful Jody Kane – numbed with pain, gloomy, and often ferocious. And I know I drank way more than my share. Yes, that was the case, but I'm willing to admit it. That I was aggrieved and disputatious, carrying all kinds of envies and imagined injustices. Something which I can laugh about now.

Sometimes when I look at her, the words to describe what I feel for her, they evade me and seem just that little bit beyond my reach.

Except when I listen to Hank or Patsy Cline. Then I can find 'em. If we make it through December, Merle Haggard sings – do you remember that one, Ray?

I'll bet you do.

They used to play it all the time in Heartland.

I don't think I'll ever stop loving her, Greta Mae.

My one and only sweet little wildwood flower.

Come on out and see us, Ray – you got to.

Adios for now, you hearing me OK?

Not long after the brothers had gone out to get themselves some air, Jody had felt himself coming close to giving up, he'd confided in me.

Because, although the beatings themselves had been bad enough, he'd begun to think that perhaps they had administered some kind of drug – slipped him a shot of something when he'd been lying there, out cold on the floor of the van, on the way over from the One Tree Crossroads.

Because nothing had seemed to be working inside his head.

He had repeated that many times in his letters.

In his efforts to free himself of the cable ties, one of the drums of diesel had fallen over and thudded against his toe- and was now lying on its side as a large patch of oil began spreading out between his feet, the pain of the recent bruise already close to unbearable.

As, he recalled, those slow melting rainbow colours of the expanding map of oil gradually seemed to be returning him to those faraway days in the orphanage, in Whiterock.

When we'd ramble aimlessly in the High Country meadow, just lying there admiring the endless blue and white canyon of the sky, in a rolling field carpeted with beautiful golden primroses, where our old friend Sgt Redlegs would regale us with more of his extraordinary, magical stories.

–Trooper Johnny at your service, fellers, we would hear him announce as he gave us the regimental salute, the hero of Dixie who fought for God and the gallant South. So git on over here, fellers, and let us join in prayer, as we implore the Lord to bring Sweet Death and all her emissaries to the homes of all them bluebelly dawgs – hur hur!

He had a 'drop of the tinker' in him too. I remember they always used to insist that he too was part of that same dispossesed, roving tribe – a wandering, restless, migratory soul.

–Like all of our kindred, little feller, he would tell him, you and me is brothers of the Pawnee. Yup, us'n's belong to the indomitable outlaw breed – and that's a sure certain fact, Jody Kane.

He had been all over the world, he told us, but specifically the vast and spectacular continent of America.

–That old Redleg Johnny, he don't have no dreams, he used to say, on account of being who he is, and the seed and breed of his kind that was sired under bloodied stars – no, it has been ordained that he ain't entitled to no such luxury. At least not in the way regular folks as obeys the laws of their Maker might be. Sure, that's what they'll tell you, fellers, and I ought to know – because, believe you me, I been listening to that trash for most, if not all, of my misbegotten, unrequested borned days. With the difference being, my two young compadres, that folks as toss them words into the wind, shit from shinola is what they know. Because I am going to tell you a story, boys. Yep, a little campfire yarn as we sit there together in the huge blue rectangle of the night, gazing far beyond them hills to where the horizon meets its end. And where, once upon a time, long before your innocence was ever breathed upon the air, in the aftermath of an undecided battle, there was a soldier who ploughed his way through the smoke, upon his mount. Yes, an exhausted horseman bedecked in slouch hat and gleaming black rain slicker, having now decided, once and for all, to make his way back to the place of his birth. Yes, fellers, to leave it all behind him – and, as best he could, make his way through the many corpses littered about the dead land, in order that he might, finally, be in a position to say goodbye to that little valley which had made him. And for which, in the most curious fashion, in spite of all its shortcomings, he somehow still reserved a special place in his heart. What he liked to describe as a private corner of consecrated sorrow and regret – for what might have been, you understand. And so he rode on through a hail of minnie balls, the rumble of artillery, the cries of angry men, and that war's manifold, unceasing rude alarms, placing his faith in the Captain of Salvation, who along with the rattlesnake has given life to the sweetest of songbirds. And when, at last, he arrived into that valley – so pleasant in its sun-dappled majesty that it might just as easily have gone by the name of Glasson County – all at once did he climb from his steed, that spent but still valiant Rider In The Rain. And he pushed the gate of the cemetery open before him, and immediately fell down upon his knees under the leaves of a swaying willow in that windswept Garden of Stone, observed in silence by the very few who remembered him. And who, in their innocence, assumed that with his head bowed and the slouch hat dipped down low over his face, that what he was in the course of doing was bidding goodbye to all his old friends, engaging in sweet, protracted converse with the departed. When, in fact, what that exhausted horseman was doing was ridding himself, in that moment, of each and every illusion that he'd carried with him all the way through his forty-two years upon this earth. In order to become entirely bankrupt, whenever, at last, his time would come. And at which point, my little compadres, he would possess the comfort of owning nothing only his wound.

I remember him placing his hand on Jody's shoulder but thinking nothing much of it at the time.

–I'm sorry, boys, he told us, swallowing hard, all I can say is that, through the smoke of battle we do the best we can, but with the hound of our weakness always at our heels, awaking in the night with that rain of regret still moist upon our cheeks. I'm sorry, boys, that you ever had to know me – for the truth is, from the very first day I ever drew breath, I been branded with the mark of Cain.

Sometimes we'd see him cresting the rim of the meadow, complete with slouch hat and brass-buttoned military tunic.

Another day we went visiting him in his camp up in the lower field, and right out of nowhere he came swinging down in front of us from behind a tree, starting into this whooping dervish dance as he spun two silver Colts he'd bought in Granard.

–I hitchhiked in specially to get them for my deppities, we heard him hollering, whirling his hat, looking me right in the eye and launched into this slow-as-molasses John Wayne-style drawl, hooking his thumb in the buckle of his belt, narrowly squinting as he spat:

–They lie in Boot Hills all through the west – the outlaws, the killers, the Billy the Kids and worse. Say like the feller that shot Bill Hickock in the back, there's always one like that in every time of history – but every so often there may have lived in one them … *a man*!

Rebel-yelling and way-haying as he stamped down the dirt and, before we knew it, was taking up refuge once more behind the tree, making expansive wild gestures as he whooped and hollered:

–He lay face-down in the desert sand, clutching his six-gun in his hand.

–Ringo, nodded Jody, brushing away a cloud of smoke, well I'll be damned. So whaddya think about that, Ringo Wade?

And that was the first time I heard my nickname.

–Youse'un a good feller, Trooper Wade, Johnny Redlegs grinned.

As off he went yuk-yukking with his whiskey, honking hysterically on his dented brass novelty bugle.

It can still make me nauseous, even thinking about his name, never mind actually uttering it.

But all the same I got to stick to Jody's advice and focus on the good things, 'as best you can', like he always says.

Such as, for example, that very first day we arrived up in Kentuckyland, roaring along the driveway, in Mr Monroe's fintailed white convertible.

And where – to our complete amazement, so accustomed had we become to the opposite – we found ourselves being treated like princes.

Jody in particular, of course, on account of his unrivalled boxing prowess, a skill which already was the talk of the countryside.

With WW making no secret of his plans for the future as he treated us both to a grand tour of the hog mansion with its medieval blown-glass windows, cement pond and guitar-shaped wrought-iron metalwork on its gates, high upon a hill overlooking the racetrack and breeding farm along with the magnificent wooded slopes and shallow lakes of Glasson valley. With its boggy fields patchworking the central lowlands of flat rolling brown plains of peat bogs and wild areas of spiky rushes, reed swamps, turloughs and conifer forests.

–What I intend to do, boys, he told us almost matter-of-factly, is see to it that in less than two years' time, or three at the most, what you are gonna find here among these green fields is the most admirable concentration of quality thoroughbred horseflesh in the world at the Kentuckyland yearly sale. Just as soon as those daffodils and snowdrops come into bloom, Monroeville will become the gathering place of oil sheiks, princes, business tycoons, Japanese industrialists and simple millionaires. Because if WW has his way, Kentuckyland is gonna be the biggest crapshoot in Europe. So bide your time and watch them, my dandy young fellers, those sleazy kingpins who now run the sport of kings, exult in their making WW prosper.

As he turned to us and tipped back his powder-blue Stetson, clutching those lapels as he stomped out the remains of a still-glowing cheroot, radiating untold excitement and pride as he continued robustly:

—Yes, you two young men, what you are gazing upon is the property that marks the true beginning of what they will call in time William Walter Monroe's empire, his country kingdom. But let none of this fool you, fellers, because the truth is that ol' WW, at heart he's a good old boy just the same as them whose wages he pays. Yep, the very exact same as anyone, whether it's Sonny or Red or Big Barney, Wee Hughie or anyone else. And which is why I took 'em in and gave 'em all a helping hand when things fell apart at Glasson County Meats. Because the fact is I know my kin, fellers — and that's why, even though a cloud o' suspicion hung over 'em regarding a certain little unfortunate incident that took place a long time back, I decided to give 'em the benefit of the doubt, and maybe that's why they feel they owe so much to Heartland. But, hell, them good old boys they assisted me in building it up — with Tony as my right-hand man, Hughie doing the bookings and that old jive-jumper Red rock-solid behind the bar, and with nobody likely to give Big Barney lip, and who, along with Sonny, is just about the best goddamn chucker-outer in the whole of Glasson County. Them's good old boys, and no matter what rumours might have attached to them, I am in no way regretful that whenever they were laid off, at the time I gave them the benefit of the doubt. Because, when push comes to shove, no matter what degree of good fortune I may have had, at the end of the day I look at them and they look at me, and we see ourselves. Yep, we gaze in that old mirror, boys, and what do we see: a good old boy. And who is he when he's at home, do you ask? Well he's a feller who might be a little too fond, in his way, of sometime feudin' and a little sup of moonshine, but give him a chance and he'll show you how to do things with his hands that a lot of men can't. Because he's got what is known as a 'little bit of wit, a little bit of grit, and a goddamn whole lot of motherfucking shit'. Sure, that good old boy he's funny and he's a trickster and he'll get his hand in your pocket faster than his grandaddy, the three-card trickman. He'll beat you at horse, nine-ball or poker. He's got the best hunting dogs in the region and knows where to get the best moonshine in all of the midlands, yeah, and up North too. He's been around the world once and to two agricultural shows. Some of these fellers, as is well known, don't survive. But the ones who do, you can find 'em grafting at the plumbers and the electricians, or maybe under a wreck at the bodyshop. He might work at the sawmill or learn to be a long-haul trucker and you can bet your bottom dollar that, at least until now, he ain't never gonna be found in one of them hog mansions that his wife in her dreams is always hustling for – preferring to remain stuck back among a copse of pine, close maybe to where he was born, and never far from his very own fishing hole. Now come on, boys, for you and me, we got ourselves a whole bunch o' hosses here as needs tendin'!

He had driven us down to Heartland after that, describing how it had come to him in a dream – the ballroom first, then the attached hacienda-style roadhouse, where the three of us found ourselves standing now.

As he swept his arm up towards the gleaming chandelier.

–All the way from Italy that came, fellers, he told us, and as you can imagine we didn't have too many o' them in that two-roomed cottage not three-quarters of a mile from here, that was where I first saw the light of day, fellers, and one thing for sure is – WW he ain't never forgot it. Just who he is and where it is he comes from, here among these hill-folk as has been randomly shoved by God in these fields and hollers, to hunt and to fish and to love their mamas each and every one. No, WW Monroe he ain't about to forget where he come from, not now, not never, Jody Boy Kane and Raymond, you misbegotten little hombres for whom old WW is gonna do a turn and a good one. And the reason for that is, maybe even more than most, that us good ol' boys, we got our pride. And that's why I want you, this second, to come right over here and join me by this window and keep me company while we survey my coming kingdom. For this is only the beginning of it, fellers, because after Kentuckyland there is gonna be Heartland and, hopefully, and in double-quick succession, palaces of an even mightier splendour – Roseland, Dreamland, you name it fellers. I am gonna transform this here county. So go on, take a look! Run your eyes over the coming extraordinary future …

Then we made out way back to the breeding farm in his jeep, and as we stood there, with his two arms flung around our shoulders, already you could see them, just the same as he did – all those yet-to-be Kentucky and Heartland ghosts, chic and elegant in their broad-brimmed hats, jewellery, furs and shined shoes, swarming all over every inch of the downs, and whose stately elegance mimicked in every way the immaculate image of a Kentucky bluegrass horse farm.

–Hell, either of you two boys could just as easily be Mickey Rooney in *National Velvet*, grooming his breeds for the one and only WW, and I got to say that that just suits me fine, what with you being good local breeds y'selves haw haw …

Below us, the barns were roofed in tile, the stables painted white and the stall doors a soothing shade of green, with the bridle path swept and manicured.

–Kentuckyland, we heard him hum with pride, and I could have sworn I saw him thumb a tear from his eye.

As he handed us both a smoke and led us into his Louis XIV-style lounge.

–Like I told you, I heard him remark to Jody, I knew your father back in the day – and I happen to be aware that, whatever misfortunes he might have encountered in his life, that your dad Chester, right down to the bones, he was a motherfucking thoroughbred, son. Through and through. You got to believe that.

He handed us drinks. And just stood there in front of him, pressing his fist into Jody Kane's chest as he insisted:

−And you, son of Chester, you are going to carry on that very same tradition. You got me?

With him going on then to claim that he fully intended to turn Jody into the best knuckle-fighter Glasson County, in its wildest dreams, had ever seen.

A project with which, as it transpired, he was soon to spectacularly succeed, with the name Jody Kane on everyone's lips, and those early Country Club bouts having already passed into sports and gambling legend.

As those bones kept crunching and the gouts of blood flew.

And why wouldn't we be proud of it, WW would often say, to the legendary Bone King of the Glasson Meats killing floor − the one and only:

Tony Begley.

For TB, as he called him, was Mr Monroe's right-hand man, his loyal and trusted first lieutenant.

−You got it, Mr Monroe, you would often hear Tony Begley agreeing, us old country folks we got to look that critter right in the eye. And you know what, WW? Tame that tiger − look that hungry sumbitch in the eye and then, when you get the chance, make your move and bone the fucker. Bring him to heel.

−And you're the man to do that, Tony, WW would respond, like he'd cracked the greatest joke in history.

−Yup, his sidekick Tony Begley would laugh good-naturedly, just like he used to every day in the factory. Up there on the floor of Glasson Meats, when business was flying and they'd bring old Tony no end of Holsteins.

—Yes, Holsteins, Mr Monroe, and Friesians and Charolais too. Because I weren't choosy. No way, no-how. Because as long as them bitches got four legs, Tony'll do the job. Yep, skin the fuckers, every one.

To those who didn't know him, his legendary meanness – so stingy, some contended, that he squeaked when he walked – TB would have appeared a somewhat unremarkable, perhaps conventional, rural individual – a characteristic most signified, perhaps, by an inordinate fear of offending his mother.

Who was collected by him on her doorstep every single Sabbath morning without fail.

But, having succumbed to a very brief illness, in the aftermath of which she'd unfortunately died, Tony had announced that he wouldn't be appearing in church ever again.

—Because, you see, the fact is, I'm afraid I don't like God anymore, he was heard informing his friends. I'm sorry but for me, I regret to say, that the God my mother worshipped so faithfully over the years, the fucker's dead, I'm afraid.

—As are a lot of other things, he would then add cryptically.

And then look at his associates in 'that way', as they described it.

A kind of stillness, a silence which made them feel uncomfortable, like they were being judged or something.

Especially then, when out of nowhere, he'd turn around and give you that faint, wan smile.

—Did you know that she went to church every day? he would ask.

And, before they'd have sufficient time to make any considered response, he would just look away and say nothing at all, almost as if he had forgotten the question.

And then he'd shiver just a little as he looked back and said:

—But all the same, no matter what I might say about God, sometimes late at night I'll still find myself saying the odd Hail Mary. Because that's what we used to do, me and her, together say one or two little Hail Marys.

—Kneeling together, they would hear TB whisper, so happy we might have been children again.

Chapter 15

The Secret Life of Oranges

Nobody, deep down, knew what to make of Tony Begley, so they were always talking about him.

Just like now.

–TB, complained Hughie, I wonder did he ever buy a drink in his whole fucking life?

Sonny Hackett shook his head.

–But, man, he began, you got to admit that he sure is one mean sucker. King Sumbitch, a.k.a. Tony Begley. You know who the Mean Sumbitch is, my friends? He's the one who's destined from birth to be a loner. Has never in his life had a real friend, just a coupla jerks he reckons he can manipulate easily – maybe the likes of you and me, who knows? He figures the world owes him on account of his very nature. All the bad-ass brotherhood to which he belongs they hate and despise him. But, most of all, they hate themselves. Because at times like this, they know they need him. That's TB's kind, I'm sorry to have to say. Is he out there yet?

–No, said Barney, no sign so far.

Hughie was rhythmically patting his perspiration-pearled dome, with Sonny Hackett rocking in his chair, heels on the table, back and forth

As Big Barney Grue, standing over by the jukebox, kept stealing glances out the window, before returning to gravely stroke his chin.

Red Campbell was frowning as he called across to Mervyn:

–What's so interesting about that stupid willow tree? What do you find so special about it, Mervyn?

Mervyn Walker sighed and looked right over at him, smiling.

–It relaxes me, that's all. Nothing more. For your information, I just find it calms me down. That's all, Mr Campbell.

–You're a funny fucking customer, said Red, a funny customer – that's what I'd have to say about you, Mervyn.

As Hughie abruptly pocketed his handkerchief, before announcing:

–As long as I've known Begley, there was one thing he always used to say. And that was that he made it his business to never hurt a woman. Yes, that no matter what it might be, and in spite of whatever it was she was supposed to have done, he would always make sure to do his best not to cause her physical harm. I remember him always saying that, going right back. That it's one thing you just don't do, cause unnecessary physical distress or upset to a lady. No matter what she's been guilty of.

Pausing for a moment to gather his thoughts, Sonny Hackett considered this remark for a moment before sipping once more and, with those piercing dark eyes, regarded Hughie over the rim of his glass.

–That's interesting. So, did you ever hear what he did to Tiny Smallwoods? What he happened to do to Tiny when he was going with her?

–Tony Begley was going out with Tiny, was he? said Barney, taken aback.

—I didn't know that. I never heard tell of that. I never knew he was going out with her — not Tiny Smallwoods. Are you sure about that? I mean, are you certain?

—Not only going with her — he was mad about her. In love with her, he was. But she jacked him over.

—Jacked him over? interrupted Red. Tiny Smallwoods jacked him over? Jacked Tony Begley over — no!

—Making cadence with someone else she was. I'd never have trusted her, not an inch. And neither should Tony. To tell you the truth, I'm surprised he ever did.

—So what happened then, Sonny? asked Big Barney, what happened after she jacked him over?

—He calls her into his office this night, Sonny Hackett continued, and there she is: *What, me?* You think that I did something, do you Tony? Why would I do something wrong? O please no Tony — don't think ill of me. But Begley reassures her that it's all gonna be OK. You don't got no call to worry, Tiny, he tells her. Only then he goes over to the window and says, in this real low voice — you know the one he uses. Tell me about the oranges, he says. Tell me about the oranges, Tiny Smallwoods. And Tiny, I mean, you know, she's not stupid. So she starts into all this backtracking and sobbing. Well, you would, I mean, wouldn't you. I mean you all know the way that Tony can look at you. So there he is, standing there, just looking at her and saying nothing. No, nothing at all — just the way he does. In that particular way that he likes to do. And what's she do? What is there for poor old Tiny to do, only sink to her knees and start bawling and crying. Because she knows what's coming. Because she's heard that he's done it before.

—Done what before? interrupted Barney. Done what, Sonny?

—Done what? replied Sonny, reaching for his glass.

Stroking the bridge of his nose with two pinched fingers.

—Get you up like a good girl now, he tells her, and take yourself off out and go and get them for Tony. You'll find any amount of them in the supermarket. Go on now, sweetheart – away off with you and get the oranges. And so off she goes, just like she's told. I don't know how many she got in the end – maybe six or seven pounds:

—Six or seven pounds of oranges? mumbled Red. Oranges, Sonny – six or seven pounds?

—Yes, spat Sonny, what the fuck do you think I said, Campbell – teeth? Pounds of teeth – is that what I said?

Red Campbell swallowed and looked away, saying nothing.

—And it was after she came back with the bag that he did it, Sonny elaborated, yeah that was when he set about his business.

—Was that when he did it? gasped Wee Hughie, fearing the worst.

—Did what? stammered Barney. Did what, Sonny?

—Told her about the oranges.

Big Barney's eyes blazed and he tore at his whiskers.

—Told her what, for fuck's sake, about the oranges? What can you tell someone about oranges that they don't know already? What about fucking oranges – that's what I'd like to know. Outspan, Jaffa, there's sweet fuck all to know. At the end of the day, there's not much to know.

—Barney is right, nodded Hughie, I don't know what you're talking about, Sonny. Making a big deal about—

—Maybe apples, Big Barney laughed loudly, there might be something you could say about apples. Eh, Hughie?

—Aye! chortled Hughie, eager to develop this more lighthearted turn in the conversation, maybe something you could say about Granny Smiths or Cox's Pippins!

But, in this regard, Sonny Hackett gave him absolutely no encouragement at all, continuing to gaze at his knuckles as he repeatedly opened and closed his fist.

−That, I'm afraid, is where you're wrong, he explained, because there are a great many things you can say about oranges and their secrets. And perhaps the most important is that, if you happen to be looking to swindle money out of the insurance, you can give someone a fierce fucking hiding and leave her with a welter of great unsightly bruises. Which ought to see you good for a coupla sackfuls of moolah − but with the advantage, of course, of not doing any serious damage to the internal organs.

He looked away with a thousand yard stare.

−Men are one thing, women another, Tony used to always say. Men are easy, but with the judies you got no choice but to adopt a different approach. You got to be nice to the judies, he always said.

−I heard she was never the same again, said Red, that's what I heard …

−What, asked Hughie, what did you hear?

−That she'd some kind of nervous collapse or something after it. And that they used to see her up at Lake Wynter, just sitting there crying her eyes out, under a tree.

−But you know what the funny thing is? Sonny continued, the funny thing is that, in the end, he never actually did anything at all. Because right after he'd given her that great big speech, he just took every orange and put them right back into her bag. And never went near her ribs or nothing. That, you see, is the secret of the oranges. That he never touched her − not even so much as lifted a finger. And do you want to know why? Because I love you, is what he told her. Yes, loved her with all his heart, that old Tiny, he said. And that, even though she'd jacked him over, that he'd still go on, doing just that − loving her, like he said − he still , you know, keeps her picture in his wallet. I know that for a fact. My Tiny, he used to sometimes say to me, I was stone mad cracked about her, Sonny, you know. But I guess it just wasn't meant to be, he would tell you. That's the truth about the oranges, guys. Ain't it strange?

But no one replied to what Sonny Hackett said, and all you could hear was the scratch of yet another record as it kept on revolving.

And the soft gentle sweep of the willow, sighing.

Chapter 16

I'm Mr Bonny

A dollar down and a dollar a week – that was one of the ways Jody liked to express himself. When he wanted to explain how he had managed, in the end, to find some way of facing down his demons.

It's not like it's some dam inside of you bursts, Ray, he told me, with everything coming at you in one go and that's the end of it.

No, Ray, my friend – like Johnny Cash says, one piece at a time, easy does it.

That's pretty much how I succeeded in coming to terms with it, he said – calling some kind of a halt to the grim and relentless march of my experiences at the hands of so-called Trooper Johnny Redlegs, winnowing away at whatever little part of my soul remained.

After all those years of being frozen emotionally, do you understand what I'm trying to say to you, Ray?

I did – and I still do.

And which is why I sat down and wrote right back to Sweetwater, Georgia.

Explaining how, coincidentally, that's exactly the same advice they give you in AA.

With 'incremental' being the word they prefer to use — one day at a time, in other words.

Half of what I had written by return to Jody that night had come to me almost in a blinding flash. I'm not suggesting some kind of revelation, but I had definitely slipped into some kind of blissful daze.

With me starting the letter somewhere between sleep and waking, and then letting my hand roam free in the hope of doing justice to the dream I'd just had.

And which, like I said earlier, had ended up part of some strange, dark but vivid fairy tale — mostly concerning a certain Trooper Johnny Redlegs, standing at the bottom of the dormitory stairs, holding a candle as he breathed evenly in and out.

As though trying to decide whether he would climb the stairs or not.

With his long weathered face haloed in the glow of the flickering flame, as he finally began his tortured ascent.

It hadn't, of course, been the first time that he'd done it — it was a regular occurrence way back in those Whiterock days.

—I'll look after you, little dogie, you'd hear him whisper, his smile like moonlight on a tombstone as he pressed another handful of coins into my fist. Just so long as you promise not to breathe a word about this to anyone. Do you hear me now?

And Trooper Johnny Redlegs, he would sit there half the night in the dormitory, by the light of the candle staring down at Jody, sleeping fitfully.

Git along lil dogies

Why don't you lay down

And quit your forever shiftin' around, he would croon, ever so softly — to Jody. You could tell he was drunk.

And then, when the singing and everything else at long last was over, I would look up and see him standing at the bottom of my bed — with the whites of his eyes rolling as the sound of suppressed sobbing erased all trace of the lingering lullaby.

Observing, both in terror and bewilderment, as he slowly, inexorably began sinking to his knees.

–Once upon a time, I heard him whimper, when I was a young man in America, I viewed a painting called *Southerners In Hell*. And what was upon that canvas, my innocent little partner, that I beheld was a company of lonesome rebels, all sitting there covering their ears and shutting their eyes. As they listened to Abraham Lincoln reciting his Gettysburg Address – only not just for now, but for all of eternity … over and over and over, little dogie.

–This too is to be my fate, he informed me, for the crimes I've committed, not only here but in many other places, involving the flesh and all its many lusts.

–Yes, for what I've done, little feller, he continued, and loathsome persistence of all base desires – the Almighty has decreed that I am to suffer a similar fate. But I deserve it. I won't complain.

But then, quite unexpectedly, erupting into a bout of hopelessly irrational chuckling. As he swept the blankets right off of my bed and covered himself like John the Baptist, whining pitifully:

–Yes, for now until the end of eternity, I here and now proclaim my guilt to all and sundry and shall kneel here, covering my ears as I sink before the righteous accusations of the world!

He banged his forehead against the bedstead till it bled. Then, once more, he wept.

–Help me, he groaned, please can anyone help me? Please can you help poor old Johnny Redlegs, and free him from his heartless prison that decent people call their temple?

Back in Jody Kane's own tenebrous coffin of confinement, in that packed-earth outhouse where he found himself overwhelmed not only by the pain of a badly bruised foot but also the fumes of leaking gas, he became convinced, beyond all doubt, that his captors had indeed administered some form of narcotic.

For what other explanation could there be for the startling and shockingly realistic image of Johnny Redlegs who, entirely without warning, had swum out of nowhere to parade himself, chucklingly, before his eyes.

Only to be succeeded by a dizzying flurry of a pair of merciless, flying fists belonging to an opponent from another – up until now – long-forgotten ringside engagement.

Then his head fell heavy as a breeze block onto his chest, as the generator's hum lapsed into silence.

Somewhere far away, beyond the horizonline of his soul, Elvis the King again lamented the inglorious defeat of Dixie.

At which point Jody heard his name being spoken.

–Jody, he heard.

Then it came again, so soft you could barely …

Then it came again.

–Is that you, Jody? Jody – are you awake?

Was it a tune that, perhaps, was playing in the bar, perhaps – one that had just this second come in the wake of Elvis? Jody Kane couldn't establish with any certainty.

But here it was again, moving steadily closer.

–I wanted to talk to you. Say hello to Jody Kane.

The figure kept approaching until it was standing directly in front of him.

–I wanted to make contact, say hello to my friend Jody. How are you Jody?

Jody Kane's heart might just as well have stopped – yes, given out at that precise moment.

–Are you hearing me, Jody? he heard the voice inquire once more, in a languid, mellifluous, Southern drawl.

As the visitor sighed and flexed his manicured fingers, stepping into the slanting rays of the moon.

He was plump, dignified, and his attire was striking in its flamboyance – white buck shoes, and a tailored suit that was as white as ice cream.

His fine white hair was thinning a little but, nonetheless, he seemed almost regal.

In his right hand he was holding a black-banded Panama straw hat.

–How are you, Jody? You've been through it, haven't you, you poor neglected little calf. Please don't be alarmed that I seem to know your name – Mr Bonny at your service, and rest assured there isn't any need in the wide world to be concerned. For I have nothing in mind but your personal welfare.

There was an unmistakable kindliness evident in those searching eyes, as his visitor took yet another step forward.

–Would you care for a smoke? Jody heard the portly man inquire.

Jody Kane shook his head.

–Who are you? he insisted. And how did you get in here?

–Mr Bonny, his visitor replied, my country of origin is called the Bonny Land – perhaps you've heard of it? I have travelled a long way for the two of us to become acquainted. But already I can see that I have not been wasting my time. Are you sure you don't want a cigarette, Jody Kane?

–No, said Jody, no thanks – I can't smoke it. My mouth is way too dry.

–You're certain about that? frowned Mr Bonny, somewhat disapprovingly. Because I mean surely it's bound to be of some assistance.

–I told you I didn't want it! Jody snapped. I said I didn't want it, so then put the fucking thing away.

–Very well, Mr Bonny replied, sighing just a tad regretfully as he laid a soft cold palm along the side of Jody's cheek.

—Don't do that! Jody cried sharply. Do you hear me —
don't even fucking attempt to touch me!

—I know that you're a sensitive, overwrought little dogie, his
visitor whispered, because I always find them, just like some
old cattleman wandering out on that lonesome old prairie,
softly crooning an old trail song lullaby as he searches for
them afflicted stray yearlings as has gone and got themselves
separated from their mothers. Knowing instinctively just how
easily they can get themselves spooked. Yes, that's what it is
their little hearts are most afraid of, Jody … sure as the wind
peels green, that's what them motherless strays fear most, ain't
it?

—Who the hell are you and what are you doing here?
Where is this fucking Bonny Land you're talking about?

Mr Bonny was low-whistling now — you could just about
hear him.

—*Two little orphans, a boy and a girl / Stood by an old church
door,* Jody heard.

And felt like weeping.

—Why do you have to sing that? he demanded.

Because it reminded him of the old days in Whiterock —
why wouldn't it?

Before it had all gone wrong with Redlegs, when for a
while it seemed like they just might make it through.

—How come you know about that? You hear what I'm
saying — tell me how you come to know that!

—Because I know everything, explained Mr Bonny.

As he leaned forward and whispered into Jody's ear:

—You know you can always trust me. And that whatever
complex course our dealings may take, you can always be
assured that this is the case. Understand?

—Yes, replied Jody, without realising that the word had
even left his lips.

—Very good, said Mr Bonny.

As he continued:

−Because once I personally feel convinced of that, then we both can proceed with confidence. My purpose here is to help you *see* things. And to show you how even a pair of poor orphan children, such as you and that diamondback snake they call Ray Wade − how even such low-downs in the end may redeem themselves, and live unblemished among the Immortals.

−They've given me something. My mind is gone.

He waited for a minute but Mr Bonny made no attempt at reply.

−Hush now, urged his visitor, be a good dogie and try to hush.

−Maybe it was all those fights. Could be that that's what did it. There was always going to be a price to pay − is that it, Mr Bonny?

−*Hush, little dogie, lay down.*

Lay down.

And then he was gone, with just a pool of match-flare moon shedding its light on the spot where he'd been standing.

−Mr Bonny, called Jody, please Mr Bonny − will you wait? Come back … !

With the generator's outline solid now, unchanging.

As Jody Kane, exasperated, lifted his head and stared in agony, towards the tiny, butter-yellow porthole window.

Chapter 17

The Way It Used To Be

Red Campbell was staring into the dead ashes of the fire, before lifting his head and shouting out to nobody:

–Who was it put that fucking record on?

Dolly Parton had just that second finished up on the machine.

–What did you have to go and put that on for? he complained again. Because for the life of me I don't remember requesting no tune by her.

Sonny Hackett raised his head and told him to shut the fuck up.

–I don't know if I heard that right. I'm not so sure whether I imagined it or not. Someone saying the like of that to me, Red Campbell shot back.

–You didn't imagine it, Campbell, replied Sonny, it was me who said it and I'll say it again.

Then Red Campbell started up the noise with his teeth.

–Jesus, snarled Sonny, Jesus Christ I swear I'll … !

–I know what – I'll tell youse a joke, suggested Hughie, with his cheeks florid and all his blood vessels pumping. I think that might be a good idea.

–I don't, said Sonny, as a matter of fact not at all …

—Neither do I, agreed Big Barney, now semi-comatose.

But it didn't matter, for wee Hughie Munley had already begun his story.

As Dolly Parton recommenced her quavering rendition.

—*Sing a song for me, Applejack, Applejack*, she bleated giddily.

—Turn her off. Put on some Patsy Cline, shouted Sonny, do you hear me?

But nobody did — as Hughie, his shoulders shaking, continued excitedly, making wild, extravagant gestures.

—Ah yes, you just can't beat that old paper outlaw, he said, paper hat, paper shirt, paper vest, paper boots — even paper spurs.

—I suppose his horse was even made of paper, jibed Red, you little fat moron.

But Wee Hughie chose to ignore the slight, with tears of laughter flowing down his little round face.

—As in he came riding on the trail into Tombstone. Just a second there, friend, says the sheriff coming out of his office. Just where in the hell do you think you're going?

—I'm the paper outlaw, says the rider, I can go anywhere, sheriff ha ha.

—O you can, can yer? says the sheriff. Well that is where you are wrong my friend. And why I got no alternative but to arrest ya. Oh yeah? says the paper outlaw. And, may I ask, on what charge, sheriff?

By now Hughie Munley was jumping up and down and squealing, swinging his arms as he punched the air, and looking like he was just about to burst a blood vessel, or maybe two.

—Aye. Arresting me on what charge? says the outlaw.

His eyes were bright and wide as he raced right over to the seated Sonny and cried, tears tumbling, into his face:

—Rustlin'! says the sheriff.

As Sonny's lip curled, Elvis-style, and he snorted:

—Get your hands off me, you wisecracking halfwit, and get yourself back to that knocking shop in Hickory Holler …

And such devastation as then appeared in Hughie Munley's eyes as he began to tremble and hysterically demand:

—Why can't it be just like it always used to be? For just one simple time, why can't it be like that? It's not fair.

But no one said anything, as Dolly Parton continued.

Except for Red, who out of nowhere gave the jukebox a solid thump as he growled:

—What sort of song is it – a fellow picking apples? I never heard such horseshit, ever …

The record skipped as he leaned on the jukebox, pushing against it with his shoulder.

And Mervyn called over, wagging a cautionary finger:

—Easy now, easy … that's an expensive machine!

And after that, everyone went quiet, retreating into the memory of a world that once was, that once had been, and had been called into being by the abject appeal of Wee Hughie Munley.

Who was now standing over by the window on his own, tugging and pulling at the waistband of his trousers, feeling more humiliated now than ever.

Yes, they were all there thinking of the way things used to be, and if you're wondering how I know that, then all you had to do was just take a look at the longing on their faces. I could feel it myself up there on my perch, in among those rafters – and still do.

That's how I know.

Just what it had been like, way back in those glory days of the seventies, when me and the Jode had been sixteen years old, and the rest of them were the pride of the factory.

In those golden days in Glasson, when WW's Heartland Ballroom had been at the height of its legendary fame.

Especially, they recalled, on that night of all nights, when the heavy rains had fallen on the occasion of the much-anticipated Glasson County Bareknuckle Challenge.

WW had always liked rainstorms – I remember him saying that myself. Because it added something special and unique to the atmosphere, he always used to suggest.

Regular country clubs you go in them and what you got is a polished floor, maybe a fine-looking Steinway or Bechstein piano and no end of rubber plants with all of them flourishing in elaborate earthenware pots, and perhaps a fan.

Then maybe through the window you might perceive a line of stately old oaks and perhaps a couple of gentlemen standing on the edge of a golf course, discussing business.

Everyone inside would have buffed and shined shoes, and the ladies would be sporting chic suits or elaborate evening dresses.

But Mr Monroe's country club, it wasn't at all like that – no sir, not at all.

For a start, being situated as it was in a courtyard right at the back of the bar, completely illegally.

Yep, there sure were good times to be had in back then, as the Monroe Empire continued to grow.

With nothing like his dancehall ever having been seen before – not in humble Glasson County, at any rate.

A dancehall-cum-roadhouse that could accommodate well over three thousand people?

Not a chance.

Why, it was like that old US of A had decided to come smokin' with a vengeance over the side of that primitive old mountain and kick them sleepy cracker midlands right slap bang into the middle of the twenty-first century.

With its flagship being this shimmering pink marble palace, imported directly from Miami-with a huge neon sunset surmounting a tropical facade and its name like the signature of an emancipating deity flowing elegantly past the clouds: *Heartland, where beats the pulse of our sweet love's desire.*

But as well as that little poetic touch, there was also the style of WW Monroe himself – piloting daily into town in his white fintailed convertible complete with longhorns on the grillwork, six-shooter gearshift lever, more pistols serving as door handles and screeching to a halt alongside the plaza sounding his horn that made the sound of stampeding hooves.

And, as always, sporting his trademark powder-blue Stetson and Irish Republican bootlace tie with tricoloured clasp, making sure that he was the very first out of the traps with whatever the latest pub craze might be, whether a honky tonk hardwood floor, a shooting gallery and – his pride and joy – a bucking mechanical rodeo bull.

With a gaudy hoarding twenty-foot high: *It's Country Nite At WW's!* proclaiming a forthcoming Pop For Peace extravaganza – featuring Brendan 'Turn Down The Lights' Shine, Big Tom and the Mainliners and, 'Direct from Dublin', the 'All-Star Showband Hootenanny', including the stars of television and stage – Big Chief Flaming Star from *The Indians*, and many other show-stopping stars, including Samba and the Philosophers, Magic and the Swallows, Telly Savalas and the Bionic Men – and, all the way from the USA, a Red Sovine tribute act showcasing all of the C&W superstar's greatest hits, including the novelty hit of loneliness and abandonment 'Teddy Bear'. Which drunk men used to say reminded them of the little boy in the Woolworth's picture. I wonder is he a real boy, they used to mutter on their way to the lavatory, the poor, misbegotten little bastard.

Yeah, those sure had been great old times in Glasson County, with WW having seemed to make it all somehow possible. There would be prayers and invocations and hymn-meetings too, many of which were scheduled to take place in a marquee specially erected in the car park of Heartland. And over which Austin 'The Diviner' Price, the seventh son of a seventh son, leading the service as the music started up from an array of guitars, tambourines and an accordion, praying not only for an end to ringworm, cow pox, back pains, leg pains and joints which creaked and twisted with age, but also, at last, a conclusion to the Troubles in Northern Ireland.

Which, in fact, each week appeared, if anything, to be increasing in their ferocity. As the congregation – comprised of worshippers from every end of the country under the banner of *The Totus Tuus Peace Crusade* – sank as one to their knees in the car park, pleading for an end to 'misunderstandings' between Christians, along with drug-taking, sexual misdemeanours and the general collapse in morals worldwide.

–Where is my Lord, wept The Diviner at his regular gatherings in the Heartland car park. That merciful God who made the world out of one blood. Lead me, Lord, way I want to go … how I can feel his quickening power!

Throughout the ceremony, some continued kneeling, others raised their hands high in supplication, or pressed their hands viciously to their foreheads in order to shade their eyes from the world and its persistent unholiness.

And such a peace as descended when, trembling in that strange way he did, The Diviner began reciting the Johnny Cash monologue for which he was celebrated, dedicating its words to all the sinners of the earth.

–*Why me, Lord*, he began, *what have I ever done?*

However, few of those occasions – spectacular though they were, almost shocking at times, indeed, in their passionate outpourings – could have claimed to come close to the performances now being delivered every Saturday and Sunday night in the Heartland ballroom – by none other than Glasson's own stunning Rockabilly Queen, yes, the one and only Dawn 'Kit' King, the kick-stomping legend – *all the way from Arkansas!* – fronting her very own whip-cracking outfit.

Who always made it their business to announce those weekend gigs with a fanfare unprecedented, arriving in their glossy white ten-seater minibus, with *Kit & Cahoots* scripted in metallic blue along the side, coming roaring through the streets followed by a fleet of station wagons honking like crazy.

In the aftermath of a billowing smoke bomb, the band, appearing as if by magic onto the stage, with Dawn King practically busting her lungs as swung the mike and hollered: *Are you ready?*

—I want to sing you a song about the badlands, from way out there among the fields of wild azaleas, columbine and flowering dogwoods. Poor country, where they'll tell you folks was always poor but happy. Well, I don't know about the second part – but this song is by The Band and it's called 'Tears Of Rage'. I sure hope you do all enjoy it. For me, it's kinda personal.

With her tremolo-infused soprano, long slender limbs, big brown eyes and sunlit hair that fell past her shoulders, there was no likelihood of any shortage of punters willing to pay the price of a ticket just to get a look at what the Rockabilly Queen might get up to, especially when Dawn had been on the juice – to which she was no stranger.

As they watched her weave unsteadily beneath the lights, bathed in their blushing pink glow and speaking in tongues to warm herself up – sometimes, if she felt like it, picking me out personally from among the punters – and delivering one of our special favourites, Merle Haggard's 'If We Make It Through December', and giving me that smile she knew could turn me inside out.

Before continuing, those liquid keyboard teardrops falling behind her, and with that same Haggard-style trademark wrinkle of ache in her voice, in her mind wandering back up in the hills and hollows of her childhood, with the Arkansas river flowing close by.

Other times, then, it could seem like she was a completely different person – like the night she ran riot, climbing down off the stage and mingling among the dancers, shredding her throat out, like someone possessed.

As the pile-driving Southern rock, with its heavy riffing, sweeping slide fuzz guitar, continued at a jangling, coruscating lick, and the breathless drummer pounded up a storm, accelerating the rhythm as the volume swelled until the tensions in the ballroom almost reached bursting point.

With the cymbals crashing wildly as she hugged the microphone, speaking wildly in tongues about desert freeways, cavernous skies, the eyes rolling in her head as she seemed almost delirious, intoxicated by the rise of the music.

While the feet of the dancers flew thick and fast as reels, cotillions and waltzes all seemed to be so mingled and blended together that it might well have been described as a dance without a name.

–Let me tell you about the last days! they heard her cry. You want to know about the last days, my friends? Why – don't you know? These are those days, the ones we're living through this minute – right now!

After which she'd scaled the steel supports of the balcony and performed a swandive right into the centre of the floor.

Before landing in the middle of Ricky 'Big-Style's astonished, awaiting lap.

But, a hoot and a holler though she could be on those occasions, one thing you didn't do was to think you could take Dawn Kit for granted or do her down, in any shape or form.

Nope, that was something you did not do.

As the unfortunate Teddy 'Buckfast' Carson was to discover, one Saturday night in the Heartland bar, after hours.

When he had sidled up to her standing at the counter and spat sourly out of the side of his mouth: Way I hear it, Miss Kit King, you ain't much more'n a honky tonk whore – a backcountry Jezebel, that's what you are and all you'll ever be.

And about which she seems to do nothing at the time – nope, absolutely nothing at all – only to give him this look like he's hurt her real bad, slipping away as she cradles her round of drinks.

Only the next week, there he is, right in the middle of the crowd again, with the whole place out of their brains as usual, and those buzzsaw chords from the electric slide fuzz guitar threatening to burn the roof off the hall as the heavy percussion continues thundering away.

And what's Dawn doing only stalking the stage, punctuating the tense, erotically charged air with a series of syncopated, rapid handclaps, prowling like a panther in her black leather rhinestone-studded jacket and low-slung, stonewashed blue denim jeans, wiggling her tongue and shaking her ass, trawling the floor for a sighting of Buckfast.

–You got a mind to offend me, man?

And she's whirling the cable way over her head, shoving the mic into the faces of the audience as she urges them on in a call-and-response.

–*I said yeah!*

–*I said yeah!*

–*I said: you got a mind to offend me, man!*

–*I said: you got a man to offend me, man!*

And then starts bouncing from one end of the stage to the other, sneering and chewing her gum, covered in sweat, as the drums keep up their chicka-boom rhythm and the rubbery bass continues on rumbling, rumbling ...

–You wanna throw your weight around, shitkicker? You listening to me, Carson? You got a mind to dishonour a lady's pride and disrespect her dignity? Because if that is the case, and it sure does seem to me like it is, then you can take it from me that you are making one big mistake. Yep, embarked on a course of action that I would have to say is very much erroneous and inadvisable. So maybe you ought to consider switching horses, fucking loser. Before it is way too late, my friend! Because you may not like the consequences, fuck. You attending to Kit, you brainless cunt?

As out went the microphone above the heads of the dancers again.

−*I said yeah!*

−*I said yeah!*

−*I said: go down old Hannah don't you rise no mo'!*

−*I said: go down old Hannah don't you rise no mo'!*

Then she slipped into one of those odd personal trances, with those big brown eyes rolling back in her head and on one knee declaring:

−Low-rate this girl and offend her dignity − offend it yeah!? I said yeah, you low-rated it, offended it, yeah. But that dog won't hunt and that cock won't fight. Hullo girl, said my daddy one time, how is my little girl today? I walked miles of motherfucking barbed wire, use a cobra snake for a necktie − yeah! You listening, numbnuts? Carson, are you listening?

As she fanned the guitarist's instrument with the broad grey brim of her Confederate hat, throating hoarsely:

−Git down, Old Hannah, git you away on down!

Fanning some more, before sinking to one knee as she declared there was a dedication that she would like to make, focusing in on Teddy Buckfast.

And then:

−O, Teddy! she's squealing, why did you have to go and do it, lie to your pretty baby? Because you told me last week you could fuck like a stallion − and now I'm damned if I can feel a whisper of your little tinkle inside o' me here at all!

As the place erupted.

Before she moved in to deliver the coup-de-grace:

—But then, she hollered, maybe that ain't no bad thing, loverboy. Seeing as you got a face that's ugly as a stumpful o' spiders!

Putting paid, once and for all, to the foolhardy impertinence of Teddy 'Buckfast' Carson – who was never seen back in Heartland again.

But Dawn 'Kit' King wasn't finished or anywhere near it.

—I'd like to see you all out on the floor now for this one. It's a slow waltz which means a great deal to me, on account of it happens to have been written by my father. Who's dead now, God rest his soul, but in his time was a wonderful musician – you name any instrument, yep any Goddamn instrument at all and hell, could my Daddy wring a tune out of it. He could of been professional but he turned his back on all that because he wanted a simpler life for his kids and for his wife. Yeah, that was his dream, our own personal Paradise back up in the woods. And so what if it didn't work out that way, if he turned into just another junked-up hippy. Because that's what happened, ain't it father? Once upon a time there was a genius who dreamed. You had too much to dream last night, Zachariah my man – way way too much.

She takes fits, some of them used to say.

You ask me, she's a couple of bubbles short of plumb.

Then she faltered for a moment and just stood there, saying nothing, twisting the mic cable and staring out at nothing, like she'd forgotten the words or something. Before starting up again only this time with her delivery being trip-hammer fast, like her thoughts were getting way ahead of her.

—Yeah, you might think that's dumb, like I do – leaving the place of my birth in Serenity, Ohio and going up, into them Ozark hills, with nothing. When he could, just as easily, have headed somewhere else – such as Nashville, maybe, or even the West Coast. He could have made it there, you see, more likely than most. They all used to make the journey out to the Ozarks to see him, the honchos. So many of 'em, when I was a little girl – with all of 'em trying to coax him back. You gotta give it one more shot, I always used to hear them say – but it was always the same, he'd just wave it away. Nope, he would insist, because I got everything that I want right here. And if there was one bad day, then what the heck. What you think, that it's gonna be perfect all the time in Paradise? I know that's what they tell you but …

She lowered her head and got all choked up, looking around as if she had, inexplicably, gone and forgotten her name.

Then laughing uproariously and shaking her head as she wiped her eyes.

With the drummer light-heartedly striking the snare as she started up again as if nothing at all had happened.

–As a matter of fact that's what the actual song is about, you know? That particular day one of the most important people in the record industry at the time – Straight Arrow Montgomery was his name – he had come out to see us in the mountains to give 'one last shot' at persuading my father to come back to Nashville and lay down some tracks. Montgomery was short-haired and blocky and thick-necked. He had pinkish, freckled skin and was in white socks and ankle-high work shoes, the leather soft as lanolin, and he seemed to shuffle them along the ground rather than to take actual steps in them. He had thin white wispy hair and there was a ridge of deep tan across his forehead, where the brim of his perforated ball cap stopped. I know you can do this, he said, because you, more than anyone, understand the simplicity that's at the heart of country music, Zach. And that what it is is just stories told my ordinary people except in an extraordinary way. Thwarted ambition, that abiding sense of failure and being foreclosed. But I know you can give it a certain modern – sophistication is the wrong word – but levels of musical texture and complexity that are often missing, without ever losing the passion that makes it special. Let's ride them big wheels in the moonlight together – and if it don't work out then you can come back and everything will be the same, just as before. No harm done. Whaddyou say, Zachariah my friend, will you sing it one last time – that high lonesome sound, for your old buddy Straight?

–I'll never forget it, she went on, as they listened, rapt, because at first it really had been so pleasant and peaceful. But then my father, he went and took one of them weird and fucked-up turns of his. I could see it coming. For he'd only just finished cold turkey the previous week and was a trembling trip wire for a bomb, I swear to God. He's out there, he kept on repeating. Who's out there? Straight Arrow had laughed, under the impression, in his innocence, that it just my father's idea of a joke. But he sure wasn't long finding out that it was a damn sight more than that. When Daddy left down the guitar and picked up an axe – I swear to God, I'll never forget it – started swinging it in these wild arcs then above his head. Before stumbling over to where Montgomery was sitting under the spreading elm, but with his face now the colour of parchment. You wanna know something? my father said – I remember that skullface and those eyes like dead meat – Well then I'll tell you. You think I live where you do, record man? Is that what you think – because if it is, you're wrong. Because I don't live in Mendacity, Ohio, councillor. No, I don't live there, Lording it behind some felt-covered desk.

She paused for a moment to gather her strength-before eventually continuing.

–No, I don't happen to live in the shadows with some crested piece o' big business college bullshit on a frame up there behind me. Because where I fucking live, it happens to be called the truth, you digging me? Yes, that's where I

pitch my tent, motherfucker. Ri
in Truth County, Arkansas. So wh
off my property and take your off
with you. You wanna know about
that what you wanna know, our lit
tell you. He don't understand what
in the stillness. Because where he
of brass-and-glass. Hello, Montgomer   ou
reaching out to find and comprehend .. ueep, brooding
loneliness and desolation of the vast river? Well, that's
good, I'm glad to hear it. Because maybe when you find it
you can put all the money that you intend making out of
it back into your ugly motherfucking teat bars and casinos.
Cos the fact is that me and my family, and especially my
little girl Kit here, we don't want no part of it. Because
our quest is pure – you listening to what I'm saying? Pure,
you got that? And if we gotta endure a century of isolation
out here in the lonesome hollows to snare the ache and
the heartbreak of our forebears, here in the land of sultry
women, moonshine, hollers, sweet taters, romance and
good old boys, corn whiskey, Cajun crazies, snake handlers,
coon dogs, bizarre genealogies, outrageous mythologies,
and hot rods tearing up circular asphalt tracks, then that is
what we are motherfucking more than prepared to do. So
get the fuck out of here, Mendacity, Ohio!

–And we never did see that old Montgomery again, she
chuckled, he was out of there quicker than a cat can licketty-split!

–But, all the same, it's something no girl, at any age,
ought to see – her father in the night-time trembling like a
leaf. With her mother at her wit's end as she tries her best
to make sense of his drug-crazed delusions. I know what
they're saying, Kit, he used to say to me, that boy, somehow
his traces they ain't hooked up right. But it ain't so – I love
you, don't I? I'm not so lonesome, girl, that I could cry, am

y keep on saying, like I know they're doing –
I got going on inside of my mind is some kind
smic conspiracy against reality, in favour of romance
then all I got to say is, just wait till I pen my masterpiece,
you'll see. Become aware that it's you, and not me, who's
got their brain all wrapped kind of loose. I'm sorry to have
to be the one to tell you this. I can only hope that maybe
you'll understand. That where we, and my beloved family,
we are going to abide in that sweet and Bonny Land, where
nothing can ever hope to hurt us again. And there we shall
remain – *forever!*

–Look away, Zachariah! I can remember her hollering,
loud and clear and vivid, dropping to her knees at the front
of the stage. Zachariah, I implore you, look away!

Dawn said nothing for a long time and then laughed, a
little strangely – continuing to be so preoccupied that, at one
point, she almost fell right off the stage.

–But we never did get there, we heard Dawn King
explain, and never would. He just sat there watching the
green water lap at the pilings, and telling me that one day,
we would all of us sail to a country of our own, far beyond
the stars, and there live forever, up on some golden and
empurpled morning.

She remained in what seemed the remains of her self-
induced trance before, abruptly, appearing to come back to
herself as she shoved down a bottle of beer by the neck.

With the audience remaining close to hypnotised.

–Sorry for rambling, but by now you know what to
expect when you buy your ticket to a Dawn King show.
Anyhow, this one's called 'Sorrow, East Of Arkansas'! And
it's for my father – wherever the fuck you happen to be,
my lovely Daddy, and all them delirious dreams that kept
you going. With my sincere thanks to Lee Hazlewood and
Nancy Sinatra ...

—Whoever the fuck they might be! hollered Ricky 'Big Style', moonshine-whacked again as he stumbled past the stage on rubber legs in pursuit of a half-eaten hamburger, with his face completely covered in ketchup.

There were persistent rumours of a sauna and brothel operating upstairs, and WW's place had even been investigated by *The Sunday World*, a new newspaper dedicated to blowing the cobwebs off sleepy old Ireland and kicking it smartly into the middle of the modern world.

With it even carrying a front page photo of WW in his customary bootlace tie and Stetson, flashing that winning shit-eating grin over the top of a picture of a scantily clad model blowing a word balloon inquiring: *Are you getting it every Sunday?*

Whether they were or not, WW Monroe made it pretty clear that for him, personally, it was of about as much consequence as a popcorn fart in hell.

For he himself had made nothing out of the sauna, he would often be heard to insist, to compare with the return that the Country Club was bringing in.

And which had, with the acknowledged appreciated assistance of his young protégé Jody Kane, always been the jewel in WW Monroe's crown.

Especially during that blistering summer when the illicit fighting and gambling den they had mischievously nicknamed the Country Club might have been said to be at its height.

Everyone wanted to be seen there waving their money, always well after midnight and, hopefully, in the rain.

Because that was what WW Monroe liked most – you could see it in his eyes, especially if there happened to be lightning.

Then the stakes would be high, and ascending by the second.

As WW upped them by the hundred every minute on his boy.

Like I say, it wasn't a proper country club at all, nothing more than a nickname for the crudest of canvas rings, with a rude tarpaulin hoisted above and Windy Phelan the trainer hopping from foot to foot in his boy's corner. With his eyes like fireflies, pummelling the air like a man possessed as he repeated the name of Jody Kane one two three four five times and then the same all over again.

But this particular night, you could tell by the atmosphere of anticipation that it was already destined to be epochal.

High summer, it was, the hottest day of the year so far.

When Jody Kane looked a dead-cert to retain his title.

Yep, the 'Glasson Bull Calf', they'd taken to calling him – there just wasn't gonna be any way you could stop him.

With all of WW's supporters on hand to cheer him on – Los Locos Pistoleros, as they called themselves.

Whose number included such other near-legends as the formidable, taciturn Long John McNulty.

And who was, in fact, a genuine weapons and explosives expert, unlike a lot of the self-styled swaggering rebel compañeros.

Every one of whom was watching Jody Kane intently now – as indeed they might, for they all stood to lose a helluva lotta moolah on the bout – spitting though his gumshield as he squared his fists and glared from his corner like a chained-up pitbull.

–Once upon a time, announced WW, standing there in the centre of the ring, as the roving spotlight did its best to locate him, sweeping his hat flamboyantly as the shaft of light finally found him. Yeah once upon a time you heard it said that the rich were smart and that the poor man was a fool.

And that the rich men congregated under cover of darkness in the privacy of their uptown clubs. Yeah, the country club, gentlemen, that's where we belong. But what if the poor man suddenly he becomes rich, what then? Yeah, them as value honest labour, loyalty, independence and fairness over the false values of them other vulture-faced opportunists, social climbers, snobs, materialists and the well-to-do whose lives are backed by undeserved wealth and white-collar crime. Then the hell, I say to you, with the private country club of golf and swimming pool. Because tonight, good people, we are here where we belong, in WW's Heartland. Yep, right here in Glasson County which has always had its own ways and laws – and ain't at all, like they'll tell you in other places, some backland that is fitful, stark and way out of whack. A nowhere-place where folks got no choice but to lead barren and meaningless lives. Because what we got here, and always have had, is a separate world with its own seasons, weathers and a daily rhythm in which each hour has always had its own characteristic part, in this place where change, at least before now, has always come slowly but which at no time, ever, was anything but *home*. Where, unlike the city, *everything* is home. Where the rhythms of home and heartland can reverberate through the entire town. Yeah, this so-called great city that we hear so much about, which they'll tell you we spend all our time longing for, pining for success and all its dreams. But that what, of course, we lack when it comes to getting our hands on their dangled prizes is the talent, the shrewdness, the brains and the ruthlessness. With the result that we ain't never gonna be destined to be anything when compared with them, never gonna be looked-up-to, weighty men like them, whose words are always reckoned to count. With no choice open to us but to roll home roasted, again sick and defeated, hurling defiance at the moon and the roofs of our own little home, and all who have the bitter misfortune to be close to us. But not no more, my friends – no, never again. So come on board the WW Special, for this rig's riding right into the future. You hearing me, soldier? Come on – hit it, the fuck! Let's see some sparks spit from these here wheels – whoop!

As the percussionist from Kit & Cahoots commenced a furiously incessant, almost epileptic beat, with Bronco Meers coming running along the ramp to the sound of frantic applause and uproarious cheers, as every soul was released and granted latitude to run wild and raw.

–*Kill kill kill*, was all Jody Kane could hear as his opponent went straight for him, head down like a Brahma bull.

They had given Bronco Meers a name – the Cobra.

Yeah, the Cincinnati Cobra was the handle they had given him.

Even though he wasn't ever in Ohio, or Cincinnati.

Had never, in fact, been to America in his life.

Hailing from Mullingar, Co. Westmeath.

It was just on account of that famous look that he got in his eye, whenever, just like the snake, he had decided to go in for the kill.

Regarding his hapless opponent unswervingly.

Fixing him with a lethal, prideful stare.

The Cobra was hungrier than ever now, and was figuring on showing Jody Kane a thing or two.

–What's goin' on? Jody Kane provoked him, swinging and all the time dancing around.

–It ain't what's goin' on, smoke-and-horses, it's what'll soon be coming off – your face.

Leading with a double combination to the solar plexus then one two three four five to the side of the head.

And after which Jody had bled, real bad.

But had somehow recovered, and coming towards the end of the fourth or fifth round, had effected it.

That is to say, the pile-driver punch for which he was justly famous.

As the Cobra went down.

But it still wasn't over, with the Mullingar stalwart rallying – with it soon becoming apparent that the fight was definitely going to go the full distance.

As out came the Cobra.

You could tell by his expression that Jody's trainer was worried bad, for this had never happened before, not to someone like the Bull Calf Kane.

Not to Jody.

Not to the reigning champion.

With more furious combinations and one two three four five above the kidneys.

You could physically feel the pain.

But then the Cobra did a bad – and, as it turned out – an extremely unwise thing.

Kneeing Jody, slyly, in the groin.

And whispering:

–Daisyboy.

Because it was after that that the reigning champion saw in front of him ...

Yes, it was after that that the sneering, slavering visage of none other than Johnny Redlegs, rose up out of nowhere right in front of Jody Kane.

His abuser!

Filled with fake remorse and contrition

–Shucks, he heard Johnny Redlegs bleat pathetically, for all of the bad things I done in the long ago. Please forgive me and say that it's all right – will you, little feller? How can you ever forgive me, my own sweet lonesome little dogie?

After that, Jody struck the Cobra – hit him hard.

Once.

Twice.

And then again.

−Come on then, smoke-and-horses, is that the best you think you can do? Is that the best you got to offer − or is it, maybe, that you're afraid?

Jody Kane would just as readily have walked away there and then, but the Cobra just couldn't seem to learn.

No, he still kept coming.

−I'll fix you, you low-born gypsy no-good, that spent his life under canvas along with rats. I'll beat you, pikey, to a living pulp, I swear …

And that was when Jody did it − completely and utterly lost it, really.

First giving him a little jolt under the chin, just a little tap with his fist, as the Cobra grunted.

But his face went white as he tapped him again. Around the heart, down in the kidneys, and up on the wishbone. He held him up with one hand and fed him those little jolts with the other.

With the Cobra's face seeming to turn from white to green and his tongue slid out from his teeth.

And it was at that point Jody went for it.

Repeating to himself like someone possessed:

−Trooper Johnny, who is he? Trooper Johnny, who is he?

With his fists then flying out in front of him − one two three four five and then after that, the same again.

Before landing a special bulldozing right into the centre of his face.

As the Cobra howled and fell in a heap.

With the referee beginning to count him out.

But he never got there, for something was wrong. Because his trainer had already climbed in through the ropes.

−I feel so guilty, Ray, I remember him saying many times after that, I'll sometimes just be closing my eyes and then he'll be there, getting ready to come out of his corner and …

−You're a thoroughbred, Kane, that's what you are, WW had reassured him, just like your father before you was. And don't you ever disappoint me by doubting it.

Maybe I alone knew just how vulnerable he was, and how much he personally had changed.

−I'd do anything to quit, he had said one day, just get away and travel the world.

−So would I, I'd nodded eagerly, to realise the dreams that kept us going in our imaginations. Eden's uplands, back in Whiterock.

−Amigo, he said, and I said:

−Compadre.

So we'd been turning the possibility of departure over in our minds for a long while − long before the Monroe tragedy. All that did was bring it to a head.

It breaks my heart when I think how I fucked it over.

It really and truly does.

I hope you believe me.

Sometimes whenever I find myself writing, if that's what you want to call it − more like delving deep into the well of what, I suppose, is your soul − I'll often just let myself scribble away, thinking about nothing only getting the words down on paper.

Especially whenever I'm listening to music.

Although I really don't really know why that might be.

Maybe because all I really own in this world is a stack of second-hand records, or LPs as they used to be called.

Just now I was playing 'Crazy' by Patsy Cline, which was recently named the number-one jukebox hit of all time.

−*Crazy, I'm crazy for feeling so lonely …*

I don't know how many times I've listened to it, with the tears just erupting out of nowhere, of their own volition flowing down my face.

There are times when I can find myself so overwhelmed – particularly when I'm listening to tunes of that quality – that it's all I can do not to fling down my pen and go off to the pub or the off-licence and just get myself a bottle of – I don't know, *something.*

Just to bring myself down, you know? With the ferocity of the images sometimes coming so thick and fast that, at times, on occasion, it can actually be *frightening.*

I mean, I swear to God, there were times when I thought I could actually *hear* them.

The heartbeats below me in Mervyn's Bar, I mean,

–We don't know for sure he killed himself! cried Wee Hughie, on the verge of hysteria. Because when all is said and done, we've got no proof.

His face was raw and red as he poked the wooden surface of the table with his finger and kept obsessively tugging at his sleeve.

–We can't say any of that with any certainty, he suggested shakily, and anyway Mr Monroe, he wasn't that kind of man.

–Like it or not, he did it all right, died by his own hand, said Red morosely, so don't go making things worse now, you hearing me, Hughie?

–Yeah. Strike it, Patches, warned Sonny Hackett, you got nothing important to say, strike your scrake. The boss is dead – he's a goner, done deal.

–I object to that, snapped Hughie, I resent those words, you calling me Patches. Would you like to know something? I think you are a very ignorant man, Sonny Hackett. No wonder they're always saying you're moody. They say you're a moody bastard so they do. That they can't depend on you

– that you never know what sort of humour you're going to be in.

That made Sonny laugh, he said.

And Hughie Munley didn't know what he do, so he looked away.

Mervyn Walker's eyes seemed to say, It's going to be OK, fellers. Just relax.

Or maybe I'd imagined that. But it did seem to do Hughie some good. At any rate, you could see his lowering slightly, just a little.

–What's that grating sound? said Sonny. Is that you at that shit again, Campbell?

Red Campbell said nothing, staring vexedly across at Hackett.

Sonny, in his turn, matching him with a filthy look.

Before looking around at all the others.

–Am I missing something here? he wondered, is he looking at me? Wake up there, Grue – I said, am I mistaken or is Red Campbell giving me the bitter eye?

Big Barney got up in his chair and shook his head.

–No, Sonny. He's not. You're imagining that.

Red just stood there and nobody said anything. But then Wee Hughie surprised everyone by shouting out:

–Yes he is. And I wouldn't blame him, to be honest. For having to listen to people like you, Sonny Hackett, I sometimes I think in this life that we'd be better off at the bottom of Lake Wynter.

Once more, nobody said anything.

Before Sonny Hackett pushed his chair back and responded:

–What was that you were saying there, Patches? Because I didn't quite hear it.

–I think it's all stupid, behaving like this when we're waiting for TB. That's all I'm saying. And why I just tried to get it back the way that it used to be – except you had to laugh and make fun of me, didn't you?

–But I thought you were a comedian, Patches. That's why I was laughing. Because I thought you were being amusing and trying to crack wise.

Sonny nudged Campbell.

–Isn't that right, Red? Of course it is, amigo.

Then he slowly began to cross the room.

As Red's eyes followed his path resentfully, watching as Sonny Hackett flicked his forelock back and tapped Hughie Munley, playfully, on the shoulder.

–It's all right, Hughie, they heard him say, you can tell us about the old times. You go right ahead. You can tell us now. It's gonna be all right.

Hughie choked up, just a little, reaching for his hankie to give his moist dome a wipe.

–Whenever I think, he commenced in quavering tones, whenever I think, Sonny, about WW and the effect he had on the whole county – and how, somehow, way back then, we all used to be the closest of friends – and how we looked out for one another, it makes me feel kind of regretful and sad. Whenever I think of how we all used to go down to his place every night, just to drink ourselves stupid or dance, like now, to the record machine. Because we sure did have ourselves some good times – I think because he taught us, in some way, that we could. To kind of believe in ourselves, or something. Because WW, he thought big. Do you remember the day we transformed the whole of Heartland into the United States of America?

–Yeah! grinned Sonny. I sure do, Hughie. Heartland, America. USA!

–I remember it too, chimed Big Barney, leaning across the side of his chair, we did it to celebrate the Fourth of July.

–WW, he sure did have him some ideas, nodded Sonny, that you sure can say about William Walter Monroe.

–It was one of his best ideas ever, stammered Hughie, with everyone having to act as a different state!

–I was Michigan, Big Barney cried.

–And me, called Red, call me Campbell, Nebraska, haw.

–All o' them states, remembered Hughie, fantastic.

Then Mervyn called over, from the far side of the counter:

–He gave me a message – sent me all the way to Dublin, so he did. Where he'd had the American flag specially made. The stars and stripes – he dispatched me to get it.

–And man, shrieked Wee Hughie, did that old banner look good on the ballroom ceiling. Hooray for William Walter. But I hate it all now, now that he's dead. Because people like him, they're not supposed to ever leave the world ... not folks like WW Monroe, no sir.

With them all turning around then, scarcely able to believe their eyes, as that old Mervyn Walker, what did he do only climb right up there on the counter of the bar and deliver, to their astonishment, a note-perfect impression of the greatest man who'd ever lived in Glasson County – the one and only William Walter Monroe himself.

Closing his eyes tightly and lifting up those two long slender arms exactly the same as WW had done on the occasion of that fabulous Fourth of July celebration.

There had never, ever, been a night to compare with it – which the barman, quite magnificently, was giving them the opportunity to remember now.

When, to yet another tumultuous roll of drums, WW had eventually appeared onstage, whirling his Stetson as he called out to three thousand people:

–That mongrel breed, that's what they used to call us, friends. The ferocious backsettler, lawless and unsociable. Who live in sloth and know little of beauty. But that's where they're wrong, because from this day forward we live whatever way we want to, by our own backcountry codes ...

Then Mervyn, at last, gave an extravagant bow and left the stage of his own bar counter.

–Ah. Them was days, lamented Wee Hughie, they were the best days ever in Glasson County.

–Before it all went wrong, Red Campbell spat bitterly, exploding dramatically and crying out, hoarsely:

–It was Wade, from the start, who set the whole thing up. I sometimes wonder if that poor gypsy bastard Jody Kane even knew what he was getting into. But that other unreliable self-serving sumbitch – not one inch of him would I ever have trusted, and now it's come to this. Pulling a Judas on WW, ripping off all he'd got left, his bonds. The best man this whole backcountry has ever known, and him lying still warm underneath the clay of Glasson Mountain, the place where he was borned and reared.

–And a place he loved, maintained Wee Hughie Munley, more than any other, because he told me that himself.

–It's that smug sweet-talker by the name of Dawn 'Kit' King that's at the back of it all, mumbled Sonny Hackett with unconcealed malice, it was her more than anyone who turned poor WW's head. Because he took a heart-burning for her, and there ain't anyone in Glasson who doesn't know it, and that's a fact.

–That might be the case, but I'm still gonna cut that snake and cut him bad whenever I see him.

–You ain't gonna cut no-one, Campbell. Anyhow you wouldn't have it in you. We'll leave all that to a certain Tony Begley. It's Mr Begley'll do any cutting. For we want no repeats of what happened with Wilson Gillis – so we'll leave it to someone who knows what he's doing!

–What happened that night was an accident, protested Hughie, you got no right to go bringing all that up again.

–That's right, cried Barney, awaking sharply from a semi-slumber, why would we want to harm Wilson Gillis?

Then he fell right back into the chair, like all the air had escaped right out of him.

Mervyn Walker was busy searching underneath the counter. It was a fishing rod, he had resolved to tell them, if they ever got around to being sober enough to bother inquire.

Something, considering their advanced state of inebriation, he considered extremely unlikely indeed.

In any case his little parcel didn't look at all obtrusive, with his having taken the precaution of discreetly wrapping it in jute, binding it with twine in a number of places.

Nudging it with his knee, manoeuvring it securely out of sight.

As he wiped the counter and smiled across benignly at every single person, each in their turn.

By now they had all returned to a game they had already been playing, involving the naming of various American states and towns. Just like they'd done on that night long ago, on the Fourth of July, in the Heartland ballroom, 1976.

–Saginaw, Michigan.

–Kalamazoo.

Then Hughie Munley got up to his feet and shouted ecstatically:

–But, best of all, Paragoul, USA.

With Sonny, even, showing some enthusiasm – laughing his head off, in fact. As he outlined his share of names and then, suddenly, swept a heap of glasses off the table.

–Hey, called the barman, what in the heck?

But, fortunately, none of them broke.

Wee Hughie started picking them up.

–I'll look after them, Sonny, don't worry …

But Sonny didn't care whether he did or whether he didn't.

For 'Sunny' Sonny Hackett, he had other things on his mind.

You could barely hear him as his knuckles turned white.

—One thing I don't like is Indians coming around. Whether living in caravans or anything else. Because me and her – we used to be happy.

Then he went over and stood on his own by the side of the fireplace.

As Wee Hughie Munley said to Red Campbell:

—It's a pity that this had to happen at all.

Red Campbell looked at him, running his fingers through his copper curls and nodding.

—I have other things that I could be doing, at my time of life.

Wee Hughie nodded and after that, said nothing. Before Red became aware that he was gently squeezing his arm.

—I was wondering would you like one of these?

He was offering him some nuts from a bag.

—KP, said Hughie, they're better, I think, than Planters, Red.

—Yes. I think so too, Red Campbell replied, his overwrought face like a map of rough road.

—I wish, to be honest, all the same, that I could go home.

Wee Hughie nodded.

—Red, he began, do you mind if I tell you something?

—No, said Campbell, go right ahead.

—You were the only one who was ever half-decent to me in the factory. I've always had a mind to tell you that.

—That's OK, said Campbell, you and me always got on fine. Anyhow, I could afford to be nice to people, because that was before we got roasted and let greed get the better of us, terrorising an innocent man. And then, to make it worse, pretending that it was something to do with freedom and politics, instead of the moolah, which is all it was. After that, it could never be the same. The fairy tale was over – and, believe you me, that was exactly what it had been like, in the weeks and months after me and her had won the Kentuckyland prize, after we scooped the Dance-Off trophy. Me and that old Anita, we sure were some team. I used to call her the Kid, did you know that?

−Red and the Kid, smiled Hughie fondly, I sure do remember that OK.

−She looked real good that night, wearing that swirling flamenco skirt. The band were playing 'Y Viva España' as we swept and wheeled and dang near lost our minds. 'The Toast Of El Paso', they all started shouting up. Up until that time in Glasson County, there had been no Spain, because everyone used to holiday at home. Man, that little bolero jacket she made me, I never thought I'd have the guts to wear it. But there you are − that was the effect the Kid could have on you.

He hesitated as he searched in his pockets for his matches. Then he swallowed hard and said:

−Hughie, can I tell you something?

−Yes, replied Hughie, yes Red you can.

Red Campbell looked frightened, and almost regretful he'd ever made the offer. But Hughie's eyes looked so hopeful that they provided him with the encouragement he needed.

As, hoarsely, he continued with his story.

−I was sitting in the bar one night with Mr Monroe. Back in the days that used to be. Yes, sitting in the bar along with WW, except for one thing.

−For one thing? said Hughie.

−Yes, Red continued, except for one thing. It isn't him.

−It isn't him?

−No. It isn't him. It isn't Mr Monroe. O he looks the same all right − in that he's wearing the very same suit, with the hat and the boots and all the rest. But just as soon as he opens his mouth you can tell.

−What can you tell? demanded Hughie, holding a single nut in a pincer-grip between his left forefinger and thumb. What can you tell Red? Please.

The colour was beginning to drain from his face.

–That it isn't WW, said Red, like I said, it isn't him.

–O God, said Hughie, looking away, reaching in his pocket to produce the enormous handkerchief, patting at the sweat that was gleaming on his crown.

–O God, he croaked, I don't know if I want you to go on.

But Red Campbell couldn't have stopped himself even if he'd wanted to.

He too looked queasy, almost faint.

–But that isn't all that happened that night. Not by a long shot, Hughie. Because then the lights come up and who arrives in through a side door only the Dawn King. Yes, the lovely Dawn 'Kit' King, the singer, she comes sidling in. Almost out of nowhere, it appears, it seems, as she climbs onstage and starts performing this little swaying dance with the microphone. But – and here's the strange thing – the very same as with Mr Monroe, you can tell somehow that it isn't her. Not the real person, the actual Dawn King, if you know what I mean. O it looks like her alright, in almost every way. With that tawny hair tied up in a ponytail at the back, that lovely slender frame, and those big brown eyes. But when you looked real close …

Campbell faltered, saying nothing for a long time.

Then he resumed, seeming pale and agitated.

–And it's then that it happens – she comes right down off the stage, and like in a dream, only one with no sound, over she comes and sits on his lap. And starts talking, like you could see they'd been doing, about this whole new life they'd been planning to share together. In a place, she says, our beautiful valley, where the dawn will come breaking over the mountain and it'll be like the very first dawn ever imagined. Some velvet morning, my love, she whispers in that smoky voice, some velvet morning when we wake …

–Some velvet morning, moaned Wee Hughie Munley, some velvet morning, Jesus Christ!

As Sonny suddenly barked, glaring fiercely into Red Campbell's face:

–What'n the fuck you talking about, Campbell? You're raving, so you are – talking loco!

Then he turned away, rocking back and forth on his Cuban heels, closing his fist.

–One of these days, warned Sonny, one of these days, Red Campbell, I swear, you and your raving and those dumb fucking choppers … !

He went over to the jukebox, draping his lanky frame across its front.

–*The way it used to be*, sang Englebert Humperdinck.

As, without even realising they had spoken at all, Wee Hughie and Red Campbell murmured in unison:

–The way it used to be. That was always on in the canteen long ago.

–I remember it too, said Barney Grue, stirring.

–Let me rest on peaceful mountain, Mervyn Walker whispered softly behind the counter, recalling his old friend standing, as had been his custom, in the very front pew of Glasson village chapel, praising his Maker with his Good Book, page open at Galatians 6:7.

Thinking to himself about the many walks they'd shared together along those quiet country lanes, and those Saturday evenings when they'd stand side by side on the bridge overlooking the lough and sometimes, even, at dawn.

As the sun's pale rays lanced off the surface of Lake Wynter.

On that morning, long ago, when all had seemed as quiet as the breath of a bird, without a cloud to be seen in the sky.

When two old friends, spin-casting their lines, looked down from the arched stone bridge into a field where they could see a horse nudging a foal on spindly legs. As a woman hung out her washing on a line and her husband whistled a low little tune, from underneath a propped-up car hood, leaning over an engine block.

With it, albeit unspoken, occurring to both men that it somehow didn't seem to matter how many highways or shopping malls they built in their beloved Glasson because nothing could ever interrupt the unchanging rhythm of the life that both of them had known as boys.

Wilson Gillis and Mervyn Walker: ageless, almost − like two tall stately pine trees themselves, it had somehow always seemed.

−What is Time? his friend had, abstractedly, inquired on that occasion. Can we ever really say what it is, Mervyn Walker − plumb its essential nature? Some say that it tends to move forward. Others, both forward and back at the very same time.

−Who knows, he remembered saying, who knows Wilson? All I care is that, out here, for you and me, it always stands still.

As their lines were played this way and that beneath them − almost, just like Wilson had suggested, the very same as Time itself.

Chapter 18

In the High Country

The very last letter I found myself receiving from Jody, I just can't tell you how tender it was. Or how sweet and wonderful I felt when I got it – just for having received it, I mean.

With my only regret being that he felt he had to leave in the piece that he wrote about the dream.

But I can understand too why he might have felt the need to say it.

Initially, I remember, after reading that first page, I had found myself in a state of peace, kind of like I was back in the imagined, breathtaking wonderland of our boyhood.

Because I had never actually known that Jody Kane was capable of writing that way.

Except there it was, right there in front of me on those blue-lined exercise book pages, in that very same spidery longhand scrawl which I remembered from the classroom when the two of us would have been in third or fourth class, in Glasson Primary.

O man, Jody wrote, it feels so good to get all of this off my chest at last, and to be able to share these personal memories with you, Ray. Not just about the trauma we both experienced that night, but everything.

Because, he went on, although I've met so many special and wonderful people since arriving here, nonetheless there's still something private and unique and irreplaceable about the experiences you've shared with the folks from the place in which you were born.

I was thinking only the other night about the time we skipped out of the orphanage and headed back up the mountains to the waterhole where we just lay down and laughed there, for hours, with our fishing poles dangling there, over the water. Do you remember that Ray? All the things we were going to do. So many things, Ringo – so many things we found it hard to keep track.

My wildwood flower tells me I'm sentimental – and that the way of the world has always been for human beings to keep on shedding their pasts the way locusts do their shells, moving across the plains of history, and that what I got to do is to learn to be more like them if I'm to survive.

Because that's what the human spirit requires, she says.

And I know that it's true, like so much of what she says. But there's a part that holds fast and, no matter how you try, just won't seem to let you go – do you find that Ray?

Like it's there when you want it or feel the pressing need of it, a kind of sheltering harbour of nostalgia, I guess you might call it.

That would be one way of describing it.

Sometimes when I think of Glasson and the fields and rivers and hills all around it, it's like it's the centre of the universe itself.

For there are few nights that go by when I don't feel it coming again in my mind, with all of its small bridges and sheds, its letterboxes nailed to trees and lonely petrol pumps, and the river winding through it making its way westward across a pattern of little lakes and hills, as the shadows and the strong scent of the pine trees reaches out into the water.

Every night, believe it or not, in one way or another, that scene drifts right in front of my eyes – gleaming bog pools and the peal of a distant bell, coming drifting across the sleeping countryside from some old churchyard, winding through the pine-fringed mountains and forest lakes.

I love it, Ray – in some ways that's crazy, for sure, and no one knows that better than me.

But nonetheless it's true.

And I keep on thinking of those childhood days, especially of the streets on a hot summer afternoon, watching the men in the livery stables, joshing and chatting and smoking by the wagons, yuk-yuk-yukking and guffawing the way they used to do.

Which brings me, Ray, to what it is I want to talk to you seriously about – this dream that I had the other night. And which has affected me, I got to say.

So much that my flower insisted that, sooner or later, I would have no choice but to have it out with you – or, at the very least, tell you about it.

And, having done that, hopefully, minimise its effects. Possibly even, somehow, end the whole thing.

You see the thing is, Ray, what happened was, I was standing there in the dream whistling and mucking out the stalls, the same as I always used to do in Kentuckyland. And thinking to myself just how fortunate the two of us had been. When I heard a soft , low voice behind me and a couple of hesitant steps approaching. And then I saw him – but not the same way we were used to, with that second-hand shop military jacket and his dented brass bugle. But looking like his whole body had been drained entirely of all its blood, and with that greasy combover falling down across his hunted eyes. As he gave me one of those sickening smiles, and said: Yes, you've been fortunate, you and Ray Wade. But me, I'm afraid, I haven't been quite so lucky. And which is why you owe me one last favour. So, come with me now, little dogie, there's a good little feller …

That's what he said – yes, those were his words, Ray – as a matter of fact, I'm actually trembling as I write them.

–Because you and me, I heard him repeat, you and me is going to a garden country. We are going to the Bonny Land, my friend. That place which is known as the Southland of Forever.

And then, whenever I looked again, the two of us were making our way across the High Country Meadow, and he was already pushing the door of the big haggard open.

–All of our whooping, long-gone lonesome games, little dogie. You had better be sure of it, the South is a-gonna rise again!

I was hesitant about going in, Ray – you can understand why – and just stood there listening to him muttering and singing to himself inside.

–*Tramp tramp tramp the boys are marching!* he hollered and whooped.

He must have been in there for well over half an hour, Ray – at least that was how it seemed in the dream. Over and over and over and over – *tramp tramp tramp, tramp tramp tramp,* determinedly marching on the spot.

Until, at last, he appeared once more in the doorway, only this time wearing not so much as a stitch, whirling a bloodied garden shears above his head. As he wailed and shrieked and appealed for me to forgive him, to show him whatever little morsel of mercy I might be able to muster.

On account of what he had just gone and done – 'harvesting his tackle' – which was how he described the act of self-evisceration in which he'd just been engaged.

That was when I saw it, Ray – the black blood coursing in long twisty rivers down along the insides of his legs.

–See what you gone and done, little feller, I heard him chortle. You've only just gone and made me harvest m'godarn tackle!

And, after that, Ray, he was gone.

As was I.

The following page of the letter was blank. And at first I thought that was the end of it. But then I discovered two other pages in which Jody did his best to explain his confused feelings.

I don't want to overstate it, Ray, he continued, but the truth is that ever since having that 'tackle' dream – it's been having a really bad fucking effect.

And what I want to ask you now is this – and if you choose not to respond, be assured that I'll do my best to accept that decision.

But I know, you see, that you followed us up top the haggard that day, as you did on many other occasions. With the result that you knew practically everything that was going on. Regrettably, however, deciding to say nothing. Because that's your nature, isn't it, Ray? Wait till you see what's in it for you. Because you're a watcher, Ray – an uncommitted, selfish copperhead, like they say. Except that it's even worse than that, ain't it, Ray Wade.

He paid you, didn't he? He bribed you, Ray – bought you and convinced you not to breathe a word.

So you put yourself first. As usual, Ray.

Why did you have to do it, old friend?

Because – and here's the hard part – no matter how anyone advises me, even my love, my sweet beautiful wildwood flower, no matter what they say, I'm still not sure I can do what it is they're asking. And by that, I mean, Ray, as I'm sure you've already guessed, is grant you the the forgiveness that you've asked for.

But I'm trying, Ray – please believe me when I say that. And I just pray that, in the end, it will all turn out good.

My beloved is one hundred per cent certain that it will – insisting that all that matters is we all do our best, at this time, to be strong.

On another note, Ray, I was thinking just this morning about the very first day that the ballroom went up – do you remember that, Ray? Like some beautiful new dawn had arrived in Glasson County.

Like the one that's coming to you and me, old friend, at least I hope so.

I don't know how many times I've read and analysed those words – time after time after time – until they're little more than a blur in front of my eyes.

I don't like to dwell on it, but my doctor tells me he's certain that the relapse I experienced recently can be directly traced back to my receipt of that letter.

And which is why Fr Conway keeps on asking me what was in it – or, at least, to give him some small indication.

But the truth is, I can't.

I actually couldn't.

Because I don't even want to remember it now.

Why, you ask?

To that there is one simple and regrettable response: that never, in the whole of my life, have I ever felt so awful.

And which is the reason I decided I'd no choice but to go out and have a drink – just one.

Perhaps just a pint of beer, I thought.

Because, of course, it's only the hard stuff that you really have to worry about, I kept on telling myself.

And which, of course, is the fatal error – one made by many similarly afflicted survivors long before me.

Whatever might have made me think I was any different?

In any case, that was what I did – I did it anyway.

And whenever I got back, almost as soon as I came in the door, I found myself in such a state of elevation that, straight away, I got out a sheet of paper and pen and sat down to pen my response to Jody Kane's letter.

One that would be straight-talking, I had already decided, direct and honest, with no punches pulled.

Inquiring as to how he might have thought it was easy for me, and that, at least, he'd had the privilege of knowing his parents, even if only for just a little while, which was a hell of a lot more than I'd had.

At least, compadre, that was something to help you to make your way through life, I scribbled furiously, my brow covered in perspiration.

Before going on to explain how, insofar as I could, I had done the best I could to look out for myself, at least not ending up like my poor unfortunate mother and father, killed in a road wreck, mangled beyond all recognition for all I knew.

Yes, just like my mother and father, I continued on writing.

You getting me, Jody? You know what I'm saying?

OK, so I'm sorry – I fucked up our plans. I screwed it over. I admit that, friend.

But – and you had better listen to this, amigo – at no time was I trying to pull a Judas.

Because I didn't, and never would.

Not on you. Jody, old friend.

Not you.

All that happened was I'd got so roasted after the funeral that I lost precious time trying to remember where I'd stashed the bonds.

I accept it all – it was the screw-up of the century.

And another thing, Jody – as far as all of that business with Redlegs goes, if you want to know the truth, he threatened to fix me with those shears if I said anything, if I opened my mouth to anyone. So it isn't as simple as you might think.

You want your tackle harvested as well – *that what you're fixing to happen, little dogie?* That's what he said – and not just once or twice.

You've got to believe me, Jody, you really have to.

I know it might sound strange, but by the time I had finished pouring out all my feelings, all I can say is that I was feeling exhilarated.

Having cleared the air and put things straight as best I could.

Except that when I turned the paper over and cleared my throat in order to start reading the pages from start to finish, all I could make out from the manic, illegible scribble were the words:

YOU'LL HAVE TO LIVE WITH THIS

Scrawled I don't know how many times.

And overleaf was exactly the same.

As I shook my head and found myself starting to laugh.

Before deciding to go out to the pub.

What else could I do?

It must have been was close on 3 a.m. when I finally made it back home, still high as a kite.

Snorting as I crumpled up the letter and tossed it into the fire grate, before falling on top of the bed, like I hadn't a care in the world.

At least, that is, until I woke up.

So maybe, like the doctor says, it does all go back to receiving that letter.

But, no matter what he or the padre Fr Conway might insist, there are other memories lying in wait, patiently gauging the best moment to strike. Bringing you back, when they choose to, to that open coffin of an attic over Mervyn's, when you would happily have given everything you owned in the world, such as it might be, to be accorded the privilege of just one single cathartic scream.

Chapter 19

El Brindis Del Paso

Sonny Hackett stood up and went across to the jukebox. Then he changed his mind and walked over as far as the fire. The next thing he was standing underneath the Woolworth's picture of the little boy sitting on the potty clutching his teddy. After that, he spent a while worrying the dartboard with a couple of fantails. Then it was off to the lavatory and back again. But, try though he might, the tall brooding man just could not seem to settle or sit still. Now rising to his feet as he shot, sharply, over to the window, sparking up yet another rollie.

As Red Campbell and Hughie remained at the table in silence, with Big Barney Grue continuing with his loud, intermittent snoring.

Under which a tense and brittle silence reigned, with the jukebox machine dead, until, at last, Red Campbell looked up and said:

–You used to know her when the lot of us were young, didn't you Hughie?

–I sure did, Red. She used to live up the Backs, behind the railway.

—The Kid, murmured Red, with his mouth still all dry. One day I came and found she wasn't there.

—She didn't leave you, did she, Red? I didn't know anything about that. I didn't hear.

—No. That's right, she didn't. She didn't leave. I mean, she's there every day whenever I get home. But she isn't *there*.

—She's not where, Red?

—What I mean is – there's a stranger in her place. Do you want to know the truth about her and me, Hughie?

—If you want to, Wee Hughie said, flushing, that is if you think it's any of my business.

—I do think it's your business … she doesn't love me anymore, Hughie. She tries but she can't. And every time I look at her sitting there, I'd give anything to see them lovely eyes of hers, the way they used to gleam when she'd look back, returning my gaze. *Red*, they used to say. But now they say nothing. For the simple reason that they aren't hers. No, they aren't her eyes. I'm afraid not, Hughie. Because she's gone, the Kid. Yes, I'm afraid the Kid ain't there anymore.

Big Barney belched and shifted a little in his chair. As his mouth fell open and his words rolled around the room.

—I'm sorry for what we done that night on Wilson Gillis …

Then he woke up, looking startledly all about him.

—It's all the gypsy's fault, bawled Sonny, only for him none of this would even be happening.

As Wee Hughie Munley lifted his two arms, leaping into life.

—It's gonna be OK, Sonny, he insisted, because any minute now Tony will be here, and after that we can all go home. Whaddya say?

The phone rang and everything went dead.

—It's Tony, said Mervyn, he says twenty minutes. Or half an hour, at the latest.

He replaced the receiver in its cradle and smiled, and then returned to wiping a glass.

–There. Didn't I tell you? We'll soon be on the last train home, declared Hughie.

As Sonny turned pale and erupted in a fury.

–What are you talking about, last train home? What kind of lamebrain shit you talking now, you fucking dwarf. Guffing out of you the whole night long – sit down and shut your stupid fool mouth. Sit down, you hear, or I'll fix you, and a coupla them sisters o' yours along with you.

–Here, said Red, easy there, Hackett. For there ain't no call to be talking like that to Wee Hughie …

–There ain't no what? returned Sonny. No what?

Then he rounded on Hughie.

–You think he's right? You think I'm treating you disrespectfully?

–No, said Hughie, I think you just said it. I don't think you meant it. Did you?

–That's good, Patches, I'm glad to hear that. Because that's not something that Sonny Hackett would be inclined to do, disrespect Patches the world-famous comedian. The funniest man in all of Glasson County. Ain't that the case?

–Yes, agreed Hughie, yes Sonny. If you say so, then that's the situation.

–Screw you, grumbled Campbell, screw you, friend. In any case, he might be a midget, but at least he's got a wife that's happy to stay at home with her child, instead of running out to caravans every chance she gets.

Sonny raked his fingers through his glistening hair and snarled viciously, swinging on his heel:

–You ever talk to me like that again. You ever dream of saying the like of that to me one more time, and O, I swear to God, but I will hurt your lousy body oh so fucking bad.

Looking, however, like he was about to faint as he stumbled towards the nearest wall in an effort to support himself.

—Don't say that to him, Hughie Munley pleaded with Red, standing beside him, looking into his eyes.

—Because I don't want no hassle with him. You know what Sonny Hackett can be like!

Red nodded and grunted, saying he didn't care. Lifting his glass and staring over at the small man, emptily.

—Not now that I'm living with a stranger. Not now that the Kid is gone.

As Big Barney snorted and his chair gave a screech.

—Sometimes I think *I'm* a stranger, they heard him say.

He seemed groggy, still half asleep.

—What? said Hughie. Sometimes you what?

Big Barney got up and tossed back his chair, sleepwalking across to the table beside them.

And just sitting there, in silence, for quite some time, his fleshy chin propped up on his soft broad hand. As his enormous prize-fighter's shoulders sagged dramatically and they heard him murmur:

—Sometimes, out of nowhere, I'll just get the oddest feeling, and find I'm kind of beat, becoming completely miserable and way kind of down, you know? Not knowing what to do with myself — with the strangest thing being the way that it just somehow comes, like I say, completely out of nowhere. Maybe when I'm just sitting at the table eating my dinner, or it could be when I'm watching TV. Like it did that day when Foghorn Leghorn appeared on the screen.

—Foghorn Leghorn? asked Red Campbell. Who's that, Barney? Foghorn Leghorn — because I don't really know.

—He's a rooster, interrupted Hughie, a great big yella fella. Isn't that right, Barney?

—Yes, that's correct, Barney Grue affirmed, you'll sometimes see him on the evening TV. But anyway, I was telling you: it's whenever you least expect it that this feeling I'm talking about will arrive. This truly awful black mood which is really beyond words. I hope youse don't mind me saying all this …

They heard Sonny Hackett loudly clearing his throat.

—I don't know what you're talking about, he shouted, and if I did — if I did happen to feel like that — I think I'd be inclined to keep the information to myself.

But Big Barney ignored him and continued in a dozy haze. With Red starting up with his teeth again, even worse this time.

You could see Hackett wincing.

—I told you, he bawled, I warned you to stop doing it.

But Red didn't.

Stop, I mean.

As Barney proceeded, with his heavy eyelids drooping.

—It's the kind of mood that's nearly impossible to describe, he said, one for which you'll never, not properly, ever be able to find the words. The more I try to describe it to anyone, the harder it always seems to get. It's like a kind of great big emptiness, so it is, that just comes floating right down out of nowhere and then — *boom*. You could be anywhere, like I say, even watching Foghorn Leghorn, absolutely anywhere in the world when it happens. I hate it. I really do. Hate it more than anything. I suppose youse must think I'm mad.

—No we don't said, Hughie, shaking his head, we don't — do we, Red?

But Red too now seemed lost in a world of his own, trying his best to come back from it by grinding his teeth.

Except it wasn't working.

—Kid, he was saying, where did you go? Did I ever tell you about my memories of Spain?

—What's he saying now? Sonny Hackett called over.

As Red poured a glass and continued clicking and grinding.

—Break his back, I swear I will, Hackett muttered sullenly, take him down, and one by one take out those teeth. Don't think I wouldn't.

As he left his chair and breasted up to the counter, grinning away at the barman.

—Right, Mervyn? Am I correct there, my man?

As the barman smiled, continuing to polish the glass, closing one eye as he lifted it up, for inspection, to the light.

—How's that, Sonny? he said, with a twinkle.

—Some people they just got a knack o' getting on other peoples' nerves! Comprende?

—Maybe, said the barman, and then again maybe not. It's not for me to say, I guess. You know what I mean, Mr Hackett? That it really ain't my place to say.

As he set about replacing the now-gleaming glass and Sonny's beady eyes narrowed into slits.

—You're a funny customer, he said, not a bit of wonder that sometimes I get these things into my head about you, Mervyn.

The barman flexed his knuckles and smiled.

—That a fact? he said. Do you now?

—Yeah, sniffed Sonny, things in my head – I get them about you.

—Well well, the barman smiled, how about that.

—Ha ha, called over Hughie, that's like my joke – well well well …

Then, all of a sudden, and in spite of his abrupt attempt at levity, seeming quite agitated as he strode across the floor, noisily pushing down a few of the flyblown slats.

—No sign, he announced, returning to the table.

—No sign? said Red.

—That's right, repeated Hughie, it's like a stack of black cats out there …

As Barney Grue seemed to sway in space, with his large knotted fists swinging loosely by his side.

Lunging forward as though just having experienced second thoughts and was doing his best to retrieve the words which that very second so passionately had been set free from his quivering lips.

With his falsetto cry frantically penetrating the air.

—I don't care what any of youse say. Because never as long as I live will I forget it.

—Forget what? asked Hughie.

—He's just drunk, aren't you, Barney? That's all it is — it's just that loco crazy jungle. It think it's getting to us all, tell the truth …

But Barney wasn't listening to a word he was saying.

Anxiously scratching away at the palm of his right hand, doing the best he could to collect his disparate thoughts, before dramatically exclaiming:

—I was supposed to meet her there, you see!

He lifted his head and looked at them imploringly.

—Please. Can any of you tell me? he continued. Can any of you please help with this? Have any of you ever been in an airport at midnight? Give you the shivers so they would. But especially this one, because it was completely deserted. Although a couple of planes were still coming in. I was just looking out the glass of the observation bay, staring out right across the tarmac. I had never seen it before, ever, looking the way that it did. You'd have thought the moon was going to plummet right out of the sky and land right there in front of you, right out there on the runway, I swear to God. But it didn't. It just stayed where it was. Quite a ways away, you could see the city — well, not see it so much as feel it, you know? I still don't know what it was that made me think about the electrisms. I wonder did any of youse ever hear about them? Hmmph? Well did you, guys?

He waited, hoping that someone, anyone, might chance a response.

But no one did.

So, blindly, he proceeded:

−Years ago, when I was a little boy, don't ask me what age, maybe eight or nine − the electric men came to Glasson County and they brought the electrisms with them. Which came from the water, the old men said − many's the time I heard them talking about them. Yes, they came from the rivers and there was more of them in the waters of Glasson County than anywhere else in Ireland. These were the men who brought power to the valley, the very same electrical impulses that I could feel now, travelling through thin air, as I waited alone in that airport. Watching. All the electrisms of the world be's in them wires, I remember the old men saying, so I do. Before looking at one another, scratching their heads and saying: but what are they? What *is* an electrism? No one could say. Not then, not back in them days. And it made me shiver all over again thinking about that. Because I could see the fields under the mist spreading towards the city … over there in the air, many miles away.

He waited again to see would they speak.

They didn't.

−And then, as well as that, the ticking of street lights, and gas lines hissing. I tried my best to shut my ears but the sweat was already streaming all the way down on my forehead and neck. To tell you the truth, I felt like crying. Because there were just too many sounds at one time. That's why I sometimes pull up my collar, to keep out electrisms. I know that sounds stupid. But, I'm sorry guys − what was I saying? Yes − right then, very close by, I saw this rabbit. Just standing there, watching, with his ears pricked up, hunched right there, in the middle of the tarmac. Dead in the centre of it, alert and waiting. And when I seen it I became all choked up. I suppose, because it was just the two of us there now. And because, all of a sudden, it had seemed to go so cold. All I kept thinking was that maybe the plane I was waiting for had crashed. You see, an even heavier fog had started coming down. As a matter of fact, now that I remember, it was already well down. Like a great big massive grey sheet that was covering the whole airport. And it was then I heard it – the low drone of an aircraft making its way in, approaching the landing strip. You could see the windsock blowing this way and that, real slow, you know the way they do. And then, sure enough, I could make it out real plain. Yes, there it was, banking as it made its approach, coming on down the coast.

Sonny struck the wall with his fist and announced that this was more than enough. And that if Barney Grue didn't shut it then he might very well come over and give him some encouragement.

–No threatening, called Mervyn Walker, you got that Sonny Hackett?

–Well well, Sonny grinned, if it ain't the big-talking barman. Who asked you to interfere?

–I said what I said, replied Mervyn, quite genially, that's all. As Wee Hughie Munley looked anxiously around him.

–Well well well, he chuckled hopefully.

And, in that instant, deciding privately that he didn't give a damn any longer about being funny, or being called a 'gas ticket' or 'the flower of the flock'.

Or any of the other stupid names that they used to describe him.

–The hell with this, he shouted, why should I have to do it – put up with it?

–Put up with what? hissed Sonny Hackett, shut your dumb little stupid dwarf mouth. Go on home to Hickory Holler and put some patches on your clothes. And while you're at it, tell one of your sisters to switch on the red lamp. For I'll be coming up to see a squad of easy judies, just as soon as we're all done here.

But Hughie Munley didn't respond.

Having privately resolved not to bother caring.

And, maybe, never to do so again.

Irrespective of whether it was about patches or sisters or anything else.

As Barney Grue continued with his aeroplane story.

—Yes, he elaborated, with its port and starboard lights showing and then the winking light below the fuselage went on as it swung out to sea in a long lazy turn, coming in once more before it banked, and …

He hesitated for just a second, seeming somewhat alarmed, continuing to scratch at the palm of his hand.

—You could tell, do you see, that the rabbit had seen it too. It seemed to take an age, with its landing lights – they kept on flickering, on and off, on and—

—For the love of Christ will you get on with the fucking story, broke in Sonny Hackett, and quit this accursed around-the-house rambling.

But Big Barney heard nothing, or chose to ignore it.

—It landed all right, he went on to explain, it did that OK. But as soon as the doors of the aircraft opened … when they opened and I looked out …

He lowered his head. By this point everyone was hanging on his every word.

—She wasn't on board.

—Because it wasn't her aircraft, he nodded as he explained.

—Yes, you see, because it wasn't her plane. It was the wrong one – the completely wrong one.

With Red Campbell, unexpectedly, suddenly reaching across the table and, finding that the bottle was empty, calling out in a hoarse, dry voice:

—We need some more o' that jungle over here, Mervyn. Because if I don't get it, I think I'm going to get the horrors.

—And we wouldn't want that, now would we, ha ha, laughed Mervyn, in the middle of tying up his long grey ponytail.

He leaned across the counter and smiled as he said:

—But you don't got to worry your head about it. Nope, you don't got a thing to worry about on that score, Red — because it's coming right up.

—Gracias, said Red, giving the barman an appreciative thumbs-up.

Big Barney's pupils were as wide as ever again, as he began a near-desperate trawl inside his pockets.

—I know I have it in here somewhere, he gasped, because I always carry it around with me, you see. You can still see her name at the bottom of the likeness. I know it's all creased and dog-eared. But nonetheless you can still make it out. Because it's right there at the bottom of the picture. Mercedes Starrs, that was her name. Yes, that was her beautiful name, fellers. But here, what am I doing? Somehow I can't seem to find it anywhere.

Then he laughed, a little oddly, and announced that he had to go to the lavatory.

—Mercedes, he repeated, tripping over a rubber mat, where are you Mercedes? O God how I love you … !

—Easy, called Meryvn, easy there, Barney.

After that, a silence followed.

Before Sonny Hackett brayed like an ass.

—Mercedes motherfucking Starrs, he jeered, well I've doggone heard it all now so I have. Because there'll be snow in July, and that's for sure, by the time that big goon ever gets himself a woman, called Mercedes or anything else. To tell you the truth, I doubt if he was ever even *in* an airport. For he hasn't been out of the county in his life.

—All the same, suggested Mervyn, you got to remember that them old rabbits, they'd be safe up there.

—Rabbits, scoffed Sonny, who wants to talk about stupid cunting rabbits. Why don't we talk about something that might be interesting — like that night in Heartland when

Los Pistoleros took the floor, man that was a gas. And I have to hand it to you, Red Campbell old buddy – you sure shut the mouths of them as swore that you didn't stand a chance. Because you saw them all off, didn't you? So that was one night at least that Red Campbell was useful for something.

–Him and the Kid, they scooped the Heartland Dance-Off Trophy. Which seems to me more than you ever did, Sonny Hackett, shouted Hughie.

Seeming astonished by what he had just said but exhibiting no indication of intending to recant.

–Get back into your shack, little man, just walk away and crawl into your hole before I come over there and do some serious damage.

–I don't have to listen to this shit, spat Red, because what Hughie says is right. Me and the Kid, we *did* scoop the Dance-Off. While you were there muttering to yourself in the corner. Which is all you seemed to ever do. Not a bit wonder she left you for the Indian.

–She didn't leave anyone – wait. Where are you going? Sonny Hackett called.

After Red, who was already gone, with the door swinging out behind him as he made his way down the short flight of steps into the outhouse.

Where, unmoving, a single bulb dangled directly in front of Jody's face.

Before Red caught a hold of it and sent it sweeping off in a series of wild, unpredictable arcs.

Laughing his head off as it did so, erupting once more into another verse of 'Y Viva España', shaking an imaginary maraca, chuckling at the very absurdity as the vast black wingspan of the bulb's shadows enveloped first the walls, the damp packed earth floor and then the corrugated galvanised roof and the small porthole window.

With Campbell craning his neck as he leered into the bruised, swollen countenance of his still-defiant captive.

–Boy, he taunted, are you gonna get what's coming to you tonight.

The skin around Red's eyes seemed white as he ran his nicotine-stained fingers through the younger man's blackberry curls.

–So what you looking at, Kane? You got something that you want to say to me? You got reasons for giving me a look like that?

Jody winced in anticipation of a blow. Before snarling back:

–If there was just you and me – if that's all there was, just you and me, the pair of us right here – I'm telling you, Campbell, you would be one regretful sumbitch.

–You know what I think, Jody? You want to know what I think, travelling man?

–I don't know or care about anything you got to say, Red – there ain't so much as a single chance in the world—.

Red sank his fist into the middle of the boxer's stomach.

–That a fact? he said, grinning.

And grinned once more as he reassured him that he didn't have to worry, and that all of his pain would be over very soon.

–All I'm doing is fooling around here, Jody. But then I figure that you understand that. I'm just joshing – nothing more.

He folded his arms and his upper gold incisor gleamed.

–Yes it ain't nothing more than a game to pass the time. You been listening to our little party in there upstairs? You been lending an ear to our little hoedown? Maybe you heard what Mr Hackett had to say. Because if you did, then you will know how prone he is to jealousy. Because he is, you see – jealous of many things. But, in the main, of me and the Kid.

With his face creasing up, Campbell released a mournful cry and struck him desperately – a combination of one two three blows.

–I'm living with a stranger now, Kane. A stranger, do you hear? So that isn't her name. She isn't called the Kid anymore. Say that, Jody …

Then a howl issued right from the pit of Red Campbell's soul.

Before sinking to his knees on the earthen floor as he gripped Jody Kane by the torn leg of his jeans.

–Don't you ever low-rate me, smoke-and-horses, he warned, don't you even think about doing it.

Before clambering to his feet and sinking his closed fist, one last time, into the centre of Jody's stomach.

As the door to the bar swung shut behind him.

And silence reigned once more in the darkness.

At least until Mr Bonny emerged from the shadows, in a soft white blur.

–Is he gone? the gentleman in the suit whispered quietly. The Toast of Old El Paso? Because I was beginning to think he might never leave.

Lowering his head, fanning his face with the black-banded Panama.

–El Brindis Del Paso, Jody heard him whisper, such pitiful baubles as they covet …

Chapter 20

The Memory of an Old Christmas Card

Same as Big Barney Grue, having come close to breaking his neck on his way back from the lavatory, Wee Hughie decided there was nothing for it but to stop for a moment as he passed by that old counter and order himself a coupla pitchers of sobering-up water.

−The natural mineral, he explained to the smiling barman.

−After all, Mr Walker, he laughed, we don't want to end up doing a Jimmy Buffett.

−What's a Jimmy Buffett? the barman wondered, leaning back and contemplatively stroking his chin.

−O! That's when you get yourself the head-scalds, interjected Sonny, sounding like his humour had, at last, improved somewhat.

−When you been shoving that juice way down just a little too much and the next thing you know, without realising it, you're on the fast train down to Margaritaville. Except that by the time you get as far as the station, seems like you're finding it kinda problematic remembering your own fucking name.

Ain't that a fact, Red? Yep, that old Red Campbell standing there, he knows a thing or two about doing a Jimmy Buffett. Matter of fact, the last time he got the head-scalds he must have been three whole days on the juice. Before they finally ran him to ground, snoring his head off in the doorway of Apache Pizza in Ardagh. Ain't that a fact, Campbell? How long ago is that, you reckon, now?

–Dunno, Red replied, I couldn't rightly say. Could be, maybe, a coupla years.

–Yeah, a coupla years maybe. All I know is that you and Teddy 'Buckfast' Carson had been on the beer a coupla days until Buckfast decided he couldn't take it anymore. Way I heard it, Red, you were sure in some goddamn-it freaking state whenever they eventually come upon you lying in that doorway. Three whole days on the moonshine – that's an almighty session for a married man. Now why, I wonder, would a feller go and do something like that?

Big Barney raised his hand and tugged a little at the ends of his beard, before heaving breathlessly as he hoisted his britches.

–I got the answer to that, he announced, or at least, if not me, Hank Williams and Merle Haggard and maybe Patsy Cline have. Because there comes a time, for all of us, when a man gets to feeling that he kind of ain't able to stand too much of this anymore, being hemmed in everywhere, every which way that he turns – boxed in at every turn by other folks' codes. And that's what gets to him, when he most gets to feel the urge to run kinda wild and raw, and I guess to pull on the jug just that little too much.

–Yeah, well hell that old tooth-grinding sumbitch over there Sonny he sure tied one big one on that day. Lying in the doorway sweating and howling his heart out, with the head-scalds getting at him, man, real bad. The squeals of him, I heard you could pick 'em up as far away as Glan. O, them old head-scorchies – you ain't seen anything like 'em, no sir.

Sonny snorted teasingly, shaking his head.

—And it wasn't the first time neither, was it Red? As a matter of fact it was the third. Or maybe even the fourth. When that old Red Campbell he goes right into that old post office and cleans out his entire account, and then sets off with a crate o' jungle and causing holy hell in the town of Longford — in a dispute, way I hear it, over a simple bottle of cola.

Wee Hughie Munley thought this was really funny, pressing his palms like a bellows beneath his oxters as he rocked back and forth, with that round rosy head almost turning a whole three hundred and sixty degrees.

—Well I'll be damned, he chortled, his whole body shaking, such a handling over a bottle of poor old cola!

—That's what I'm telling you and I ain't hearing Red deny it. O boy, I reckon he must have faced seven different kinds o' hell-shit when at last he made it home.

—Ah but here, argued Hughie, still laughing, what kind of crack was it that started this row about the bottle of minerals? What kind of feller, dammit, bothers his head about a stupid dumb coke?

—Well, I don't know, Munley, Sonny Hackett continued, but spittin' worse than a goose shittin' by moonlight, is how he was. Then went and told the barman that he'd stiff him right there where he stood. You think that there's something the matter with Glasson County Cola? he says to the barman. You reckon that down Longford way you got it all worked out when it comes to Coke and that there's something not quite right about us upcountry mountain folks? That what you think, Longford? he says, and then goes on: Well I got news for you, my friend — back where I come from we don't quite see it that way, and maybe you ought to get to think a little bit, and maybe have the courtesy to stock our fucking top-class produce. And so the next time I might have occasion to come around these parts, I won't feel it necessary to come by these premises, and separate your fucking head from your shoulders.

–He's lucky, I say you're lucky, Red, that he didn't call the cops, said Hughie.

–Hell, you sure are some loco down-home boy, Red Campbell, for to go and do a thing the like o' that, chortled Barney, sobering a little now with the water, but if you don't mind me being somewhat impertinent, the way I see it we got more pressing matters to talk about right now, seeing as Begley gonna be here at any moment.

–Not that he doesn't like his share o' jungle too, remarked Sonny, TB I mean. I seen him knock back a bottle or two in his time.

–That's right, agreed Hughie, especially when his mother died. Woah boy – talk about the head-scalds then.

–Do you know what, Mervyn? called out Wee Hughie Munley, still rocking away merrily. I reckon this water is just about doing the trick, because I don't feel too bad at all.

–I'm glad that you like it, Barney, Mervyn responded, nothing but the best for solid gentlemen like yourselves.

–Because we gotta do our best to keep it all together, suggested Hughie, considering what has got to come yet.

–As sure as there's water in Lake Wynter, agreed the barman, folding his arms as he repeated the observation a number of times:

–As sure as Lake Wynter it's got it's share of water.

Before lowering his head to inspect his tightly wrapped, jute-covered package, and in the process permitting himself what might be described as a smile of contentment, if not even bliss.

Being satisfied that everything was safe and sound in that department, with absolutely nothing to worry about in that regard at all.

Nonetheless, he gave it another little nudge with his knee – just to be on the safe side. Double sure.

–Because there ain't no need or call to go taking unnecessary chances, he told himself.

As he returned his gaze to the willow's brushing leaves, drumming a gentle tune on the countertop with his fingers.

One, perhaps not uncoincidentally, that his old friend and neighbour Wilson Gillis had used to like.

'Let Me Rest On Peaceful Mountain', it was called – a gospel tune.

One he had liked to sing every Sabbath morning, right there in his appointed place in the front pew.

Prior to his murder.

Before being done to death in the privacy of his own home.

One night, a long time ago.

–Give me over that jug of water, the barman heard Sonny Hackett shouting at Hughie, because I want to be one hundred per cent sober for Begley. I don't want him giving me any of those looks, saying things about me. Complaining, criticising, the way that he always used to.

–Aye. You have to make sure to be on your guard and at your best whenever Mr Begley is around – and that's for sure.

Hughie came over with the half-full jug.

–Here, he said, and poured some out.

–I reckon we're all in pretty good shape now, he enthused, and that we ain't got a whole lot to worry about. And then, soon as it's over, we can just up and go and forget that it ever happened. But, wait a minute, what's happened to the twins?

–To tell the truth, I forgot all about them, Sonny said, but I think maybe Shorty said something about going out and getting themselves some fresh air. That Runt, he takes turns. There was always something …

—Something not right wrong with him, snorted Red, that's what you mean.

—Only for their father, they'd never have been invited by me to come anyway, said Big Barney.

—What addition are they, said Sonny Hackett sourly. Not much different, when all's said and done, to that fucking idiot old man o' theirs, Trampas, blowing his nuts off out in the woods.

—You don't got no call saying that, said Barney, I reckon it ain't right.

—Whether or not it is, it's the truth, said Sonny.

—Well they had better get back here soon, said Barney, because any minute now he's gonna come walking right in through that door. Tony Begley …

Sonny released a low, protracted sigh.

—I'll just take a look out the window and see, he said.

He pushed down the slats.

—Nothing, he said.

And then sat down.

—I'll put on a song and we can play another hand, he said, that'll maybe take the edge off this waiting. Because, let's face it, it can't be all that very long.

—He'll be here shortly, said Barney, for definite.

As the cards fluttered, one two three four five.

—I wish you hadn't done that, said Red to Hughie Munley.

—What's that? Hughie replied.

—It's just that song it brings back memories from childhood, Red explained, the one with the beautiful red sleigh in the snow.

Sonny Hackett impatiently stubbed out his smoke.

—I know that it isn't anything special at all — and that everyone has them, their memories of the old times — especially at Christmas. But I used to just sit there looking at it for hours.

—Looking at what? queried Barney Grue.

—The old Christmas card. With that lovely log fire burning away and the snowflakes falling ever so slowly through the pines.

As the phone rang piercingly and the barman picked it up.

—It's Tony, he called out, he says he'll be here in less than five minutes …

Chapter 21

The Tackle Harvest

Deep in the bowels of that acrid, suffocating dungeon, Mr Bonny released a doleful sigh, standing in the match-flame glare of the moon, smiling at Jody.

−You know what their problem is, don't you, little dogie? You know what their enduring difficulty is and − being of the upcountry breed like yourself − always has been?

He knitted his brows and moved in real close.

−Tell me that you know, that you are aware of their dogged and persistent inadequacies. If you please, relate to me what it is you might know of this conundrum, Mr Kane, he repeated.

−I will, if you tell me just who it is that you are. And that, once and for all, you agree to stop playing games. Who the hell are you, Mr Bonny?

But his visitor refused to say anything − in fact, made a point of ignoring the question completely.

Before coolly examining his nails and proceeding once more into the shadows, whispering softly from behind the humming propane tank.

—Those sad little fellows, them good old boys. Are you telling me you don't know what it is that their all-pervasive difficulty might be?

Jody Kane shook his head.

—Very well then, replied his visitor, in that case Mr Bonny will take the liberty of telling you.

As he whispered ever so softly, smiling across at Jody.

—Ah yes, he elaborated, their unfortunate predicament is that ever since birth, they have it within them, in their nature, to be wilfully disputatious. Much too in thrall to the emotions, with their poor caged souls ever-straining to fight free, seeking solace in either sweetness or wildness, getting drunk and cutting loose on the world. Prone to taking offence at what are often slurs of an entirely fictitious nature. Yes, I would have to insist, Jody, that they are only too ready to commit themselves to violence, generally over some imagined grievance. Such a waste of valuable energy, I have always thought, and the curse of heartlands everywhere. Do you know what I am going to tell you, my little dogie? That those unfortunate fellows – that they would dispute the ramblings of two flies wandering up a wall. Unhappy men? Primitive? Maybe. Everything that civility deplores, that's for certain. But at the same time I got to acknowledge they got within them their own style and grace, if that may be a little loosely defined. Mainly in the way the air that they breathe stores power under the hot sun of August and is liable to explode at any time in a thunderstorm, in a violent outburst of emotion. One that is far removed from the church-steepled civility of the village, and which can make them seem ferocious and unsociable at times. Craving, as they do, above all, the wilder, freer side of life. Which they most of all find in the squeal of rubber and crunch of metal on the stock-car circuit. The cockfight, the bloodstock races, the football games. All them things they get to argue about. And what else? Ah yes, their relationships with the sweethearts – do you think that they might, in the wind-up, be afraid of women? Perhaps they are, perhaps not. But one thing you can be sure of – that them good old boys out there, they sure do love their mommas, don't they?

–I don't know, but I do know this, choked Jody, shaking like a leaf, tough as I might have been in the past, I know what that sumbitch Begley is capable of. I know just exactly what he can do. You don't know what he's like, Mr Bonny …

This appeared to amuse his visitor no end.

–I don't know what he's like? You're telling me that I don't know what people like him are *like*? But, just one second, Jody Kane, ain't you gone and got me straying off the subject now. Because what we were talking about, if you remember, was the subject of them good old mountain boys out there. And how they love to hunt and fish and pull on the jug and raise Cain whenever they get the chance, whenever the opportunity for whooping comes by.

Mr Bonny smiled and flexed his fingers.

–I mean, even take music. All night they been arguing about that. Hell, they're even in dispute about someone as sweet and wholesome as Jim Reeves.

–Who's that? Jody Kane asked. Who's Jim Reeves?

Then, perhaps the most extraordinary event of all took place.

As Mr Bonny whispered:

–Gentleman Jim …

Before slowly appearing out from behind the gas tank, only now attired not in a suit of ice-cream linen but a neat black bowtie and a scarlet velvet tuxedo jacket. Approaching the single hanging bulb and standing behind it, smiling right at Jody as he began to croon the words in a lush, baritone voice, ever so smoothly, just like the velvet-toned tenor himself, and with the very same blank half-smile, and that waxen complexion which could never grow old.

−*Welcome to my world*, he continued intimately, *built with you in mind* …

Now Mr Bonny was facing him again, squatting akimbo on a plastic crate − in white, as before.

−Do you ever dream about your parents, Jody? Your father and mother, do they ever come into your mind?

−I don't remember them enough to dream. All I ever really see whenever they do come are the faces of his followers around the pit as he gets himself ready to face another opponent in the woods. I was born under canvas, you see, Mr Bonny. Into a tribe that were the outlaw breed. Born fighters, they said, arriving like some ancient tribe of warriors, unannounced, into every village, with their long fur coats and wagons and wooden pipes.

−I see. I understand. But of course you don't remember them. Because they took you away when you were still little more than an infant, and put you in behind those high forbidding walls.

−Please don't bring that up. I don't want to talk about that infernal place …

And, just for the briefest of moments, Mr Bonny began to fade − but didn't, in the process, become a velvet-voice crooner in a red velvet jacket with black bowtie, or anything else.

Because right now he was sporting a butternut military tunic, complete with a row of brass buttons along either side.

As he winked and lifted the dented brass bugle.

−Ta ra! This is to announce that I am here on behalf of the Southland for the purpose of bringing contentment and happiness to all who are fortunate enough to encounter me. And why, on my trumpet, I'ma going to play for you now the anthem of the forever dispossessed, those for whom the

Cause is always lost. And why they live their lives in a world that is close to dream, where somewhere faraway the hounds they always seem to be baying in the morning, while nearby the doves they have already commenced their mourning. In this hallowed place of hot earth and pinewood, where the imagination holds forth unchecked. Enabling us, in its own special way, that cosmic conspiracy against romance, throughout so many centuries, to endure. But, before I perform my little tune for you. I got to sing a paean to that other special wonder of the Southland – and it is to her those rawboned good old boys must pay their constant and abject homage – those who profess to live by feud and moonshine and the ancient code of the hills, but before whom they will happily abase themselves as they lift their cup and howl to the moon: O woman, lovely woman of the Southland, as pure and chaste as sparkling water, as cold as the gleaming ice, we lift this cup and we pledge our hearts and our lives to the protection of your virtue and chastity …

As he raised his instrument and parped it a few times before Johnny Redlegs – for it was he – produced a gleaming shears and began to set assiduously about his person, right there in the fork of his britches.

Until his lap had become saturated with blood.

–Tarnation, he erupted, if I ain't gone and harvested m'godforsaken tackle all over again … what a to-do … !

As he flicked some warm wet blots at Jody's face, and then, in a whirlwind of raucous, hysterical laughter, was gone.

Chapter 22

The Glasson County Electrisms

Looking back on it all now, I often think that maybe it's just as well. That, drunk though I might have been during the course of composing my numerous replies to Jody – and, believe you me, they were indeed many – it's salutary, perhaps, that I never did actually get around to disclosing the whole truth about Johnny Redlegs and what I'd seen during our time in Whiterock.

Especially that night when he arrived into the darkness of the dormitory, and it's not all that surprising that I mightn't choose to speak of it, considering the negative effect it also had on me.

Having preyed on my mind, on and off over the years, affecting me very badly.

To tell the truth, I'm not entirely sure he'd have got it, or understood what I was trying to say.

Because not many do – with that being the reason that I ended up sustaining what they call, in the organisation, a 'minor setback'.

As a matter of fact, whenever I happened to mention it to the doctor, he didn't register anything approaching shock, and in fact as soon as he'd chatted to me about what it was I had to do, went on to talk about something else entirely.

As if it hadn't been anything at all unusual, just something any doctor has to deal with on a daily basis, particularly someone as specialised as him.

And who, in the course of his career, has pretty much seen everything – fellows coming in weeping and crying like children, with all sorts of stories about seeing things and encountering figures from their past and all the rest of it.

Just a standard relapse by people who have reached rock bottom in their time. Folk, in other words, just the very same as myself.

Except that, I am happy and grateful to be able to report, that particular situation is now, happily, in the past – bearing no comparison at all to my present circumstances.

Thanks, I am glad to be able to say, to a couple of very significant people – certain individuals, as I say, who just happen to have bothered to have faith in me, when it mattered.

Something which, once upon a time, I genuinely wouldn't have considered possible.

I didn't even think that I'd ever get to sleep again.

It used to be like having these tiny fragments of glass moving around just a millimetre under your skin, only all the time.

But then there were the more spectacular episodes, which, now that they're all history, I see no point in going into now.

To be honest, they're pretty much too unappealing – if not, at times, terrifying even.

The 'head–scalds', as Sonny Hackett called them.

Sonny Hackett, who, somewhere in the recesses of my mind was moving like a shadow across the floor of the bar, as my heart continued accelerating, erratically, under the roof among the rafters.

–I can definitely see something moving out there, I heard him announce, and I swear to God, I think it might be you-know-who!

As the door swung open and we saw the twins holding one another up – in their hoodies – looking like death.

–We were going to go in for a swim, gasped Shorty, but our boy started raving and pointing at things. He says he saw Colonel Sanders on the water.

–I know what I saw, his brother stammered, I know what I saw and I'm not going to fucking lie. He was standing there pointing – and he was laughing!

–I told you before and I won't tell you again: shut the fuck up with saying the like of that! You're only making a fool of yourself!

–Colonel fucking Sanders, snorted Sonny Hackett, just when you think you've heard it all.

–It's finger-lickin' good, said Red, deriving very little amusement from the effort.

–This has been the worst mistake of my life, wept Shorty.

–I could see him clearly – just standing there, in shadow. I know what I saw.

Then the phone rang, and the barman lifted up the receiver.

–It's TB, he nodded, definitely this time. Five minutes, he says – this time for definite.

Then Hughie Munley announced that he thought he might tell a joke.

As a soft gentle tapping was heard at the door.

–It isn't five minutes yet, said Sonny, as the door swung slowly open.

Tootsy Corrigan would have been past her forties, blowsy and big-bosomed.

She sometimes did secretarial work for Tony Begley, and drove for him.

–Hi, she said, giving them all a little wave.

She was wearing a shiny blue-and-white Glasson football jersey, stretched tight across her front.

—Hi, she said again.

—Hi, said Red.

—Hi, said Sonny.

The twins said nothing, just stared straight ahead.

Big Barney couldn't take his eyes off her nipples, prominent underneath the acrylic material.

—I'm sorry I'm late, she apologised, jangling a bunch of keys.

For no reason he could identify, Hughie Munley kept on slapping the table.

—Hi there Tootsy! Hi hi hi! he shrieked, beginning to chatter trip-hammer fast, with beads of sweat lining up on his crown.

—Glasson County has a great fucking team this year, so they have — and I don't care what anyone says! he squealed.

Tootsy smiled but didn't respond.

Then she said softly:

—Mr Begley says he'll be here very shortly. I'm sorry to have to say he was unavoidably detained.

The eyes of Big Barney were still fixed on her front.

Electrisms, he kept on thinking.

—Up Glasson! shouted Big Barney Grue again. Yes, for sure! Hip hip hooray! They'll win the cup, without a doubt!

—There's nothing wrong with women wearing football shirts, they heard Hughie Munley assert, nothing Miss Corrigan! No, not a thing.

But when they looked again, she was gone.

Chapter 23

A Life, Shredded

I really am glad that, after having put it off for so long, that at last I've finally taken the time and done my best to set down my story – for it really and truly has benefited me a lot.

And I can understand clearly, just by examining the sequence of events, how hasty and intemperate I've sometimes been, and how poor my judgment, at times, could be.

Among those errors being what happened that night when, yet again, I had stumbled home, full of vodka, from the pub, and started into writing yet another ill-considered missive.

But if you reckon that one was bad, then you ought to have seen what I came up with next time – when I got back after burying a bottle of whiskey, roasted beyond belief. Even by my standards in those days, knocking over furniture and hauling out all the letters he had sent me up to then. And tearing the whole lot of them, without exception, into pieces.

Laughing like a crazy man as I was doing it.

–So long then, Jody Kane. Vaya con dios, my one-time motherfucking friend. Estar viendo que en el otro lado de la luna! So what if you're happy to have been so fortunate as to get yourself a lovely partner and a beautiful place to live – you think I care about Sweetwater, Georgia? Because if you do, that is where you are wrong, my one-time friend. For, as far as I'm concerned, you and I never knew each other. As a matter of fact, I'm finding it difficult to remember your name. So long then, compadre, whoever the fuck you are – for all I can say is that you're no fucking friend of mine!

Only to find myself the following morning, waking to a blaze of sunlight hammering on the shutter, lathered in an icy-cold sweat, consumed by self-loathing as I pulled on my clothes and made my way out as fast as I could.

Where else, but to the counter of some anonymous bar, don't ask me where, taking the torn-up pieces of one of his letters from an envelope and doing my best to put them back together.

It's obvious that I shouldn't have ever sent him what I'd written, because I never did get to hear from him after that. So, drunk or sober, now I had nobody.

Angie having finished with me months before.

–I hope you find what you're looking for, Ray, she'd said, because I know now for sure it doesn't include me. Maybe she can give it to you, the girl of your dreams that you know I'm talking about.

And I didn't much care where I ended up after that – drifting aimlessly from one job to another, all of them dead-ends.

Until, eventually, I pretty much became what you could only describe as a vagrant wino.

Which is a career choice, believe me, not recommended in Ireland – certainly not these days, with all the changes there've been, most especially in little places that once would have been described as backwoods or out-of-the-way.

Not anymore, I can assure you, with five-lane blacktops cutting through the countryside and great big eighteen-wheelers burning rubber from dawn to dusk.

I don't know how many times I came close to getting killed, stumbling in a half-daze along the hard shoulder, bleary-eyed, clutching yet another can of Superstrength.

I'll never forget the night I went back to the site of what, once upon a time, used to be Mervyn's Mountain Bar, lodged between two hills backing onto Lake Wynter. All of which is completely overgrown now, with no hint or trace of what it used to be.

What I was doing there, I haven't the faintest idea – I was drunk, of course.

It must have been nine or ten o'clock at night, for Christ's sake, black as molasses in the midwinter dark, you couldn't so much as see your hand in front of you.

How long I lay there before I heard it I couldn't rightly say.
–*Kuklok!*

But I do know this – that it was a sound which shot right down into the very core of my soul.

I think I might have screamed. I can't be sure.

But if I did, I would never have been heard, with it being the kind of cry that made no sound.

Like you'd make in a cockloft after the departure of a certain Tootsy Corrigan.

And it was just at that point that I heard the same sound again.

–*Kuklok!*

–Is that you, Mervyn? Mervyn – is that you? I gasped hoarsely, in trepidation.

As I could have sworn I heard his voice, whispering softly as it came drifting accusingly, through the trees.

–*You'll have to live with this.*

Forever.

Before collapsing in a faint and remaining there, in the bracken.

With it only being by the grace of God that I didn't contract frostbite, being scarcely able to move when I awoke in the dawn, still clutching Jody's envelope and its shredded, pathetic contents. What was left of all those torn-up letters, with each one ripped as my nerves, and my body howling, beneath the sky, for alcohol.

As I fell, in a daze, along the side of the mountain, my soul a bitter, unspeakable site of ruin.

Chapter 24

The Mountain Throwback

The same as the rest of them, only maybe even more so, I knew what you were dealing with whenever it came to Tony Begley.

Principally because of that day he'd pursued me without my knowledge as far as Dawn's place out by the lake, an old fishing lodge she'd rented during her time in Glasson.

I had never breathed a word about it to anyone – but, like WW and a number of unnamed others, ever since first setting eyes on her, I had taken a bad heart-burnin' for Dawn 'Kit' King.

And, somehow, Begley had come to know about it.

I don't know how long he'd been standing there in the doorway – observing me, sombrely, chewing on a matchstick.

I'd taken the liberty of picking the lock.

–Hi, he said, and with the way he looked at me, my blood ran cold.

–I was wondering might you mind if I came in and sat down?

Before I got time to answer, Tony Begley did just that.

He was wearing a great big black puffa-style anorak with a pointed hood, his soft red fleshy face peeping out from it as he said:

—What's that you been reading there, Ray? Huh?

It was a floral-covered notebook, a kind of diary Dawn King used to like to keep.

A dream journal.

—Give it to me, he said, and I passed it to him.

As he sat there, impassively, turning its pages, smirking as his shoulders tensed.

—There is only one time I ever feel really free, and that is when I take Ophelia the quarterhorse out into the fields. Or when I ride her by the shores of the lake with nothing on me only my old cowboy shirt and wait for the water-pale sun of the dawn to come up, on those mornings of early summer when the air's so quiet you can almost hear your own soul quiver. When there's just me and her – that beautiful, gleaming mare Ophelia as we gallop without a care into the valley of the golden morning. July gonna be a burner, my Daddy used to say, and then you and me gonna go down to the coast. And we'll ride like this, just you and me along the sand, and swear to God it'll be as if you and me and the rest of our sweet lovely family, it'll be as if all our lives we have been fortunate enough to be strangers to pain. Because that's how it was supposed to be when I was your age, my angel, when you're still young enough to be able to hope and dream. We were gonna build us a whole new society in the woods, me and her – Phaedra, as I used to call your mother. Zachariah was her name for me, with the pair of us cantering, without a care, along the shore, just the very same as this – with our naked bodies painted in blue and red spirals, like we belonged in some electric, golden creation, our own special, private psychedelic western. But then things went wrong – the commune we'd planned to set up in the woods, I don't know, it all somehow fucking fell apart. It somehow just got all tore up, the way things do.

−Would you think I'm in this? I heard TB insouciantly inquire. You reckon that maybe she's got one or two sentences regarding me in here?

−I honestly don't know, Tony, I replied, I really couldn't say. Because, to tell the truth, I haven't actually read it.

−You haven't read it? he replied, incredulously. Then how did you know it was all about dreams?

−I didn't, I just guessed, Tony.

−I see, he said.

But it was clear he didn't believe me.

−They got a propensity, the judies, for writing about their dreams, don't they? he continued. Travelling along the highways of their hearts. Maybe it helps them to think things through − would you say that's the case?

−I don't know, I said, I don't know. I guess.

−You guess?

−Yes, I said.

−Maybe their thoughts and aspirations.

−Aspirations, yes, I said, without really thinking what I was saying.

Then he got up and walked over to the window.

He was wearing a baggy blue pinstriped suit, steadily patting at the glistening accordion pleats of his hair.

His expression seemed pained as his eyes creased up and he gazed out the window, into the distance.

Far beyond, towards the surface of Lake Wynter.

As, through clenched teeth, I heard him tensely, resentfully, observe:

−You think you're the only one who's special, don't you? But that's where you got it wrong, you see. Because she's done the same with me too, and others. She knows that we're dumb and she knows how to work it. Even WW − who would have believed it? She's written to his wife and it's all going to end in disaster. But I know how it happened and I'm not going to make a judgement. Because magical beauty the like of what she's got, it makes its own rules, got its own laws. Whenever I'm with her it's like the coldness inside of my heart it somehow melts and I don't want to be anywhere else except with her. And if you don't believe me, then look in there, among those pages. Because it's there, in her little book of dreams – we've each of us got our own little chapter. You think there's nothing about me? Well, that's where you're wrong. That mare she's talking about, Ophelia, the one WW gave for her birthday? This particular morning, Wade, you see, the two of us went out together. Yes, just took two horses and galloped off, side by side, into the mist. I can't tell you how desirable she was. Wearing this sweet little white lace veil that covered her head completely, except that when she turned, I swear to almighty God …

He stared at the floor and said nothing for a very long time.

–But maybe that's because I haven't had many women. None, really. I'm very inexperienced in that quarter, Raymond. I know you won't believe me, but I'm sorry to have to say that it's true.

A shadow fell across his face as, quite unexpectedly, he turned and swung on his heel.

–Did you hear what I just said? he spat. It's true!

And then, just as unexpectedly, composing himself in a remarkable fashion.

–There's a reason for that, though, he continued softly, I used to get these scruples, you see – when I was a younger man, I mean. And, fool that I am, I went and told her all about it. Yes, went and blabbed that secret too. All my shadows, she knows about them now. Maybe she'll put them in one of her songs – those dark, unknowable tunes she sings. Some velvet morning when I'm straight, I'm gonna open up your gate, Tony, she'll sometimes say to me. As she looks right into you with them big brown liquid eyes and laughs. Rich or poor, old or young, we're putty in her hands and she knows it. Especially softies the likes of you and me, Wade – because she knows the truth, that that is what we are, deep down. She told me one night that she'd heal me, did you know that, Wade? Or did she promise to do that for you as well?

He released a sad moan.

–It's a heck of a thing, it really and truly is, he continued, even though you know it ain't true there's some part of you as desperately needs to believe that she genuinely cares for you, and that you're not being played after all. I remember us that morning standing by the shores of Lake Wynter, the quarterhorse gleaming with sweat and whinnying as the pair of us held hands and looked out over the water – in spite of everything I will always treasure those few brief seconds. When she told me about her Bonnyland dream. That smoky, vegetal Paradise, Tony, that's ours for the taking, I remember her saying, our glamorous land of long twilights and hot dawns where cloud-stacks tower from the horizon and the earth-heat always seem to go quivering upward.

He produced a cigarette.

But then changed his mind and put it back inside the packet.

–Did you ever hear the story about Lake Wynter? he asked.

–No, I told him, no I didn't, Tony.

–They say that it's filled with the bones of the dead – those with no names that were dumped there during the Troubles. You wouldn't want to end up there, nobody wants to end up forgotten beneath the water.

Then he reached for his anorak and announced that he was going.

–Leave her alone, Ray, everything's coming to an end around here anyway. Get out now while you still can. There's a piece of advice for you.

He came over and gave me a playful tap on the cheek.

Then he said goodbye and was gone.

The last thing I should have done was read the passage she had written about me. But, given the opportunity, who could resist?

So I flipped the page and there it was, towards the end of the index, under 'R'.

I got to say it, I found myself reading, that Raymond, or 'Ringo' as they call him, what with that cheeky smile and those handsome boyish features, that you would have to say, to admit that he, at least, has a bit of class.

Although, she continued, in this backcountry wasteland, I got to say that that wouldn't be hard, with most of them little more than a step up from the herds of cattle and sheep they and their forebears spend their time tending. I guess there's just something kind of appealing and sweet in his personality. My own sweet handsome little dogie, Ray Wade.

But it was the line on the second last page which hurt me the most – really hit me hard, I got to admit.

With my face still burning as I put the diary back on the shelf where I'd found it.

Although, Dawn King continued, in her elegant feminine hand, in the end poor old Ray is not a lot more than yet another sad mountain throwback – no matter how good the little dogie fucks.

Such a long way from the first night we'd spent there together, after one of her spectacular ballroom performances.

When, I guess you could say, she had given me the treatment.

Little girl lost, I guess you might call it – her *modus operandi*, I mean.

We'd been drinking a lot, and I think I must have been almost out for the count, in the back bar lying slumped, with my forehead pinned to the counter.

Before I heard that soft whisper as her lips gently touched my ear:

–You're special, Ray Wade, I just want you to know that.

With the next thing I knew, the pair of us standing there in the car park and she's looking right at me, with the car keys clutched in her fist. You'll always be special, I heard her say again, and as long as I live I'll never forget the effect it had on me.

As she stood there watching me, pushing a long silky strand of hair back from her face, until her boot heels were crunching the gravel of the car park and she was opening the car door and climbing into the driving seat, looking as happy as ever I'd seen her, launching onto another of her compelling American mountain stories and telling me everything about the day the legendary guitarist Duane Allman from the Allman Brothers had come to visit them in the Ozark commune.

–'Skydog' they all used to call him – man, how they loved to see that wisecracking sucker coming. You familiar with them, Ray – you like Southern rock at all?

Then, before I got a chance to answer, she launched into a story about this night when she would have been still in her teens, when Skydog had arrived on a Harley Davison, yeah right out of the blue on a Harley rider and their campfire party had turned into an unforgettable weekend.

–They say all kindsa things about that old Duane. But I'll tell you this – I never found him nothing only a gentleman. And with great respect for the female gender, I can tell you that, unlike some of the phony rebel pussies that you get around here, if you understand my meaning ha ha Ray, you know?

Then she reached over and put on some of their music – a forward-moving, piledriving track of psychobilly rock with slide fuzz guitar-those same snappy handclaps and a stomping, forward-driving chorus.

—Yee-haw! she hollered as she vigorously slapped the arch of the wheel. Yep you go girl! Sure as night follows day. You are gonna be a great goddamn singer one day little lady, Duane that old Skydog told me, can you believe that Ray? And, I mean, it ain't every day that one of the Allman Brothers has that kinda confidence in a lady – huh?

She swerved dangerously, skimming a tree.

—They think I want a recording contract? Then they are out of their fucking minds, Ray – because I don't need those assholes, no how. You getting me here? You hearing what I'm saying? Because I'm going to do it without those motherfuckers – finish what my father started. This hillbilly opera he was working on with Duane. An electric western was how they used to describe it, a baroque backwoods comedy. Think Luke the Drifter, Kit, he used to say, think o' that old Hank and Dante getting it together over a couple of bottles o' Jack, and then you'll have an idea of what me and that old Skydog are after.

She brushed what I thought was a tear from her eye and then turned around and said:

—But like so many other of my father's many other fucking whacked-out dreams, it never came to anything. That's why I'm going to finish it, Ray. Yep, finish it, ha ha – like he finished me!

No, they had never gotten around to completing their long-nurtured project, up in the mountains – presumably, as I later discovered – because of the fact that the hard-living rock guitarist Duane 'Skydog' Allman had died in a motorbike accident in the year 1971, precisely two years before he was supposed to have paid them his visit in the Ozarks.

—He's part Indian, Ray, you know, she would confidently announce about Robbie Robertson of The Band – again displaying that troubling nervous tic which registered whenever she became excited, and ought to have warned me from the start.

–Yeah, she'd continue, that old Robbie used to take me down to the water when he'd come to visit my father ... Lake Wadayaha it was called, not far from the camp. Water of the Morning – it's Cherokee, you know?

But all her fantasy stories did was add to the mystery. And there we'd be, lying naked once again, sprawled across her scented double bed.

While she moaned ecstatically, pressing her palms hard and flat against my chest, swaying high above me, with her soft skin pearling as that beautiful bronze body shuddered and she flung back her head like someone possessed, biting voraciously into my neck as she released an almost terrifying, wanton cry:

–You'll always be him – you'll always be the only one, Ray Wade!

Chapter 25

The Wayward Wind

−I feel sick, I heard the Runt weep. Please can you help me, our boy? Because I really think I'm done.

−Steady, urged his brother, soon it will all be over.

−Why did he have to call me? Why did I have to see him, Cosmo, the boy who came from the moon?

−Hush, urged Shorty, please will you not?

−My hands are covered in sweat, so they are, Mervyn, exclaimed Wee Hughie, cautiously. Do you think I might have another shotta you-know-what?

−Coming up, replied Mervyn, coming right up, Wee Hughie − no problem.

−Where in Christ's name can TB have got to? lamented Hughie. O where in the name of Jesus Christ can he have gone?

−I think it was probably the rain that delayed him, remarked Big Barney.

−Shut your mouth about up about rain! spat Red. Because it's got nothing or anything to do with fucking rain. Why the fuck do you have to start on about that for? Fucking rain!

–How about we try and get on with the rest of the game? suggested Hughie, mopping his crown.

–A pair of deuces, requested Sonny Hackett, lighting one cigarette after another.

–I think I need me another shot too, Big Barney shouted.

–Coming right up, answered Mervyn, adding:

–Anyone else?

They all had one.

–Ah laaks that ol' jungle, laughed Sonny Hackett, doing his best to put on an American accent.

And which turned out, surprisingly, to be pretty good.

Which was why all the others began to imitate him.

–Yup. That ol' Sonny, he laaks his hooch. Ain't it?

As Sonny sat there, swaying, shrouded in smoke.

–OK then, where are we? asked Hughie.

–I think, I reckon: give me two, said Red.

–Two? said Hughie.

–Two, Red nodded.

–And how about – tell you what, give me three, said Big Barney.

–This don't look good. I think I might have to fold, said Sonny, grimacing as he shook his head.

–Toss me another, called Barney across the table, doing his best to sound confident and brassy.

But, in truth and in private, not feeling so good at all.

Feeling dreadful, as a matter of fact.

With the creeping kind of feeling beginning to take a hold of him – slowly, inexorably, getting in there under his skin.

But he had to make sure to try and keep on smiling.

At least till Begley had been and gone.

–O my God, he repeated to himself, I hope that none of them are watching me.

Then he shot forward abruptly in the chair, gripping it fiercely by the arms, as he gazed straight ahead.

He felt sure that someone was definitely going to comment.

So he steeled himself and waited.

But no one did. No, no one spoke.

As a Jack of Diamonds fluttered onto the table, landing plumb between the pair of overstuffed ashtrays.

—Well I'll be damned, Big Barney cried, with both fists squared on the table in front of him. You would have to go and do that to me. Why, at a time when Begley is nearly here, did you all have to go and do that? It's rotten, so it is. Back off, you hear? All of you – I'm warning youse.

No one knew what he was talking about.

Or thinking about, come to that.

As he gradually raised his fist and unclenched it, spreading its fingers, blinking furiously.

—Five fingers, he heard himself saying, what did someone have to go put that song on for? Whose idea was it to make that particular selection?

As they all looked at Barney fastidiously tugging each of his digits.

—Ah yes, he sighed regretfully, you'd have to do that. To remind me of those little five fingers. Thanks. Thank you very much indeed. Thanks a lot.

He appeared to be addressing himself.

As he began to tear up a soft damp beer mat, reducing it, within seconds, to a mound of tiny fragments.

—Them five old little fingers, he repeated, chuckling oddly.

—Ha ha, he said.

Before closing his fist and placing it back on the table where it had been.

—Do you know what it's like, they heard him continue, sort of like you're in a show on the telly. And where you're not really sure who's the real people anymore – like who is real and who's the actor or what's going on or what the hell.

Especially when you've had a bunch of jungle, know what I'm saying?

Hughie leaned forward and prepared himself to deliver a joke – but then, apparently, thought the better of it.

–I've got one or two things to say, began Barney, and the first is, that when all of this regrettable business is over, none of you are ever going to see me again. Because I'll be going to America too. Just like the McHales.

Then he sat down.

The McHales said nothing. About America or anything else.

Everyone around the table was still.

Remaining watchful, out of the corners of their eyes taking stock.

But Big Barney Grue didn't care, he told himself.

Not now that he'd made his decision to purchase a ticket and get away once and for all.

Now there wasn't so much as a sound.

With Sonny Hackett glowering fiercely at the freckle-faced Red.

And Hughie looking at Barney.

And Barney looking at them both.

With Sonny still lighting one cigarette after another.

As the pool balls clacked.

But, most of all, Mervyn Walker went on saying nothing – just standing there, as always, behind the wooden counter, observing every single thing around him.

Not uttering a word at his post behind the bar.

Smiling away in his neat black waistcoat and collarless grandad shirt with his long silver mane hoisted in a ponytail.

As he hummed a little tune and gazed out the window.

Like he knew something.

Or something.

With that predictable patient and inscrutable smile.

Big Barney Grue wrinkled up his nose.

Acknowledging to himself that he just didn't know what to do.

As a matter of fact, he considered, what in actual fact he felt like doing was running away out that door and never coming back.

Because all of this waiting, it was beginning to make him feel physically ill.

With no one knowing what anyone else was thinking even though they had known each other for years.

And the truth turning out to be that all they knew about each other was their names, and what did that mean?

Because what did a name tell you about anyone?

So, when you thought about it, you might as well not have such a thing at all.

As a name, he meant.

But worst of all about this night was knowing that it was only just a matter of time before they all looked up and saw Tony Begley just standing there smiling, in the doorway, in his anorak.

But there was something else bothering him.

He didn't quite know what.

Why did Mervyn keep looking over? What was he poking at underneath the counter?

Was there something down there?

Something they ought to know about?

Big Barney couldn't say for sure.

All he knew was he wished he wasn't here.

Showing tonight, on Barney Grue TV: *They Came To Kill You And Tear Your House Apart: The Killing Floor Hombres.*

Starring, of course, all the old Glasson Meats gang.

He felt like laughing it sounded so stupid.

Knowing in his heart that Big Barney Grue, in actual fact that he wouldn't hurt a fly.

Why, he even got frightened at airports, for heaven's sake, he told himself.

–Tee hee hee, he chuckled softly.

Covering his mouth completely with his hand, and praying that no one would see what he was doing.

But this time they did.

As Sonny Hackett leaned across and kept tapping his cigarette.

–What exactly are you playing at there, Barney?

But Barney Grue didn't even attempt an answer.

Which had the effect of making Sonny Hackett feel even more uneasy than he was already.

As Hughie stood up to allow himself a bit of a stretch, as he termed it.

–Ah yes, the small man observed, in another little while it'll all be over. And, boys, what a laugh we'll all be able to have ourselves then …

–Why? remarked Sonny sourly. Will you be telling us one of your gut-busting yarns? One of your world-famous wisecracks, maybe?

–There isn't need to say the like of that, said Hughie, turning red, in my opinion that's unnecessary.

– I agree, said Red, and particularly not now. Not now when it soon will all be over.

–With you it's teeth, and with him it's laughs, Sonny Hackett muttered, that's all you'll ever get from youse.

–So what do you think you're gonna do about it, Hackett? Gonna do something about it, are you Sonny? Gonna fix us, are you? The way you maybe fixed the Indian in the caravan? Because, the way I heard it, he's still out there at all hours banging his tambourine. And ain't got no intentions of shifting camp. Now why's that, do you think?

Sonny's eyes flashed as he began searching frantically inside his pockets for tobacco.

And doing the best he could to explain, even though he didn't have to.

−Look, he said, that whole thing about the shirts strangling me and that, when I had to get tested as a boy at school − it was that which gave us Hacketts our reputation, and which isn't fair. It really isn't. I mean, of *course* I wasn't afraid of the shirts in the wardrobe. Honestly, for God's sake, the idea of clothes coming out and strangling you. I was just a bit young, a little bit anxious, that's all. And in those days, anyway, they used to send schoolboys away regular for tests. So you don't know what you're talking about, Red. For it'll take more than an Indian bashing tom toms to put an end to us, I can tell you. So, back the fuck off and leave me alone.

Sonny appeared to have lost his train of thought, and just for a second Hughie was considering whether or not it might now be appropriate to intervene with a funny story. Just to lighten the atmosphere somewhat, but again thought the better of it.

−What's the big deal anyway, Sonny choked, about her going out to get herself some counselling? That's the way things are these days − things have changed. The priests are history.

−There's no big deal, Sonny, consoled Hughie, absolutely none, there isn't Sonny − and what you got to remember is, that you're among friends.

−Then what in the hell is that Indian talking about? squealed Sonny.

Looking as though he had just witnessed something terrible to which no one else in the room had been privy.

Such as his little son Cosmo with his pudding-bowl haircut, bathed in a phosphorescent glow and holding a piece of paper in his hand. As he opened his little mouth and, ever so softly, intoned the word: *Bones*.

−Indian? exclaimed Hughie, swallowing hard, Indian, Sonny?

But not knowing what to say after that.

As a matter of fact, nobody did.

So no one said anything. As Sonny flicked and flicked at his rollie, doing the best he could to collect his thoughts.

−You see, what's been happening is − Hughie, are you listening? − she brings wee Cosmo out with her every time. And that's what's making him strange, I think. You see, he knows what we did. Because he seen it in one of his dreams. He knows what we did to Wilson, I think. No, I *know* he does − because he drew another picture for me one night. And insisted that someone − or *something!* − was guiding his hand. An old gentleman, he told me afterwards, with white shoes …

As Hughie Munley stood there, grinned even more widely, swaying uncertainly as he rubbed his stubby hands and did his best to think up another joke.

Before Sonny released a high-pitched shriek.

−AND WHAT WILL I DO THEN? they heard him plead helplessly. What if it does turn out that the Indian has, after all, put a spell on them?

He lunged forward, dry-retching as he clutched his stomach.

−One day Cosmo looked at me with eyes that were more like glass, not eyes at all. Daddy, he says, is there any way out of me dying in Lake Wynter? Because that's where I know they're going to find my bones.

Shocked to the core of his being, Big Barney pressed the heels of his hands against his temples, experiencing throughout him a kind of high-voltage charge, the fierceness and intensity of which reminded him once more of the churning Shannon waters and the inexplicable mysteries of the electrisms contained within its boundless depths.

He was sorry now he had said a word about them.

As he found himself sitting there waiting for the inevitable commencement of what he thought of as the Big Barney Investigation.

Which never, in fact, came.

—I'm only trying to help, Hughie was explaining, not very effectively, there isn't any need to take the face off me. I'm only trying to help. That's all I'm doing. Did I ever tell you about the Mexican? Well, this Mexican, you see, he comes walking into a bar …

Then there was a knock on the door.

Hughie went over to answer it.

But there was no one there.

Chapter 26

The Bones of Lake Wynter

The recollections in every one of Jody's painstaking letters were so acute and considered that he could even make you see the world through Mr Bonny's eyes.

As he remained there, silently, still seated on a plastic beer crate, motionless in the tar-black darkness, not speaking for what seemed an interminable period.

Before – like he reckoned he had all the time in the world – slowly, laboriously, rising to his feet.

–They say that I know everything, Jody, said the man in the white suit, plying his Panama and gliding blithely in and out between the towers of old truck tyres.

With the generator's hum shuddering into silence.

–And I don't know whether or not that is true, my unfortunate itinerant friend. But I do know this much. That, back in the days of the early seventies, at least as far as those 'good old boys' were concerned, there weren't no such things as anxiety and trepidation. And if anyone had suggested as much to someone as powerful, indeed indomitable, as 'Sunny' Sonny Boy Hackett back in them times, hell, he'd have strung those fellers up in a heartbeat.

–Not that anyone would have had the gall, would they Jody, he explained, because you know what they were like, those old meat plant pistoleros. For you and Ringo, to tell the honest truth, being that little bit younger, you kind of used to look up to them, ain't that a fact?

He cleaned a spot of dirt off one of his white buck loafers.

–But, like I say, that's understandable, he went on, on account of the pair of you weren't nothing more'n a couple of wet-behind-the ears stablehands, only too eager to leave your less than profitable pasts behind you. And getting to hanging out with them ol' hombres, hell it didn't seem that detrimental in that respect at all. As you spent your time hunting and fishing and chucking darts with the likes of Big Barney – not to mention Ol' Red and Sonny Hackett – all them good old boys, Mr Monroe's Heartland heroes. Formerly of the Glasson Meat Plant, where they had distinguished themselves in all sorts of ways – ain't it, little dogie? Ain't that the case?

And no sooner had the words made their way from Mr Bonny's lips than Jody Kane found himself, large as life, back there standing on the floor of that very same meat factory, littered with meat by-products and entrails, with its fearsome array of cutting tools and conveyor belts, that familiar dangerous network of overhead chains and hooks.

Experiencing the sensation of the heat on his face and body and arms as the grinding roar and clatter of heavy machinery came screeching back to assault his ears and he recoiled as the shackles went careering past his head.

Seeing himself blinded by the huge rolling clouds of steam as the cutting line came rolling, rounding the corner with a cacophonous roar and shooting sharply past his face. As, somewhere in the bowels of the killing floor, yet another wretched beast met an ignoble end.

As its pathetic legs buckled and went splaying across the concrete beyond the crimson-and-pus splattered walls where the iron drums boomed and Tony Begley, wielding his boning knife aloft, set about skinning and dismembering yet another beast.

Yes, there they all were again, thought Jody, in his mind's eye watching them parade in their long white bloodstained aprons and caps – like some regiment of fierce, medieval warriors in their steamed-up goggles and white protective clothing.

–Whoop! they hollered, as another unfortunate Holstein buckled, discharging its cargo of colourful, slimy innards.

As Tony Begley snickered, softly, to himself.

It was there in the boning hall that the 'accident' had been planned.

The murder and robbery and death, that is, of Wilson Gillis, Protestant farmer.

♡

In a corner of the outhouse, Jody Kane had passed out again, probably exhausted from battling the intensity of his recollections.

Before finding himself awakened by a sharp tap to the side of his cheek.

–Well, said Mr Bonny, tracing his fingertip along the length of Jody's jaw.

–What in the fuck do you think you're doing? snarled the fighter.

Mr Bonny's expression remained inscrutable.

–Does it surprise you any, looking back, that we ought to find ourselves in such a situation?

He examined his nails.

–Do you remember the occasion of the factory dispute, Jody Kane? When the formidable Tony Begley took the liberty of informing his superior that if certain workers' grievances were not addressed that he personally would not hesitate to skin him alive, right there then, just the same as he'd do to any Friesian or Holstein. And that yes – he, Tony Begley himself, with the greatest of pleasure, would haul his 'miserable fucking arse' down to the boning hall that very minute and, with the assistance of his fellow employees, shove his 'fucking carcass' right up on there onto the cutting line. What would the plant manager think of that? he wondered.

Mr Bonny smiled as he continued.

–The day that the manager was almost murdered in his own place of work, he chuckled, as he reached in his pocket and produced a linen hankie.

–With whatever few bits of him as remained being tossed to the bottom of Lake Wynter, I surmise. After all, another coupla bones ain't gonna make a whole lot of difference in there, Jody Kane …

After dabbing his forehead, he folded the handkerchief and replaced it in his pocket.

–So then, Jody, Mr Bonny went on, do you really think they would have done it?

–Done what? What are you talking about, Bonny – done what?

–Disembowelled the plant manager – eviscerated him, I mean.

Jody spat bitterly.

–Go to hell, he said again, how in hell do I know what he'd have done.

–Hush, urged Bonny gently, don't go getting yourself in a muddle. Because, when it comes, you are going to require all your resources and strength.

He thought for a moment, and then murmured equably:

–All I'm really asking is – do you really think they'd have done it – skinned him?

His visitor released a long, low whistle.

—Maybe, said Jody, I don't the fuck know. How would I know? Or fucking care, come to that.

Mr Bonny lowered his head for a second, before eventually conceding a sympathetic smile, his eyes gleaming once again.

—Look Jody, I know all of this is difficult, and not just for you. Because everyone present here tonight is undergoing their own share of private and unspoken difficulties. Therefore you needn't start assuming that you personally are being singled out. So please, do your old friend Mr Bonny a favour and don't succumb to self-pity or spurious sentiment. You do that for me – will you please, little dogie?

—You ain't got no right to manipulate me the like of this. No right, Mr Bonny.

—Yes, that is true. But how fair can it be, either, to murder and plunder the house of an innocent farmer?

—That was an accident – and, in any case, anyway I wasn't there.

Mr Bonny stroked his chin as he gravely paced the floor.

—New Orleans, he said very softly.

—What? said Jody. What did you say?

—You ever been there?

—You know I haven't. You know I've never in my life been outside of Glasson County.

—The Big Easy – that's what they call it. I come from near there, and so be assured that I know it well. So much so that I got my own personal name for it, Jody. You know what it is?

—I don't. I ain't got the faintest idea.

Mr Bonny reached in his pocket.

—You see these? he heard him say.

Two small grey bones sat resting in his open palm.

—Listen for just a moment – just attend now, for a few short seconds.

Click click.

Ricketty-click.

–The Big Uneasy. That's my own private, personal name for it. And that's where you think that I got these here little fellows, ain't it? That's where you think that I got 'em. But it ain't so, you see, because I got them somewhere much closer to home.

He came right up as far as Jody and leered, goggle-eyed, into his face.

–You got any idea where that might be?

–No I don't, Jody Kane spat back, and as I live and breathe I do not care – I just don't care Mr Bonny.

–Lake Wynter, he heard his suave visitor whisper softly, that's where I got 'em. We can only hope and pray that, please God, they are not yours. For, sure as geese go barefoot in summer, they sure do make me feel uneasy, little dogie.

When Jody looked up, Mr Bonny was gone.

With nothing but the sound of the soft wind moaning, and just the very faintest trace of his whispers.

Floating past like thin stray wisps of fog.

Chapter 27

A Delta Dawn in Dreams Embroidered

Red Campbell said he couldn't stand it any longer.

His colour was high, and his eyes way too bright.

As he flung his cards, in a fury, to the floor.

Big Barney was heartbroken – why had he ever told them anything about the airport, he said to himself, or mentioned anything at all about Mercedes and the rabbits.

Because he knew, for sure, when all this was over, that they would all just go and get drunk and laugh their heads off about it, saying poor old Barney.

In fact he could almost hear them already.

Not that it was all that surprising. Because he had always suspected that they had been talking about him.

–Look at Big Barney, he had once heard them gossiping in the factory canteen, so slow the dead lice would nearly fall off of him.

It wasn't that they hated him or anything, just that they didn't figure on him being all that important.

Sometimes, when ever they felt confident enough, they would creep up behind him and swing their arms the very same as him.

He pretended not to notice, but, in fact, always had.

—Why did I have to go and do it? he moaned. Why did I have to go and say anything at all? Why did I have to open my mouth about that stupid airport.

Or Mercedes.

Whoever *she* was.

Just a likeness he had seen in a library picture book and snipped out with a scissors to keep inside his wallet.

What sort of person does the like of that?

He hated himself now.

As he always did, whenever he thought about her hidden in there, all creased up and so faded over the years you could barely even make out her features.

His imaginary love.

Big Barney's missus.

His beloved life's partner.

His special woman.

His lady.

Every night, after a few drinks, he would make his way home in the dark and stumble up the stairs in his farmhouse until he was alone in his bedroom where he would open his wallet and press Mercedes up to his face. Closing his eyes as he heard her husky voice whisper:

—I am your one and only love, Mercedes Starrs, sweet honey-lady of your yearning and imagination, lily-pure maid of Astolat and hunting Goddess of the Boetian Hill, so pure and fragile and yet still all woman. For I, Mercedes Starrs, am the very centre and circumference, diameter and periphery of your affections. I love you, Barney Grue, and I want you to plant kisses all over my face and hair.

—Would you go 'way out of that, he heard himself protest, fearful that someone might be looking right into his mind.

But nobody, then or now, was even looking in his direction.

No one.

Not Sonny.

Not Hughie.

Not Red.

And certainly not the twins – with Shorty having enough to worry about, considering the state that the Runt had got himself into.

–Why do you go on pretending it didn't happen? he kept repeating. When I know that you seen him pointing as well? Why are you lying, our boy – what is wrong with you?

You could see that Shorty wanted to cry,

He was really devastated.

And wasn't in any position to offer any form of contribution.

Any more than the barman appeared to be, away off somewhere best described as untouchable, preoccupied by his whistling of an ineffable little tune.

As he smiled.

With the result that nobody at all was paying any attention to Barney Grue, so he could think about whoever he damned well liked, he thought, and started chuckling again.

As he reflected on Mercedes and the place where he had first encountered her loveliness. But for the life of him, he couldn't remember the picture book's name.

The one he had rented from the Glasson County library.

He went there sometimes, but not specifically to borrow books containing pictures of American beauties. Mostly just to browse or have a look through the *Farmer's Journal*.

Sometimes he'd take a look at other volumes on display but, as a general rule, couldn't seem to make very much of them.

Which oughtn't to have been all that unexpected, really, not considering that Barney had left school at twelve years of age to drive a tractor on his father's land.

Make some sense of all them big hard books?

No chance.

The very idea of it …

He found himself chortling heartily all over again.

As an invisible fragrance appeared to envelop him, and he could have sworn that he heard a familiar voice – the one, unmistakably, which belonged to Mercedes Starrs.

–Those green hills of Ireland, he heard her murmur, so different to this country with its glamorous landscape of long twilights and hot dawns, but which I know from your conversation possesses its own unique magic. And one day, as an officer and a gentleman, Lieutenant Colonel Barney Grue, when all of these misbegotten wars are concluded, you and I will travel there together.

–The green hills of Ireland, he heard himself repeat, as they both stood there on the verandah, during a gala ball perhaps staged by the city for the benefit of its gilded citizenry, looking out over the formal gardens towards the bursting sparks and tails of light sent up by the mesmerising fireworks display, as the orchestral opera music drifted out through the open French windows, gradually dissipating in the warm breeze.

As, ever so slowly, rising above the drooping Spanish moss, they watched it break like magic across the delta, a dawn that could only have been embroidered by themselves, deep in the heart of the territory of their dreams.

Big watery tears lined up on either side of his nose.

–Upon, he whimpered, that rare and special dawn.

His temples were burning fiercely once more. He pressed the heels of his hands against them.

Finding himself suddenly compelled to do something completely out of character.

Such as growing wings, perhaps, and taking a run right across the room – maybe, even, leaping right out of the window, giving a cheer.

That would be good.

—Are you all right? he heard Sonny Hackett querying. Are you OK there, Barney?

As he thrust his jaw forward, grinning as he flipped back his forelock.

—Well, are you? he inquired again.

—I don't know, replied Barney Grue.

—What do you mean you don't know? he heard Sonny Hackett's irritated reply. What kind of an answer is that?

—It's just an answer, Barney said, I don't know what kind of answer it is.

—You're one great big mountain of laughs, so you are, maybe you ought to tell us your story about the airport again.

Big Barney stiffened and was on the point of responding: You are a very cheeky person, Sonny Hackett. And maybe, instead of trying to say smart things about me, you could tell us all about when you were a boy and you used to think that shirts might come out and strangle you.

In the end, however, deciding not to say anything

Because, to tell you the truth, he said to himself, I really do not care what they have to say or think about me anymore.

With the reason for that being that he wasn't really happy any longer – and which, as he was now beginning to accept, had been the situation for a very long time.

Even though Sonny Hackett was doing his best to stop him, Red Campbell was repeating something about Wilson Gillis.

—That's enough about that, do you hear? Hackett barked. Fuckingwell more than enough already, Campbell.

But Red just continued to ignore him.

—There's no point in any of us kidding ourselves anymore, he suggested, because the facts are as follows – we broke into the house of an innocent man, and whether or not it happened by accident, Wilson Gillis is still dead. And it's us that's responsible.

—What we did is in the past, protested Hughie, and there isn't any sense in you coming up with all this now. Do you hear me, Red?

—I'm telling you that there isn't any such thing as the past. No past, no present and no fucking future. This world is a bad dream.

—Ah now, Red, don't talk crazy. You will have to ease up on the jungle there, Red. No such thing as the past. Whee-hoo!

But Red was already in a daze, looking away.

And, as a matter of fact, looking like he too didn't care much any longer.

As Big Barney Grue once again pressed his large hands against his temples, with his face this time contorting grotesquely.

And doing his level best not to think about the stylish and sophisticated Mercedes Starrs, standing on a balustrade attired in a swathe of lace as she plied a delicately decorated pink-and-blue fan.

Which she suddenly moved aside, revealing, to Barney's horror, just about the tiniest of hands imaginable.

And which, most clearly, was not that of a fully grown woman.

But one, in fact, of a newborn infant.

A little pink round one, in fact, with the pinkest, loveliest, sweet little chubby digits – five small fingers.

—Look at them, the lovely lady was whispering, aren't they just the last word? Aren't they really just perfect? Why, a freshly born infant, another of the wonders of God's many creations …

And it was at this point that the silent and subterranean fuse which had been travelling anonymously all the way along the complicated circuitry of Big Barney Grue's nervous system, elected to ignite and silently explode right there in the centre of his head. With its white light almost blinding him as those watery tears turned into a flood.

–Once upon a time, began Big Barney Grue, with everyone slowly turning around to observe him, not without a degree of astonishment, there was a beauty who wandered by herself across this mountain, and she was mine … all mine … the lady belonging to the officer and much respected gentleman, Lt. Col. Bernard at your service.

He was trembling all over.

As Hughie decided it was time tell a joke.

–Did youse hear the one about the Mexican firefighter?

–No I didn't, as a matter of fact, Big Barney roared, reaching out and grabbing him and holding him up by the collar with his short legs swinging, and I don't want to!

Before releasing him and then just sitting there, staring straight ahead.

Staring out at the willow, in silence.

As everyone waited for another selection.

–Does anyone want to hear some music? asked Sonny.

But no one responded.

So none ever came.

No selection, I mean.

–I'll just go over here now and see if he's coming, said Hughie Munley, pushing down the grimy slats.

Nothing.

Chapter 28

These Are My Mountains

Then, out of nowhere, the door swung open again – but it was just another fleeting gust of wind.

–Nothing to worry about, said Mervyn reassuringly, you know what's the cause of it.

–It's just the wind, nodded Hughie, that's all.

–Just the wind, agreed Red, nothing else.

But the Runt said no, that it wasn't.

–I know what it was, he insisted, for I seen him. Out there, standing on the water.

–Ha ha! laughed Hughie. It's finger-lickin' good!

As he clapped his hands and swept in between the two of them.

–The Mexican firefighter – did you know he had two sons? Hose A and Hose B.

–That's not funny, snapped Sonny Hackett, of all your fucking dumb wisecracks, that has got to be the stupidest yet. And that is saying something. Yes, that is really saying fucking something, Hickory Holler.

–I'm sorry it isn't to your taste, returned Hughie, turning towards the door.

–Still no sign of him, he murmured, TB.

Red Campbell went over and put on a record.

–*Once upon a time in a land made of gingerbread lived a happy girl and boy*, sang Gregory and the Cadets as the needle dropped into the groove.

–Me and the Kid used to dance to this, announced Red. Me and the Kid, we used to always dance to Gregory and the Cadets …

–Easy, soothed Hughie, patting him on the shoulder, easy now Red.

–*Once upon a time*, sang Gregory, and then again.

The needle was stuck.

–Everything's gonna be all right, said Hughie.

–No it isn't, said Red Campbell, shaking his head, it isn't gonna be alright at all …

As he stared at Hughie with red-rimmed eyes.

–They used to play regular in Heartland, he said, Gregory and his band.

Then he started laughing uncontrollably.

–What are you doing? Sonny Hackett shouted over. What the fuck do you think you're doing?

But Red Campbell had already inserted a fistful of coins into the jukebox chute, and was in the process of performing an amusing little dance – a kind of arms-up, legs-out, boogie-woogie Teddyboy shuffle.

–I told you, hollered Sonny, I thought I fucking warned you, Campbell!

Rising to his feet as he whisked a pool cue from the rack and slammed the butt right into the glass of the jukebox – first once, twice, and then three times.

He didn't seem particularly enraged or anything while he was doing it – he was thorough, however, and entirely committed.

As a spiderweb crack spread out across the machine's transparent front, before Sonny Hackett replaced the cue and crossed the floor to sit back down.

Shards of glass lay scattered on the sawdust.

Curiously, Mervyn Walker elected to make no comment on what had just transpired, none of any kind.

Just watching Sonny ambling laconically back to the table. The barman smiled and said nothing as Sonny sat down.

With Wee Hughie doing his best, once again, to mask the tension. Appearing more excited than ever, in the process, repeatedly flexing his fingers as he cried out, hoarsely:

—Gregory and the Cadets — what a band! Yes sir, a famous outfit and no mistake. All the way from the land made of gingerbread, oh man.

As the barman, whistling a soft low tune, lifted the drop-leaf and set about sweeping up the jukebox debris.

—O Jesus, moaned the Runt, these pains in my stomach, I think they're getting worse. I hope he's not out there. Did you hear that noise? Listen — there it is again.

But Sonny Hackett, or everyone else for that matter, decided to offer the Runt McHale nothing by way of reply.

And instead just remaining there, drumming his fingers, counting out smoke rings — one two three.

What did they do in the land made of gingerbread, Gregory the singer kept on wondering — perhaps built castles in the sky.

Well, of course they did, because anything that had ever caused them trouble or made them feel terrible grief or sadness — all of that was, quite magically, now gone.

That was how it had been for Gregory and his band the Cadets.

A song which I too remembered, and as soon as it came on, had hit me hard in the gut.

And carried me away from my confinement among the roof-beams to a day long before when I had first heard it coming drifting from a transistor radio somewhere in the distance beyond the high grey limestone walls of Whiterock Orphanage.

And whose sentiments Jody and myself, perhaps more than most indeed, had implicitly understood, lying there in the High Country Meadow, with a canopy of blue overlooking the world – and we ourselves, where both of us lay on a vast carpet of sweet yellow flowers.

Such were the thoughts I found myself recalling as I lay there constricted underneath those cockloft rafters, an emotional knot forming in my throat, and I had to clench my teeth together in order to keep it together.

Thinking of us dreaming, like Red Campbell, in a way, of a future so beautiful and fragile it could never, in truth, have risked coming into being.

While, not so very far away in a tumbledown outhouse which might have been a coffin stood on end, that noblest of the noble, valiant and courageous warriors found himself awakening in the dank air once again, emerging from a state of near-delirium, during which, more than once, he could have sworn that, indeed, he had died.

To his dismay and bafflement, opening those exhausted, troubled eyelids to find himself the object of Mr Bonny's renewed observation.

–I just didn't think it was fair to leave you, he heard him say, not after all that you've been through.

He plied his hat and gave Jody a smile.

–Given the extent of your ordeal, he continued, it isn't that surprising that your offended mind ought to play such tricks. Because whose wouldn't, given similar circumstances?

Then he arrived over and opened up his hand.

–I wanted you to have this, Jody heard him say.

–Please, Mr Bonny, pleaded Jody, no bones.

And then looked down to see a single, green-stemmed soft little flower.

–In remembrance of the High Meadow Country, said Mr Bonny, the primrose – sweetest of all our Creator's most precious blooms. For you, little dogie, to hold against your heart, in honour of a future that, in some other dimension or world, might have had the good fortune to be born. Goodbye, little dogie.

Beneath me in the bar, the proprietor had just now finished sweeping up.

—Don't go thinking that I'll let this go, hissed Sonny Hackett, don't for a second let that get into your stupid dumb fucking head, Campbell!

Red closed one eye and brandished a fantail.

—I'm so fucking scared, he said in a low voice. I'm terrified.

—Ah stop it now, fellers, will you, pleaded Hughie.

—He's dead, the fuck, and it's been a long time coming.

—Please, said Hughie.

—Look, Patches – this is the situation. No matter what you think, I *know* my boy wrote that piece of paper. And, unless I happen to have had my brains taken out in the night, which I don't think I have, I know that no child could ever come up with something like that on his own. So I'm sorry to have to disappoint all of you if that's the way that you've been thinking. But no young feller, at least that ever I met, just comes in from school one day and sits down at the kitchen table like he's in some kind of trance or something and invents a poem the like of that.

—Shut up, will youse! the Runt screeched hysterically. I don't want any of youse talking like this. Because youse don't know what is about to happen – he's out there, waiting!

—Shorty, for Christ's sake, pleaded Wee Hughie, at his wit's end, for the love of Christ will you do what I'm asking!

But Shorty was at a loss.

With Sonny Hackett continuing, oblivious.

–Of course, as you can imagine, that was what gave my wife her excuse. Because after that she kept on saying that what was happening to poor Cosmo was that he had inherited that weakness of mind. With which the Hacketts, down the years, had been afflicted. Or so she said. It's your crowd, she kept on saying, it's your bad blood that's made him this way.

Sonny explained that the words were getting all clogged up, somehow, in his throat, but Big Barney Grue leaned across and touched his arm – giving it a gentle but firm and reassuring squeeze.

–It's gonna be OK, Sonny, he assured him, it's gonna be alright, compadre. You's gonna be fine –don't you worry, just take your time.

Sonny's face was pale grey now but, somehow, he eventually rallied.

–Then she said it, Sonny Hackett continued, looked me right in the eye and told me how the Indian had said to her – *warned* her, in fact – that if she didn't make an effort to get away from me once and for all, that something terrible was going to happen. Something awful, he said. That was what the Indian said – something *awful*. Can you believe it?

For a moment, his eyes were fierce.

But then he laughed uncertainly.

–It's inevitable, she said. She said it was inevitable. That's what she said. *Inevitable.*

He slammed his hands flat down on the table. With his voice so high it was only just audible.

–Yes. That's what he told her about my own little Cosmo. That if we didn't do something he was probably going to end up being possessed. It's punishment. Punishment, I'm telling you …

Wee Hughie turned white.

—Ah what the hell do Indians know, he spat acidly, fucking tom toms!

Red Campbell nodded, with a vehemence clearly intended as conciliatory.

—Steady on here now, Sonny. Let's do our best to get to grip with things, if you get my meaning. I mean, didn't you tell me yourself that his sister was studying poems at school? So couldn't that be where he got it from? What do you think Hughie?

—I'd say that that's a very likely explanation. As likely an explanation as any, I would say, Red.

—There, you see? beamed Red Campbell, nodding away.

As Sonny swung around and struck the wall an unmerciful blow.

—IT'S PUNISHMENT, he cried, PUNISHMENT I'M TELLING YOU!

Then he let out an odd, irrational chuckle.

—We can avoid the subject all we like. But in the end, let's face it – murdering people, it's kind of a bad thing to do, ain't it? he said. It's just a pity that it had to be poor old Wilson. Ah, well …

Red Campbell lifted a heavy ashtray and wielded it.

—That kind of talk ain't getting us nowhere, he warned.

Throughout it all, Mervyn Walker had chosen to pass no comment of any kind, seeming content to amuse himself by whistling a familiar little tune – one which, once upon a time, a long time ago, had been associated with his lifetime friend, the respectable Protestant farmer Wilson Gillis.

—Let me rest on peaceful mountain, the barman murmured softly, and you could almost hear the low drone of a harmonium and see Wilson, as always, erect and stately in the front pew, opening his Good Book at Galatians 6:7.

Praising his God in a quiet country church.

With Mervyn Walker becoming so absorbed in his thoughts that he almost forgot completely about his inconspicuously wrapped cargo located beneath the counter.

As he remained there, drumming his fingers in deep contemplation, magisterially reflecting on all of those evenings that he and Wilson had spent walking by the river and, on Saturday mornings, spincasting their lines as the mist began to clear over the still silver surface of their beloved Lake Wynter.

I have to stop here for a little bit because sometimes it's hard for me to remember everything properly.

Not to recall particular details, you understand – more dealing with them.

Because that emotional knot you might remember me speaking about earlier, it can just, out of nowhere, swell up in you.

Sometimes they say that I have a tendency to dwell too much on the past, or at least certain aspects of it – and that, with my unfortunate history of alcohol abuse, may well have become prone to a degree of self-delusion.

And, to some extent, I acknowledge, in some fashion, that may well be true.

Because my breakdown definitely did leave a mark. One which, unless you've been through it yourself, is very difficult to explain.

As well as that, it's tedious also. I can't tell you how often I've been tempted just to get up and walk out of the AA meetings. With more interminable accounts of nightmares, agitation, pressure and autonomic hyperactivity – fast heart rate and high blood pressure, in other words – doing the rounds.

All of which are the standard symptoms of delirium tremens, and to which I won't pretend to be any stranger, particularly to the sensation of impending catastrophe and that awful feeling of something crawling underneath your skin.

–You know I sometimes think you imagine things, Ray, Fr Conway has once or twice remarked to me, or at the very least, exaggerate them – maybe you listen to too much music. All them wonderful tales and melodramatic stories …

And the priest may be right.

Except that, unfortunately for me, everything I've written – about me and Jody, at any rate – all of it is one hundred per cent verifiable. Just read the letters.

They'll help.

For, what with the valley of Glasson County always having been such a unique and special place, complete with its own insurgent vision and unique, perhaps eccentric, code of manners – it was always going to be difficult to understand this story, certainly for someone who comes from outside.

So, all I can say is that everything I've set down here in these few humble pages is as close to the truth as I can possibly get. And I remain pretty much convinced that, in general, I have managed to get it right.

I guess, just by being born in Glasson County – having grown up in the heartland, I mean – there are just some things you instinctively *know*.

You've got to believe me.

Chapter 29

Five Little Fingers

I clamped my hand hard, almost brutally, against my mouth – convinced for sure that, this time, I was definitely going to do it. Sneeze, I mean.

The air in the room below me was, bad as ever, still infected with apprehension – although Barney Grue was smirking impishly, rocking back and forth in his armchair.

Probably bringing back a fond memory of some Saturday night, when he'd been standing on the balcony sipping a cola. Thinking about who he might ask to dance, and what was she likely to offer by way of response.

Before deciding, abruptly, to pay a visit to the lavatory – only, in his enthusiasm, coming to the realisation that his three hundred pound bulk had suddenly gone drunkenly crashing to the floor and, in the process, delivered him a considerably painful bump on his forehead.

But, fortunately, Wee Hughie was on hand, assisting him with some difficulty back onto his 'throne', which was how the small man good-humouredly described it.

As Big Barney snorted defiantly and swung his enormous arm in a wide, extravagant arc, bawling out the single word:

—Fingers!

For Red Campbell's part, all that was going through his mind was:

The door!

At which he kept staring with blazing, bloodshot eyes.

More than anything he wanted for that door to open, and once and for all, put an end to this waiting.

Barney Grue snorted and laughed to himself a little as he saw himself standing in front of the stage in Heartland, the showband going through the motions of twanging out their hit, the one entitled 'Five Little Fingers'. With the lead singer in his natty black velvet tuxedo-style suit now, in Barney's memory, sinking to one knee in order to perform what they called the 'talky bit' to all the girls who were reaching up trying their best to grab him.

Once or twice, the singer had even pretended to sob as he spoke the words – every one of which Big Barney remembered, something which made him want to laugh out loud, when you considered the amount of pain that they brought him each and every time he remembered them.

–Yes, lamented the lead vocalist, I knew only too well that night just what it was my own little baby was trying to say to me, in its own quiet and little special way. That she was trying to love me – that's what my baby was trying to say. And it only took five little seconds for those five little fingers to reach out and tell me all that I needed to know – I love you, Daddy.

Barney well knew that if any of his colleagues somehow got to know what it was he was thinking about just now, whether it be showbands or babies or fingers or anything else, they would probably have fallen off their chairs in hysterics.

Being well aware that Barney Grue, principally on account of his built-for-diesel girth, had very little experience to speak of in the world of romance.

Except that that was where they were wrong, you see.

Because there was one particular person about whom they knew nothing.

And while he mightn't be Elvis Presley or anything, this person herself had privately confided her affections to Mr Grue.

For it was her – yes, none other than the radiantly beautiful Mercedes Starrs – who had insisted that what was most important was what you found inside a person. And whether or not you could depend on them to be there.

Whether or not, when it came to it, they would let you down.

And whenever he heard those words from Mercedes Starrs, Big Barney Grue shifted just a little on his throne and murmured:

–That very first night when I laid eyes on Mercedes Starrs, what I can only describe as a light that was almost unearthly shone upon me. One that glowed like no other before or since. And underneath which stood a creature pure and sweet as the clearest of spring water, and in whose blue eyes the virtues of selflessness and charity shone out clear as the glassiest ocean. And provoked in me, yes in big old bumpy-head fat Barney Grue, a sensation which no man in this world has got no right to expect. To even entertain the notion for one second that the Queen of Appomattox, the brightest jewel in old Virginny, she might ever consider even passing him the time of day, much less accompany him onto the ballroom floor.

Where he would lead her – how vivid it seemed! – in a quadrille as the Palm Court orchestra struck up the piece she had come to know and love, 'The Green Fields of Ireland', her long black eyelashes keeping time with the swayingly elegant sweep of the violin.

As her lips murmured: *love* – for that was, he knew, the emotion she was experiencing.

Finding himself quite overcome, his extremities started visibly trembling as he suddenly shot forward and loudly vacated his seat, robustly announcing that he felt a pressing need to visit the bathroom.

As, arising and trailing his way across the floor – and crashing headlong into three chairs on the way – he found himself calling her name out loud, and just as the door of the lavatory swung open before him, briefly caught a glimpse of her standing there, large as life, reflected in the ochre-stained porcelain surround.

–Mercedes, he choked, through the lattice of his fingers, my one and only Mercedes Starrs – that I among men should be so chosen. To be so privileged as to carry a flaming brand for your special beauty. And why it must be, in humility, one last time I utter your name, unique among women: Mercedes, gentle woman, as pure and chaste as sparkling water, as cold as gleaming ice, and to whom alone, from this night out, I pledge my heart and life to the protection of our love.

He was never to know just what it was that happened, and neither did any of the others. Because the door had already closed when they overheard the unmerciful cry and ran inside to discover Barney out cold on the tiles, but with a deep cut three or four inches wide on his forehead, bleeding profusely.

–He must have lost his balance again and slipped, Wee Hughie suggested, and with Red Campbell's assistance heaved him back inside the bar.

–Here. Let me, said Sonny, dabbing the livid gash with a towel.

As Mervyn arrived over with a rudimentary bandage – a scarf, basically.

Which they knotted around his head.

–I'm sorry I don't have a first aid kit, said Mervyn, I do apologise.

–That's all right, said Sonny, as he dabbed some more water on the big man's protuberant lips.

As Barney Grue awoke once more, howling with the pain, which he said was unbearable.

–What happened? he repeated. Please does anyone know what happened? Where's Mercedes?

Looking all around him but, hardly surprisingly, finding his surroundings nothing more than a blur.

With no sign of her anywhere – Mercedes.

But then, of course, as they all knew well, there never had been anybody by that name.

All it had been was a vision in an airport – one which now came blindingly back to him again, in an eruption of prismatic colour.

–Give you the shivers, sometimes, these airports. I was just standing there looking out the glass of the observation bay across the tarmac. When, all of a sudden, it seemed to go cold. And all I kept thinking was that maybe the plane she was on had crashed. Mercedes, I remember crying, my Mercedes. You're here.

Then he looked up and realised what he'd said, looking ashamed.

–Oh Jesus, he moaned, oh Jesus Hughie, can you help me? Can any of you do that – pull me out of this trough?

With the actual truth being that, in recent times, Big Barney had been experiencing violent, periodic blackouts.

About which, however, he had never breathed a word – and as a result, he had started to become seriously concerned that he might, in fact, be in danger of losing his mind.

And had already resolved – long before the accident in the bathroom had occurred – that, definitely, just as soon as all this was over, that, once and for all, he would foreswear alcohol.

Then, quite out of nowhere, and entirely in spite of himself, yet another striking memory returned.

And he found himself thinking about a great big rooster, or chicken.

Foghorn Leghorn was the big fellow's name.

What am I going around thinking about him for? Barney Grue wondered.

Then he remembered – but of course he did.

That, on the day when he'd paid a visit to a certain labour ward in Midford Hospital, the rooster in question had been playing on the television. Yes, going through his antics:

–*Ah say. Ah say, that boy!*

Yes, that was what he kept on saying, in that distinctive Southern drawl, as he stomped around with those great red rooster feet.

–If ah happens to discovah just who has been pokin' around mah hutch, then believe you me there gonna be a raisin'.

Now, as they looked at him, everyone in the bar was astonished to hear Big Barney bawling:

–I bloody hate that Foghorn Leghorn – I fuckingwell hate him. Hughie, do you hear me?

As that great big wounded bear of a man then lifted up his head, looking out with blazing eyes through a great big forest of whiskers into the long grey face of Sonny Hackett, now entirely distorted.

–Are you there, Big Barney? he heard Sonny Hackett repeat, tapping him solidly on the head.

Barney Grue, then, was swallowed by an entirely unnamable dread.

Because, just the very second that Sonny Hackett had spoken, he could have sworn that he'd heard the sound of a baby.

And then, after that, the squawking of a big giant chicken.

–You got no friends, you great big built-for-diesel tubba grease, it was saying as it stomped around, and that's the way it's a-gonna stay.

After which the rooster gave a callous impatient cackle and tossed back its flapping comb before glaring at him, ferociously.

−Yes, ah would say that that boy Barney − why that he ain't got hisself no friends at all! he screeched.

And that was the reason why the sobbing had begun again, even if no one could properly hear him.

Because Big Barney was, however reluctantly, beginning to accept the strident assertions the chicken, or the rooster, or whatever the fuck he was.

And which made him feel just a tiny bit better − confirming as it did, that for probably everyone alive, when you got down to it, there wasn't really any such thing as what we call a 'friend'.

There's only you and the person you love.

That's if you're lucky enough to have someone.

Someone called Mercedes, maybe, in a long dress of calico, wielding a fan. Over which she might look at you, fluttering her upturned lashes.

A woman you could call your own precious lovely sweetheart.

No wonder he used to love going to the Heartland ballroom every weekend to spend his wages from the factory, to drink and look at women.

Such dreams as he used to have up there, on that pink-painted balcony.

Heartland: Where beats the pulse of love's deepest desires …

Then another night came back to him − a special one, again.

When he and Mr Monroe − yes the one and only Walter, the King of Country − the two of them had retired alone to the quiet of the back bar, with the floor swept clean, and the chairs all neatly stacked.

There wasn't a sound.

With the dance long over as they treated themselves to a couple of well-earned shotsa juice.

−You're the best bouncer ever, he recalled WW complimenting him, because roundabout Glasson County there ain't no one dumb enough to give much grief to Big Barney Grue.

They talked about this and that. About WW's further plans to make the very bar in which they were having their well-earned, late-night shot into a watering hole the like of which no one could ever have conceived, bedecked with money, state-of-the-art cocktails, airline stewardesses, college sweethearts.

And to hell with Austin Price 'The Diviner' and all of his jumping Jesus friends – around-the-clock working judies.

Then, after a while, somewhat unexpectedly, they had gotten around to discussing those kindsa things that no men ever get to talk about.

Not much, at least.

Including love affairs.

Yearnings.

All that kinda stuff.

–All those hidden secrets, he remembered WW remarking, that come to us all when our head touches the pillow last thing at night.

Monroe had been drinking quite a bit that day, and as a result had confided something quite unexpected to Big Barney Grue.

That he had fallen in love recently with a woman who wasn't his wife.

–It's Dawn, WW Monroe had admitted, eventually, it's her – the singer Dawn 'Kit' King.

But Barney had just nodded, mainly on account of he hadn't really known what to say.

–I love her, Barney, WW continued, every day when I awake she's the very first thing that comes into my mind. When I think of her smile, it's like the very first morning that has been breathed upon the world. I know that sounds stupid, but that's the way I feel. It's crazy, I know. But that's just the way it is.

–The very first morning in the world, Big Barney had mused, staring towards the rooftop with its irradiated, inspiring pink heart.

–And now she tells me she's going to have a child, lamented WW.

Who would ever have expected that, thought Big Barney – a showband singer, making cadence with the likes of WW Monroe?

But everyone knew that Dawn was something special. An *enigma*, he remembered, was what WW had called her. Having arrived in the valley out of nowhere and disappeared just as mysteriously, leaving nothing behind her but a string of unpaid bills in the Lodge, which she'd left a wreck, filled with empty bottles and a barely legible note covered in stains, which read: *reality is nothing but a fucking conspiracy – see you whenever, love you Dawn.*

–I did some digging on her background, Barney, he had informed him, and although I didn't find a lot that was of very much use, I did establish this. That she doesn't come from anywhere near Serenity, Ohio. Or anywhere in America, come to that. She's from someplace down the country, far as I can make out – Mayo, maybe. I heard Crossmolina mentioned once or twice. Having spent a while in a coupla children's homes, and has constructed this magnificent lie around herself. But you know what's the strangest thing? It makes me want her even more.

Someone with such a beautiful, respected wife and with so much – so much to lose. How could it happen? puzzled Big Barney.

How?

–If I lose her – if I lose my Connie, Barney, so help me God I don't know what I'll do. But I can't seem to able to give

Dawn up. I just can't stop thinking about her, and that's the truth. I'm worried, Barney, real fucking worried. My heart is close to broken; if you want to know the truth.

He was cold all over, in his chair, remembering that. Still lying slumped in the chair with his improvised bandage as Sonny Hackett tapped his head.

–Earth calling, Grue – Big Barney, are you there?

Big Barney didn't answer, now almost grateful for the constant throb of pain, distracting him as it did from the memory of that night with WW.

Because he knew what it would lead to – directly to his very own memory of a certain other girl who went by the name of Bridie.

Bridie Cullen, who used to live not far away from him, in 17 St Martin De Porres Terrace, Midford.

And who had spent a summer working the line in Glasson Meats.

And with whom, on one shocking occasion of which he had never spoken to anyone, he had found himself in the act of 'making love' in a hay barn just a little outside of town, one Saturday night after the dance in Heartland.

And upon whose countenance – without ever daring to consult or confide in her – he had taken the liberty of conferring the astounding features of the incomparable Mercedes Starrs, his own sweet lovely calico Southern belle.

Yes, Bridie Cullen, even though she was only just gone seventeen, she was already everything that a man could ever need.

And who, subsequently, had given birth to the sweetest of little baby boys.

But who, unfortunately, had been fated to spend most of his very short life confined to a hospital incubator, in the children's ward of Midford Hospital.

Although it was considered highly irregular by the authorities – given the circumstances, the secretary informed Mr Grue that it had been agreed he would be permitted one single visit.

And he remembered so clearly standing there alone that morning, staring into the small glass case through which, although a little fuzzy, nonetheless provided him with a view of five little fingers.

Moving slightly – just a tad.

Yes, just a little.

First one, then two.

Two barely perceptible twitches.

There was a television set beside him on a shelf, with the volume at the time turned way down.

On the screen, carrying on, you could see the big rooster, Foghorn Leghorn, stomping around in the dust, complaining.

–*Ah say. Ah say that boy,* he kept on repeating.

Very shortly after, the little boy died.

As he left the hospital that morning, Big Barney had made it his business to seek out the nun who had interceded on his behalf – to thank her.

The same sister who, incidentally, had registered no discernible hint of affront or displeasure whenever she had encountered Big Barney standing there waving his large knotty fist.

Bawling, quite hysterically, at the TV screen:

–Shut your mouth, you big fucking stupid big chicken – why don't you try shutting your mouth for a while? Maybe, for once, you ought to try doing that, huh?

–Try your best to put your faith in the Lord, the nun had urged, taking him by the hand in the corridor as he departed.

–I'm sorry, I really am so sorry, Big Barney had apologised, stumbling as best he could out into the devastation of the early afternoon.

After which he had made his way into the back bar in Heartland and remained there all day, drinking himself practically into a coma. But, just before his eyes had closed and his arm had slipped off the edge of the counter, what had come on the jukebox only Frankie McBride – yes, his favourite band playing his favourite song, 'Five Little Fingers'.

–*Give me one reason to live,* the melody continued somewhere in the distance, *give me one reason to live now that my darling has died.*

He knew that, in a way, he too had betrayed WW – by not having shared his own personal pain that intimate night.

When he knew he ought to have opened up his own heart and divulged his secrets like his employer, with such candour, had done.

To have been open and honest and genuine with WW, just the very same as he had been with him.

And told him all about Bridie and the night that they'd spent making love in the haybarn.

And the baby.

And those five little reaching-up fingers.

But he didn't.

Because he couldn't.

Just couldn't manage to bring himself to do it.

Even to admit that there had never been a proper woman in his life, apart from the imaginary Mercedes of the South.

Something he knew was never likely to happen again.

Not after this.

He had met Bridie Cullen a couple of times after that, but they didn't know what to say to one another.

Someone told him that they thought that she'd got married and had bought a house in Dundalk, so far as they knew.

Remembering all that – and, indeed, properly admitting to it for the very first time – had more or less knocked the stuffing out of Barney. As he began to laugh at the top of his voice:

–Ha ha, we sure did have some good times in Heartland!

Chapter 30

The Arrival of Tony Begley

But nobody was paying him the slightest bit of attention –
Barney Grue, that is.

Being much too preoccupied by the subject of grinding
teeth.

–It was the last time I was gonna warn you, thundered
Sonny, I thought I told you, fuck!

–Your wife is right, Red Campbell taunted, everyone
knows there's a weakness in the Hacketts!

Sonny walked over and whisked out a pool cue.

–Easy, cautioned Mervyn, laughing just a little as he
nodded towards the jukebox.

–Ha ha, he continued, I can't afford any more damage.

–I'm afraid of the likes of him? I'm not afraid of him, spat
Red Campbell, kneeing his chair out of the way as he strode
towards the centre of the floor, entirely ignoring Wee Hughie
bleating loudly:

–I got to tell you about the night with the Crackaways! O
man, I swear, it was it the night of all nights!

–Easy now, urged Mervyn, cautiously approaching Sonny,
we don't want no more damage, do we? My poor Rock-Ola!

Sonny said nothing, ominously turning the stick in his hands.

As the barman sighed and gave a broad grin.

You really had to hand it to Mervyn Walker.

–NO ONE HAS THE RIGHT TO SAY THE LIKE OF THAT TO ME! bawled Sonny Hackett. YOU HEAR?

Before flinging the cue away and taking refuge in the bathroom, loudly slamming the door behind him.

Far in the distance, I could hear the roar of the flush.

Laid out across three chairs, the Runt released a drawn-out groan.

–We're finished, he said, that's it now. We're done.

As Mervyn brushed up what was left of the few remaining fragments of glass. And as he did so, keenly observing his clientele – one by one.

Those men who had been busy one night, a long time ago.

When they'd paid his old friend a nocturnal visit.

–Amber days, he smiled contentedly to himself, amber days.

Before Hughie announced he didn't care about Begley, or what he did. Shaking his head as he emptied a quarter-glass of jungle.

–Yes! he hollered. That old Meester Señor Begley he might have thought he was the great big motherfucking shot back in the factory, but I'm sorry Señor Beggs but zat was a very long time ago. Hey Tony! Tony, did you hear the one about the Mexican who walked into the bar?

He was so drunk now that he didn't hear the door gently closing behind him, or notice Sonny Hackett waving his arms and trying to warn him. No, he didn't – because Hughie the comedian was once again in full, irrepressible flight, rubbing his hands vigorously as he welcomed everyone to 'Hughie's Comedy Evening'.

–Yes, I am here to help you put that sad right back in the bottle where it belongs, he announced, and especially for that

Big Shot Mr Tony Begley, wherever the fuck he has decided to get to!

–Please, said Sonny, lowering his head.

But Hughie Munley already had his eyes closed, forcefully slapping his thighs as he continued, with his high-pitched voice now close to hysterical.

–Did youse ever hear the one about the Mexican who walked into the bar? He says: I am looking for my compañero Senor Begley. Yes, I am looking for ze leetle greasy motherfucker who thinks because he is WW's big special amigo that he can walk around telling everybody what to do. Except, you see, zat is not true. Certainly not where a Miss Tiny Smallwoods is concerned, at any rate. Because she write to Tony: Dear Tony, fuck off!

Barney Grue was looking unbearably pained, and, like Sonny Hackett, doing his best to capture Hughie's attention. But without success.

As the rotund comedian feverishly continued, now closely observed by the mute figure standing directly behind him.

TB.

–So what you gonna do about it, Señor Begley, Hughie went on, send me some of your famous oranges, maybe? No wonder Miss Smallwoods was seen sitting crying above at Lake Wynter, chain-smoking cigarettes with her mascara all running – probably thinking about how lucky she'd been, getting away from someone like him, that everyone knows has got a tile off!

–Hi, said Tony, his voice barely audible, sorry I'm late.

–O Jesus, Sonny Hackett said. O Jesus.

Tony's clothes as a rule seemed just that little too big. His mother had always been scolding him about it, he said. Those clothes you wear – they don't fit you, she regularly used to say to him.

He had told them that a number of times.

And, looking at him now, standing in the centre of the floor of Mervyn's Mountain Bar, you would have had to agree that she was right.

With that oversized anorak and the ill-fitting suit underneath.

He draped the anorak across the back of a chair.

Sonny Hackett was drinking like a fish.

–For God's sake Sonny, take it easy! urged Wee Hughie, wringing his hands, still reeling from shock.

But his advice only seemed to make Sonny Hackett worse.

Then Red Campbell started doing the same, shoving down slug after slug of jungle.

And then calling out for more.

Begley was standing underneath the Woolworth's picture, saying nothing as he stared up at it.

–Poor wee fella, they heard him murmur.

TB was short and blocky, with the glistening, accordion-pleated waves of his hair shining underneath the light.

He was wearing a pair of brown, elastic-sided boots, which he kept on looking down at.

–I was wondering what youse might think of the elaborate detailing on the uppers? he asked.

Nobody had any opinion – or if they did, they elected not to advance it.

–Kind of like Oxford brogues, he went on, not that I care, to be honest. Because it'll be a long time before I ever go to Oxford, won't it Hughie?

–Yes, replied Hughie, looking around him uncertainly, I suppose it will. It would be, yes.

–Would you like something to drink, Mr Begley? called Mervyn from behind the counter.

–Thanks a lot, Mervyn. But no thanks, if you please.

–Very well, said the barman, right you be.

Begley hoisted up his loose blue pinstripe trousers and, somewhat out of breath, sat down on an upended crate.

−You don't have to sit on that, Mr Begley, offered Mervyn, let me bring you over a chair.

−It's fine, the other man replied, I'm perfectly comfortable sitting here, believe it or not.

−That's no problem at all, smiled Mervyn.

Then, adjusting the oversized knot of his tie for a moment, TB lowered his head and rubbed his two hands together. Before looking up, and smiling again, winningly observed:

−So here we are then, gentlemen, eh?

Scrutinising each individual in their turn before releasing a protracted sigh.

−That it should come to this.

Subsequent to which, he lapsed once more into silence.

After a long time, raising his head.

−I was thinking, before I came over, about names.

Nobody said anything − as Mervyn Walker folded his arms and watched the willow, with its leaves as they swished this way and that.

−What I'm trying to say is, Tony Begley went on, if you weren't called the name you are, would you still be the same person? Hughie, what do you think? Your opinion of a statement like that, what would it be?

−I couldn't say, Hughie Munley replied, I'm not even sure that I know what it means.

Tony Begley stood up and, after gazing out of the window for some time, cleared his throat and looked back at Hughie.

−Say your name was Poindexter Rufus Gallantry. Ichabod Kiernan, Vanderbilt Coyle. Would you still be the same person − as the one you are now, I mean.

He looked across at Red.

−So − what do you think, Red?

−I don't know. I really couldn't say.

–You don't really know. You really couldn't say?

–That's right – I don't really think I could honestly say.

He turned to Sonny.

–Mr Hackett. Your opinion?

–I don't really have one. Not now. At the moment, anyway.

–Poindexter, Bigelow, Begley repeated softly, Bigelow, Poindexter – all those names. Tommy Squidge.

Begley shook his head.

–Would we all be the same people, that's the question.

He went over to Barney and laid a hand on his shoulder.

–I just don't get it, he said.

–Which? said Barney, which is that now?

–The world, he explained, I just can't seem to grasp it.

Before walking over to Hughie Munley and, standing right behind him, beginning to gently massage his shoulders.

–You know what it is I'm trying to suggest? he said.

–I don't really think … not for sure, I don't think.

–Say that the world is a very strange place, will you Hughie?

–What?

–The world is a very strange place – say it.

–The world is a strange place.

–The world is a strange and extremely forbidding fucking place. Say that.

–The world is an extremely strange and forbidding fucking place, complied Hughie.

–It is indeed. It certainly is that. Thanks for saying it, Hughie.

He looked over at Campbell.

–Isn't it, Red?

Red Campbell looked up fearfully.

–It is, Mr Begley, they heard him reply.

As Tony Begley gave Red's little thatch of beard a sharp sudden tug.

–*Ow!* squealed Red, *what the fuck!*

As Begley went over to Big Barney and sat down beside him.

—I'm sorry to have to tell you this, Big Barney, but certain complaints regarding your behaviour have recently reached my ears.

—My behaviour? stuttered Barney.

—Yes, elaborated Begley — as regards my assistant, Tootsy Corrigan.

—I know nothing about Tootsy Corrigan, spat Barney sourly.

—Except that you were looking down her front, continued Begley, except that you happen to have been seen doing that. When she was only coming here for the purpose of delivering a message. I'm sorry to be the one to have to tell you that, Barney.

Barney Grue lowered his head, with a dribble of saliva falling onto his whiskers.

Begley stared for a long time at the floor.

—I think these boots of mine need a polish. What do you think, Hughie?

—Maybe, Mr Begley. I don't know.

—We should never have come here, sobbed Shorty McHale, I don't care about my father's dumb memory. All I only want is to go to America.

—I think I'll get a brand new pair of loafers. Will I, Hughie?

—If that's what you want, Mr Begley, yes.

—I'd prefer if you called me Tony. Will you?

—Yes, Tony — if that's what you want.

—A brand-new pair of loafers, he went on, not these dumb fucking out-of-date things. You know something, Hughie, I'm a disgrace.

—Yes Tony.

—What — you think I am?

—No, Tony. I didn't say that.

—Well, to be perfectly honest I wouldn't blame you if you did. Seeing as I went and made the mistake of trusting that sumbitch fuck that you got tied up out there in that shed. Because I got better things to be doing that coming here. I got pressures, Hughie. Pressures, I got to tell you, that I don't need. Pressures I could gladly be doing without. Pressures I thought I'd left behind me a long long time ago. You know what I'm saying here, Barney, do you?

–Yes, nodded Barney, I think I do.

–But then it's always been like that, right from the start. I guess you didn't know I spent time in a seminary. Four years, as a matter of fact. A spoiled priest, it used to be called.

He was walking around the pool table, circling it, abstractedly, as his fingers danced along the edge and he said:

–There were times, though, I got to tell you, when I really did enjoy it, I mean. But, in the end, however, I just couldn't seem to cut it. That's how I ended up in the factory, you see. That was all they said I was good for, to such an extent I started to believe it myself. People like Begley, they never finish anything. It's a pity, all the same, about the shame it'll bring on his mother.

He sat back on the crate and began poking at the heel of his shoe.

–So what would you have to say about that, Hughie?

–About the shoes, is it Tony?

–About me not being able to finish things, I mean.

–It's wrong, Tony.

–Yes, it's wrong, agreed Begley, as he added:

–And right now I'm going to show you how wrong it actually is. So let's set up a nice little game of cards. One final round before skinning that old smoke-and-horses.

But before anyone could make a response, he signalled to Mervyn and a tray of drinks arrived within minutes. With the barman replying that it was his absolute pleasure, whistling a jaunty little tune as he crossed the floor.

–Nothing but the best for Mr Begley, announced the barman.

–Now isn't that much better? said Begley, as the game proper got underway.

With his eyes still twinkling, as he looked over the rim of his cards.

–So what you reckon, Sonny mi amigo?

–We're doing good, Mr Begley, it sure is real good to see you.

As every drop of colour drained from Begley's face, and he rose to his feet, looking every inch a living corpse:

–THAT IS NOT MY FUCKING NAME!

He looked at everyone around the table.

–How many times do I have to say it? he demanded. Or can you tell me what the fuck is wrong with the people in this room? Tony, I told you – Tony, or didn't you hear?

Then sat down quietly.

As, through the gap in the floorboards, I caught the narrow, upraised eye of Mervyn Walker – squinting surreptitiously as he lifted his head, pressing a cautionary forefinger as he did so, to his lips.

Chapter 31

Moonlight and Roses

As to whether, like Fr Conway has suggested, I'd actually misinterpreted, perhaps even *imagined* Mervyn Walker's sly admonition on that occasion, to this very day I can't, really, honestly, say.

And maybe part of the reason I'm leaving this little journal behind me is that, somewhere deep down, I'm hoping that in some small way it might be of some small benefit to anyone who happens to come upon it, particularly someone with a soul as punch-drunk and compromised as my own.

For, believe you me, I could have been doing with some direction what with the way things went in the years after Mervyn's Bar.

The sad part is that, for the first year or so after having the good fortune to meet and move in with Angie, it had all really begun to seem as if at last I was actually going to be able to get it together.

But all of that, too, turned out to be a delusion.

Much of what happened in those days – directly after our break-up, I mean– is shrouded in a drunken haze. Something which I don't mind a great deal, considering how painful it can be to remember it.

One particularly bad night, I recall, I'd gone and lost it completely – driving the flatbed all the way out to the One Tree Crossroads, and almost crashing the fucking thing twice on the way.

And then just sitting there, heaving down yet another gutful and laughing to myself with abandon, what with it being the first proper drink of good jungle that I'd had in months, treating myself to what Barney Grue might have described as 'a good big motherfucking bellyful of electrisms!'

As I emptied that sucker right down to the bottom, cheering as I tossed the bottle out the window.

Because what did I care – about the whole fucking world, or anyone who lived in it.

Not so much as a rat's ass did I give.

And it was then that I heard it, loud and clear – the lilting strains of a familiar, old-time waltz.

As the dashboard – I swear to God, and with no help from me at all – lit up suddenly, filling the cabin with a rainbow of lights, a riot of flickering, living neon.

And a warm, lush baritone gradually began enveloping the cab.

–*Moonlight and roses*, I heard the soft voice croon, *so this is where you are, you little fucking snakeyed Judas!*

You can imagine how I panicked when I realised what it was I'd just heard, as the mellow orchestration continued swelling out into the night.

And that was when I heard the tinkling of the bells.

And turned around to see his face against the window – placid, blank, with that waxy complexion you knew would never grow old.

–I've been looking for you, said Mr Bonny, yes. I've been looking for you everywhere, you mischievous little dogie.

I concealed my face – when I looked again, he was gone.

Whenever I got back to the dive I'd been living in, an old overgrown stone cottage at the edge of town, I was still badly shaken, and profoundly unnerved – consumed entirely by this sense of what I can only describe as an overwhelming ... *need*.

For the warmth and security – yes, and privilege too, I won't deny it – that I'd always experience when sleeping alongside Dawn.

And when I saw her before me that night, as in a vision, it was exactly the same as it had been the very first time we had been together.

After which she'd stood by the window of the Lodge, entirely naked apart from that long-billed airman's cap she often wore, transfixed by an evening sky the colour of burnt copper, conversing with herself in that distant, disconnected way she had.

With those narrow shoulders tensing as she lifted the cigarette hesitantly to her lips, relaxing at last and releasing that fragile, nervous, short-lived laugh. And then continuing, taking rapid-fire, frantic drags, in pursuit of her fevered, recalcitrant thoughts.

Sometimes she'd be talking for close on two or three minutes without a break.

–Look away, Montgomery, because I know that you ain't gonna like what you see. Why did you have to come here today – did you really think my father would make it in the industry? Once upon a time there was a new Gram Parsons who liked to bang his box up there in the hills. Look how the campfire plays orange among the stones, where his lady smiles in Dreamland and that electric cowboy sings her his tune – yeah, yet another song all got up in that special new kinda Ozark Mountain way – all for her, who in her damage had somehow believed him. Yep, you and me and Phaedra, we are gonna be away from all that as we make our new lives high up in the mountains in the Arkansas hills. And when I come down in the morning, you know what's gonna happen? You gonna be sitting there waiting in the kitchen, sweet as any princess in your gingham and ruffles, as you lift your eyes towards me just as appealing and as beautiful as any God in His wisdom ever saw fit to bestow on one of His creatures. And you're gonna be my one and only Rock Angel – because you and me, we are a chain that ain't never gonna break apart. So, go down, Montgomery, and don't you rise no mo' – you hearing me, old Hannah? Haw, fuck you bitch!

At first I didn't like it – those strange, disjointed outbursts of emotion. I guess the truth being that I felt completely out of my depth.

But after a while I used to long for her to do it, because it had started to sound, in its own strange way, kind of like some weird poetry or something.

—*If we make it through December*, she used to say, *if we can somehow make it that far, Ray* … and her voice would just sort of trail off.

Just as often, she'd sigh ruefully and softly whisper as she sat there by the window:

—There are times, you know, Ray, when I look out here, across the lakes of Glasson County, where the reeds are bending and you can hear the wind coming through the pines in what seems like a spatial, continental vastness, where I can almost feel it – sense my soul stirring right here inside of me. It's almost like the very sound of the harmonica itself, the orchestration of the journey of the soul of the wayfaring stranger. And you know what it makes me think about? One of those Sunday mornings when it seems so lonesome it can feel like everybody they're already dead and gone. The way the breeze when it fans and quivers the leaves it makes you feel mournful. Yeah, melancholy, Ray, because you feel like it's the spirits whispering. Spirits that have been dead for oh so many long years.

It was just impossible to take your eyes off her as she stood there, motionless, with the long-billed cap cocked pertly on her head, and that tawny brown hair flouncing underneath in a jaunty ponytail.

As she smiled – *O, what that did to me!* – and came across to the bed and sat there beside me, leaning right over as she whispered into my ear:

–They call me a song thrush don't they, Ray. But the truth is – and I want you and me to know this because I don't want any misunderstandings between us – that the person you are beginning to fall in love with is a hawk. Like I say, I wouldn't want you, in any way, to be misled about that. Because I like you, Ray. Knowing as I do that the two of us, in our separate ways, have endured bad pain.

–Pain that makes you feel numbed inside, she went on, and that you don't want to share with anyone else. Not unless you sense they might understand – like you do, Ray. Because only the afflicted can heal the afflicted, she whispered.

And it was then that she gave me the facts about her father.

Or what she insisted were the facts.

And how he'd put her in the House of the Merciless Angels, as she called it.

Just like you, she smiled, just like you.

–There was one thing he got right, all the same, one piece of knowledge that he took from all o' those Eastern do-it-yourself books that he read, Ray. And that was that this world we got here is rough and surly and will not mind drowning either man or woman, and will happily swallow your ship like a grain of dust. But I didn't really learn that till my teenage years and watched the only two people I'd ever loved or cared about in the world break right there in front of me – like a pair of helpless china fucking dolls, taking all of their dreams and promises along with them. Even if, to be fair, it probably wasn't their fault. Because I guess, like so many of their friends back then, in their way the two of them were, in their own deluded way, sincere. That's where they say I get my music from – having grown up there, in that desert of loneliness. O she sings like an angel, they'll tell you, listen to that distinctive mountain-minor twang, the spring purity of her haunting voice. If the angels were to elect a singer on earth, it could only be the magnificent little 'Kit' King, for no other can come close. Thrown back upon yourself alone, they'll tell you, confined within the solitude of your own wounded being, that's where it comes from, that high lonesome sound. From having to abide in those raw and hurting hollows of the heart. But what they're not getting is this, and I want you to know it: that I'd just as soon wring an angel's neck, if I thought it suited my purpose. Because I'm a little dogie too, you see, Ray – except that, to survive, I growed up to be a bird of prey. The 'Dawn' who takes no prisoners, you know what I'm saying?

Then she laughed and returned to the window, sparking up a rollie and tossing her head flagrantly as she aggressively released the smoke.

I've never heard singing like it, before or since.

–*If we make it through December*, she began to croon in that tremolo-infused soprano, *got plans to be in a warmer town come Summertime* ...

When she was finished, she came over and told me that she wanted to do it. Because nobody can fuck like you, she murmured, nobody Ray. You're the only one, Ray – the only one ...

As a shudder of trepidation ran along my spine – for I could have sworn I'd seen a sly smirk at the corner of her mouth, a kind of strange, discomfiting half-smile.

But you don't want to dwell on things like that.

–You're the only one, Ray. You know you can believe me.

–Do it, she said, as she mounted me again.

–Harder.

–Many miles, I heard her groan, gleaming with sweat as she shivered high above me, and plunged her tongue deep inside my mouth and, kissing me so hard I could feel the metallic taste of blood.

–Daddy, she wept, daddy loved timber, that dirty old egg-sucking dog. I'll tell you about psychedelic western, I'll tell you about hillbilly opera. About motherfucking Phaedra riding into eternity along golden sand. I'll tell you everything you want to know about it. Talking fucking crazy after all that junk, just laying there banging his beat-up old flat-top guitar, cursing the Man and the record contract he'd never sign. Yeah, that was the wonderland he'd promised us, and for which we had forsaken Serenity, Ohio. A shabby rundown so-called farm with a grassless, junk-littered yard, a cow, a few chickens and a couple of acres of fruit trees and two or three more of truck crops. When he'd take his rages, me and the rest of us, feral ragamuffins all, with tangled hair and our clothes just rags, we'd cower inside the weather-beaten house. How I remember those bare warped floors and boarded-up windows, and the enormous wood-fuel range, into which he'd shove all them fucking accursed logs that he'd chopped, as he cursed and spat, yeah just like them pieces of broke-up burning oak, as his Phaedra pleaded please don't take another swing. But he sure as hell did. O Daddy, with all your dreams and promises. He whipped us for going. He whipped us for not going. He whipped us for lying. He whipped us for spending money. Now – fuck me, cracker, like it's our very last day on earth. Screw me like you're going to end my pain.

–Do it, fucker, you listening to me, Ray?

So I did.

Till I wept, with the result that for days and weeks after it, I couldn't stop thinking about anything else. Sometimes, she'd just arrive out of nowhere and come walking right in, without saying a word.

And, just when I figured she couldn't stun me anymore, the bouquet arrived.

Eighteen yellow roses, read the little card, *a bloom for every time we did it, Ray.*

P. S. Missing you like crazy, as 'The Queen', Patsy Cline, might say xxx

It was probably around then that my pattern of sleep began to be significantly disturbed – and there definitely had been a marked increase in my drinking.

So maybe my problem stems from then.

Could be that that's when it all, in earnest, began.

Because one of the things I can remember is just arriving out at the waterhole, close by the One Tree Crossroads, where Jody and I used to fish in the summer – not having the faintest idea what time it was, or how I got there or where I had been drinking.

I don't know how many glasses of whiskey I'd had, not to mention the half-drunk bottle of jungle in my jacket.

It was dawn.

–Dawn, I said, and started laughing.

And it was then I saw it – just a fleeting glimpse, like a white blur upon the surface of the water.

I can remember my blood suddenly turning to ice.

Because I could hear my name being spoken through the trees, and no matter how I might try to dismiss or make light of it, it still persisted.

–Ray, it said, *I'll be seeing you soon. We have so many things to talk about. I'm really looking forward to it.*

And when I felt something touch me – so hastily, it was barely perceptible at all – I didn't know where to turn, and felt sick.

So consumed by dread and a sense of ... I don't know, because no matter how I tried, I couldn't seem to name it.

All I can say is that, just standing there staring at the still surface of the water, the sensation I was experiencing, it became so awful it made what happened in the cockloft seem almost inconsequential.

–*Ray*, he said again, and then, like the spin of a pearl, he was gone.

With nothing, then, but the whisper of the trees.

Chapter 32

El Dorado

Curled up in a ball, I was covered all over in a dry, stinging sweat, with my knees drawn into my stomach and the calves of my legs pressed tightly against my thighs.

I could hear the rushing sound of the lavatory, and Begley reappearing, folding his hankie as he put it away.

–So what's it gonna be, then, Hughie, do you think?

–What's that, Tony?

–Cards – how many?

–Two please, Tony. Tony, I think I'll have two.

–Two it is, then. Here you are.

–Good times, said Begley, good times, Sonny.

Two red spots coloured Hackett's cheeks.

–What's that, Tony?

–The good times, in the old days.

–Ah yes, that. The factory, said Sonny.

Begley leaned over the table and looked right into Wee Hughie's eyes.

–Good times, Hughie.

–That's right, Mr Begley – the good old good times.

Begley's face darkened and he threw down his hand.

−You're doing it again. Why do you have to do it?

−Do what, Mr Begley?

−What you promised. Call me Tony.

−I'm sorry, Tony. Tony, I'm sorry.

−It's all right, Begley said, it doesn't matter.

Then he said to Shorty McHale:

−What the fuck is wrong with you?

−I'm afraid that my brother might be going to die.

−You sure are some basket of fruit, said Begley, nearly as bad as your so-called patriot old man.

He turned to Hughie and shook his head.

−Poor old Trampas who went and blew his bollocks off.

−Please don't say that, will you not? pleaded Shorty.

But Begley had already walked back to Sonny Hackett.

−Ah yes, the old Killing Floor Hombres. They sure did look up to us back in the good times. Ain't that a fact, Sonny?

−Yes, agreed Sonny, them old Killing Floor Hombres.

−Is he right about that, do you think, Wee Hughie?

−He's right for sure, Wee Hughie nodded, they were known far and wide, them old Killing Floor Hombres.

−What you reckon, Mervyn? The men in the good times, you reckon we got 'em here?

Mervyn grinned from ear to ear, rubbing a glass as he called back, good-naturedly:

−There's ain't no doubt in my mind about it. You had to hand it to los locos pistoleros!

−Well I'll be damned! Begley laughed heartily as he tossed back his head. If I ain't heard it all now, that old Mervyn speaking Spanish!

−Estar viendo que en el otro lado de la luna, amigo, laughed the barman, raising himself up to set the clean glass on the shelf.

As Sonny Hackett groaned and shot to his feet.

—Please, he broke out hoarsely, can we just please get this over with?

Tony Begley said that that was a laugh.

—Why? What's funny about it? Big Barney demanded. Tell me anything that's funny about it!

Tony Begley completely ignored him.

—I always knew that he'd do it, you know, Mervyn – WW, I mean. Because right from the very beginning, that old Walter he always used to promise that one day he would bring the good times to Glasson County. And that he wouldn't be long showing them city boys where to get off. And which is why, I guess, when that very first digger rolled in to start up on the building of Heartland that he didn't make all that much of a fuss about it. Being already on the way to the next important project. What a guy, Mervyn. Mervyn – what a guy.

—How right you are, agreed Mervyn, a wonderful human being when all is said and done. One of the good ones, Tony, one of the good ones.

—Sometimes it could be like already being in heaven, said Red, out of nowhere, in Heartland, I mean. That's what it was like on the night that my wife and I – that we won the Dance-Off Trophy. Because when that music started, 'Y Viva España', it was like it was me and her wasn't there on that floor at all …

—Then where were youse, snapped Big Barney, angry at being ignored, because if youse weren't on the floor, then where the fuck were youse?

Begley placed his boots on the table and snapped a match.

—That's the very same question I was asking earlier on. If your name isn't your own, then who the fuck are you?

He laughed till he was almost sick, wiping the tears from his eyes with his hankie.

—O boy! he said. Who the fuck are you? Who the fuck is any of us?

But Red Campbell, like the rest of them, gave no answer – no indication whatsoever that he'd heard a word he'd said.

Being way too busy recalling the swimming pink neon light of Heartland, being shed in his mind from that enormous rooftop fibreglass monument to love and romance, vertiginously dappling the brown blanket bogland – the wooded slopes, swaying reeds and shallow lakes of the expansive wetland that went by the name of Glasson County.

–Heaven? Is that what you were saying just now? Big Barney faintly murmured. Because that's what I used to think about it sometimes too.

–So did I, they heard Begley murmur, that's why I wanted to become a priest. But when I couldn't finish it, my mother said that I got what I deserved. Dismembering animals and sweeping up shit, surrounded by entrails and cattle faeces. That's what you're worth, she said. That is all the likes of you, now, will ever come to.

–No she didn't, Tony, said Big Barney, scarcely able to bear the thought.

–Yes she did, nodded Tony Begley, because my mother didn't like me, you see.

As he looked across his cards and murmured softly to Wee Hughie Munley:

–It's been hard but I think I can finally accept it now.

He paused for a moment and gazed at Red Campbell.

–That's why I don't really like this kind of music. As a matter of fact, Red, I would go so far as to say that I actually loathe it. Country and western.

–I'm sorry, Tony. I didn't know that, said Red

–Because when it comes to music I like something that's got a little more class. You ever hear of Sidney Smith, Red?

Red Campbell shook his head.

–No? said Begley.

He looked at the others.

Sonny Hackett covered his eyes.

–You ever happen to hear of Sidney, Sonny?

He shook his head.

–I'm sorry but I haven't, he said. No, Tony, I'm afraid I haven't. Sorry.

–That's no problem. There's no law that says you have to. I used to listen to him in the seminary – during my first year, it reminded me of home. Do you know those feelings that you have when you are young?

Red Campbell perked up.

–When you're young, he declared, you're full of piss and vinegar and afraid of nothing on earth!

Tony Begley nodded and said that he agreed with that.

–Now, in the dark, we're afraid of everything, cried Campbell, morosely, everything chills us …

Then Begley continued:

–Because when you're young you're full of the joys of spring and one thing for sure is, you gotta love your mother. And that's the reason, most of all, that I came around to liking that old Sidney, and became, yeah, became partial to that late-night radio. My Sidney, she called him. A piece of his that I especially liked was a piano solo by the name of 'Le Jet D'Eau'. That was the one we always played when the two of us would be finished saying the rosary. And anytime I hear it now, whenever I'm listening to them escalating octaves, it can still somehow give me that same familiar and still astonishing feeling – where I see waterfalls, you know?

He looked at Hughie.

–Waterfalls, he sighed, waterfalls Hughie.

–Yes, choked Hughie, waterfalls Tony.

–You think there's something wrong with me saying that?

–No, Tony, there isn't. There isn't anything – wrong, I mean.

—You know what it looks like? That you don't care a damn about Sidney Smith – or his music or anything else to fucking do with him. As a matter of fact what I'm getting from you right now is that, so far as you're concerned, Sidney Smith couldn't pour piss from a boot.

He lifted his head and sternly arched his eyebrows.

—Is what I'm suggesting in fact the case, Wee Hughie?

—No, Tony, it isn't. It isn't, it's not the case.

—Then say it, Hughie. Say: Sidney can pour all the piss he wants.

—Sidney can pour all the piss he wants.

—Fucking right he can, enough to fill seven oceans if he wants to, the fucker.

Begley's eyes sparkled and he elevated the thumb of his right hand in acknowledgement.

—Thanks, Hughie. You're a good man – I appreciate you doing that.

—Yes, Tony. Sure. Of course.

Then Begley resumed as if nothing had happened.

—Like rose petals dropping from the sun, he said, turning suddenly pale.

No one said anything.

As Begley shuddered briefly and reached in his pocket and set his gleaming knife down in the middle of the table.

Sweety, he liked to call it.

Chapter 33

A Tiger by the Tail

Fr Conway has often remarked how, in times of considerable stress, people can behave in ways that are unexpected.

And, right now, you could be forgiven for thinking that Begley had gone and completely forgotten all about Jody – or what it was he had come for at all.

The kind of attitude to which I am no stranger myself, and which reminds me of one Saturday morning back in '98, when I'd been a long time out of Glasson and living for a period in a long-stay hostel in Dublin.

When I found myself waking up to the gritty morning sunshine and reaching, as usual, for that old restorative glass of hooch and the packet of smokes that I always kept on my bedside locker.

As I scratched myself and felt the jungle scorching the back of my throat, wincing as I hauled back the curtain and looked out the window – to see what?

Why, it might just as well have been that old bluebird of happiness, coming up to the windowsill to say, *Hi there, Ray, my old friend*.

And I really can't tell you just how good I felt, surprising though that might be.

As I got myself dressed and made my way to a little bar I used to go to on the southern quays, not far from Ringsend.

Practically busting the door down, to be honest, as in I came, whistling my heart out.

Don't ask me how many shots it took – not all that many, I shouldn't imagine – one, two, maybe three or four.

With the next thing I knew I was on the phone and barking down the blower to that old Jody and letting him know just how much I was looking forward to seeing him.

Because it was only a matter of mere weeks now, I said, and once I had gathered up that last coupla bucks, I assured him, then lookout Stateside – because Ringo Wade he is climbing right up into the driver's seat of that old rig and shoving down that gas pedal-boot to the board, smokin' with the hammer down all the way to Sweetwater, Georgia, I remember chuckling.

As I rattled away twenty to the dozen, about this and that – but, always, as usual, returning to his letter and my reaction to it.

You'll have to live with this! You'll have to live with this! I kept saying, winding the flex around my hand.

With the tears coursing down my cheeks as I rambled on, I swear, till I got hoarse.

Twirling the cable, filled with excitement, as I thanked my old compadre for all the thoughts and sentiments in his letters, and everything else he'd done for me, in terms of advice.

But, more than anything, the degree of understanding and forgiveness he'd seen fit to extend to me, was something which I know did not deserve.

–Not that it should come as any surprise to me, Jody, I told him, after the strength and moral courage you demonstrated that night in Mervyn's Bar. If only the rest of us were capable of such extraordinary courage and dignity.

I genuinely felt like cheering – in fact, in my exuberance, I actually struck the wall in front of me.

–Because you squared up to those motherfuckers big time, Jody. Hell, they didn't even know what hit them.

I was laughing now. I don't think I've ever felt so good.

As on I went:

–Perhaps, best of the whole lot, Jody, is that in the end you showed them what proper pride means. And what it actually means to look that so-called tiger in the eye. Because you did it, partner, you caught that sucker by the tail and swung him right the fuck around. Then I told him to hold on a minute, so as I could get more coins, for I'd gone and dropped a whole handful of the fuckers on the floor.

–With a rope around your neck, for Christ's sake, Jody, I continued, but boy did those sumbitches go and make a mistake doing that – remaining entirely unawares of just what it was they were dealing with: the one and only Warrior of Glasson County, that's who! Something which they were gonna discover very fucking soon, my friend! Whoop!

I can't imagine how it must have seemed – doubled over there in that draughty old hallway, leaning against the black metal box of the old-fashioned phone, laughing my heart out as I reached in my inside pocket and hauled out my little packet of papers, all my scribblings from the nights when I'd come home, stoned.

–*Dear Ray*, I read, as I opened one of them up, scarcely able to hold it out in front of me I was so excited–still twirling the cable and making no attempt at all to conceal my pride in our shared triumph.

–Dear Ray, I continued, maybe you ought to try and make it out before Christmas. Just so long as you're prepared for a cold the like of which you've never dreamed, Ray. But don't be alarmed, because it's beautiful too out here at this time of year. With nothing so special, at least in my experience, as that feeling of community that you can feel in the air when you emerge from the White Chapel on a Sunday morning and hear all the voices of the ones you love and depend on all around you. Hell, if that don't beat Banagher, as Red Campbell used to always say. Have you seen him lately? But, I was saying – yes, the keen cold comes around November, blasting the land, but with lots of sunshine and an exhilaration in the sharp light and crunching snows. 'The Bonny Land', as Greta Mae likes to call it, it's like vanishing, she says, into the world of an old-time Christmas card!

Which, as you must know by now, I remember him saying, is Paradise, Ray.

Paradise.

–*Paradise*, I kept on repeating hoarsely, abruptly cradling the receiver as I folded the 'letter' and gathered up what remained of my change and stumbled dazedly back into the bar-before raising my hand to order another, still snapping my fingers as I hollered at the top of my voice:

–*You got a tiger by the tail it's plain to see*, breasting up to the counter and sailing right into the middle of that old barstool.

–Someone's in good form, remarked the barman, sourly.

–Sure as a jackass likes its briars, I told him, on account of I just been talking to a certain old compadre, that's why!

As I swiftly downed what remained of my glass of vodka.

Before he turned, disinterestedly, parting his hands, Merv-style, and made it clear before spreading them that he wouldn't be in a position to supply me with any further alcohol.

With the result that, as I was leaving, I made sure to hurl back a satisfactory hailstorm of well-chosen insults.

–That's fine then, my friend, you fucking do that. Yeah, you do what you gotta do, my friend. But you know something, Tonto? Fuck you and the horse you rode in on, sunshine – because you think I can't get myself another shotta juice in this town? Well then dream on, mi amigo, friend – because very soon I will be boarding a plane that's gonna take me the fuck on out of here to Sweetwater, Georgia, if you got to know.

As the barman nodded, watching me weave unsteadily towards the door, wiping a glass as I slammed it, still laughing, behind me.

—And for what it's worth, I heard him call out after me, as my skin broke out in a pinpricking, icy sweat, for what it's worth, that phone you've been hogging for the past hour and a half? It was disconnected years ago ...

Chapter 34

The Old Rustic Bridge by the Mill

Choked by the dust and the heat rising up from below, I was convinced they could hear the erratic beating of my heart.

Begley was moving backwards and forward across the floor.

Mervyn was emptying the contents of the dustpan into the bin.

Then stood by the window.

—What the hell are you staring at out there? shouted Sonny Hackett. What in Christ's name could be so important?

—It's just the willow, Sonny, he explained, I've always found that it relaxes me. But I told you that.

Then Red Campbell suddenly became excited.

—I say we go in and finish it now. It's gone on long enough.

Tony Begley stopped in his tracks.

—What's that? he said, slowly turning around.

—Finish it, I mean. I think what we should do is finish him now.

Tony Begley burst out laughing.

—Excitable, ain't he? he said, rubbing his chin.

Then his phone rang.

—Uh-huh, he nodded, listening intently. Then, without any warning, snapping it shut. As, to their collective astonishment, he said:

—OK, then, fellers. Let's do it.

Nobody moved, as Begley walked over to Shorty and said:

—Are you fucking deaf or something – didn't you hear what I said?

—It's all right, Tony, Wee Hughie interrupted, he's not feeling good. Here, I'll help him!

Begley laughed, smiling as he shook his head.

—It takes all kinds, don't it Mervyn? he said, lifting the knife off the table and inspecting it.

—It sure does, Tony, I got to admit that. We sure gotta lot o' different types in this world, nodded the barman genially, pursing his lips and looking like he was about to whistle another little tune. As the side door came crashing open and Hughie and Red Campbell hauled in Jody.

—Time to start saying your prayers, Breed! snorted Campbell.

But you could tell – it was clear – that his heart wasn't in it.

As a rope sailed high above the crossbeam, in the course of its trajectory skimming perilously close to my face, and they dragged and stood him up on the table.

I watched Begley pacing the floor, toying with Sweety and talking to himself.

—Hey, feller! he barked out of nowhere. I fear it is time for thou to meet thou maker.

He swung around and laughed at Hughie.

—A good one, ain't it? Thou maker, Hughie! That's a good crack, maybe you could tell that one.

Red and Sonny cackled for a bit, but then their amusement tailed away and died.

As Jody began lashing out, kicking like a bull, with his right leg swinging, narrowly missing the side of Begley's face.

They all looked sick.

As Jody roared and lashed out again, with a ferocity that was even greater, his torn bloodstained T-shirt hanging out over his combats as his black leather motorcycle jacket rattled its assortment of chains, his blackberry curls obscuring those hideously swollen eyes.

–The hell with you, Begley, Jody snarled, and every last fucking one of you. Look at you, Campbell, and 'Happy Days' Hackett. Not to mention Hickory Holler 'The Dwarf' Hughie Munley – and his pal the one and only Big Barney fucking Grue. What gives any of you the idea that you are better than me – with your mothers all their lives scraping a living off the side of the mountain, just the very same as the Outlaw Breed. Yeah, washing your rags in the river and pimping out your sisters – because that what she did, didn't she Hughie? Yeah, Mary 'Two Dollars' whenever she came of age. Something which my old man Chester 'Hero' Kane never would have had descended to, seeing as he paid his way by the sweat of his brow and the sheer courage and strength of his fists. In spite of having it all stacked against him, for that's the way of the upcountry code – same as every other Godforsaken fucking place, hills or city. And maybe I didn't know him much, and for certain sure not very long. But this much I do know: that I can recall him saying before the car came to take me away to Whiterock, that it don't matter who you are in this world, or in what way you might have been low-rated. Because no matter where you've ended up, what you need to get you through you got right there inside of you, waiting for the call. Because my daddy knew that, us being the wandering, migratory tribe that we are, always and ever on the move, likely as not never getting to school to do the same book-learning as everyone else – that I'd be in need of any small piece of advice he could give. And which was that nothing, none of it, none of the rest of it mattered, just so long as in here you retained that old and ancient pride of the Kanes. Something that no motherfucking freak as loves his mother way too much is ever gonna be permitted to take off of me. Yeah, or some juice-head, neither, whose wife makes cadence with an Indian in a caravan, never mind that poor old foxfaced fucker over there, whose partner don't even know that he's in the bed beside her, or care. And, as for you, Big Barney – you happen to have seen Bridie Cullen hanging around the outside o' Heartland lately? Nope, you haven't, on account of she's been a little too busy lately, in Dundalk, having herself a bunch of sweet bonny babies. Matter of fact, she had another last week. That's eight kids now. Eight little lovely bonny little babas. And she loves her husband. He buys her flowers and dinky little presents of sweets.

Big Barney sat down and hung his head in his hands.

Wee Hughie started laughing and filling up his glass.

Now it was Tony Begley's turn to make irritating, grating noises with his teeth.

Red Campbell looked as if he was about to faint.

–What would the likes of him know about my life, or anything that's got anything to do with it anyway, he said to himself. Because whatever it might be, he's wrong about it anyway. Yes, he's wrong, I'm afraid. Because the Kid *does* know that I'm lying in the bed beside her. As a matter of fact, only two nights ago she turned around to me under the covers and said, yes she said to me: Red, what was the song they were playing that night? 'Y Viva Espana', I told her, Kid. 'Y Viva Espana'.

He swung around, and fiercely waved his fist at Jody.

–It's all over with Uncle Wylie, moaned the Runt, now we're never going to see him now. Why didn't we run whenever we had the chance?

–Because there is no fucking Uncle Wylie! shouted Jody, and never was! So you can quit with your lies, and say a prayer for your father who blew himself up!

−That's not true! yelled Shorty. You fucking tinker bastard, it's a lie!

−It's him's to blame for it all, wept the Runt, the ghost that I seen on the lake. It's him!

−You're all to blame! howled Jody, swinging his boot. And every last murdering fucking one of you knows it!

−My my, smiled Begley, looking down along the length of Sweety, quite the big speechmaker, ain't he; smoke and horses?

As Jody hurled a gout of phlegm right into the middle of his face, sneering loudly as it went trickling past Begley's nose.

Tony Begley took out his hankie.

−That was a silly thing to do, he said softly, an extremely silly thing to do, Jody Kane.

−O Jesus, stammered Hughie, o my good fucking Jesus. Look what you gone and done!

Red Campbell seemed robbed of the power of speech.

−That I ever came near this place, he eventually croaked, hoarsely.

−Bridie Cullen, Barney Grue was quietly whispering to himself, as he laughed a little oddly, I was wondering maybe would you like to dance?

Begley was standing facing Jody with the knife.

−You probably wouldn't remember this little sweetheart from the old days, Jody, he explained, but for your information it's a Wüsthof six-inch professional tool, complete with ebony handle. Sweety, I call it. Ain't that right, fellers?

−I don't want to do this anymore, announced Red, as a matter of fact I want to go home.

Tony Begley looked up and said nothing.

Then he said quietly:

−What's that you said?

Red didn't reply.

−You know, Begley continued, I don't know whether it's my imagination or not, fellers, but I am beginning to get a feeling that there is a certain troubling deficit of loyalty in this vicinity.

He looked directly over at Hughie.

—Would I be right, do you think, in assuming something the like of that?

—No, Tony. I don't think you would. No, you definitely wouldn't.

—I wouldn't?

—No, Tony. I don't think so, anyway.

—And you, Sonny? What do you think?

—I think Hughie's right, Hackett replied.

Begley swapped the blade from one hand to the other, now approaching Barney Grue.

—You've gone very quiet, Barney, he suggested.

—Yes, Tony, I know that, I don't know what's wrong with me. I'm definitely not thinking about Bridie Cullen anyway, he replied.

—You're not what? said Tony.

—Nothing, Tony. Tony I'm sorry for saying that.

—You think you'd be loyal to me, then, do you Barney?

—Yes, Tony. I do, for sure.

—That's good, said Tony, that's real good.

Then he began:

—Tiny Smallwoods used to always say I imagined things. That people were thinking things she knew they weren't.

He returned to Red.

— I suppose you know about Tiny, do you?

—Tiny, Tony? demurred Red Campbell, unconvincingly. Tiny — who would that be?

—Tiny Smallwoods, the love of my life. I know already you heard about the oranges. But, no matter what anyone thinks, the only reason I called her up to the office that day was to teach her a lesson, give her a little scare. Because, whether anyone in this room knows it or not, the truth is, you see, that I am still in love with her. And if it had happened to have worked out between me and her, I can promise you all this – you would all have been invited to our wedding. And I guarantee you, like I say, if it had happened to work out, that it would have been one of the most magical unions imaginable. I still sometimes think of us, her and me – hand in hand, walking down the aisle. Do you remember her? So small and sweet and gentle and frail that she could almost have fitted into my pocket. That's what I loved about her, I guess. But it wasn't meant to happen. Would you like to know the reason? Because she told me – yes, she wrote to me. Yes, wrote me a letter explaining the whole situation. *Dear Tony,* it began.

He was still fiddling agitatedly with the Wüsthof.

–How did it begin? he asked Hughie Munley. The letter you were telling them about? *My* letter.

–It began *Dear Tony*, replied Hughie Munley.

–That's correct, nodded Begley, *Dear Tony* is exactly how it began. I'll never forget the day I got it, because I swear to God I wept like a child. Well, I mean, why wouldn't I? Seeing as the only thing I'd ever loved, apart from mother, in my life, had just been taken from me. She said that she'd loved me all right – that much was true. But then she said that she found me way too moody and unsettling. Too unpredictable, in fact, was what she told me – and might I consider counselling. Do you know something, fellers? The truth is that if I had agreed to that, that probably in the end she would have accepted my proposal. I don't trust you, Tony, you see, she said, I think it's perhaps all these problems you seem to have with your mother. Maybe I ought not to have said anything about that. Maybe I shouldn't have told her anything at all. Yes, perhaps that was another mistake – but then that's what you do when you're enchanted with someone, you make these little errors. Share little intimacies and confidences, you know?

He stalled as he passed Big Barney and looked right at him, flicking his tongue smartly against the back of his teeth.

—You know what I'm trying to say here, Barney? he said.

But didn't bother waiting for an answer, as he continued pacing back and forth across the floor.

—We even talked about the two of us having a family. We'll be like *The Little House on the Prairie*, we used to say.

He stood beside Sonny.

—Two kids, Sonny, he quietly intoned.

—Uh-huh, replied Sonny, a small red spot forming on either cheek.

—A happy family, murmured Begley.

Before turning, unexpectedly, to Campbell.

—What's that you said there, Red?

—Me, Tony? Tony, I said nothing.

—Thinking I maybe don't have it in me? Was that what you were thinking? That, whenever it comes to it, what it takes to finish the job – I mightn't have it?

—No, Tony – I didn't say that. I wasn't even thinking it. You imagined it.

—We don't have to worry, because Begley doesn't have it in him. That what all this is about then, Red?

He looked down at the boning knife and then back up at Red.

He was shivering all over.

Then he went over to Sonny.

—So what's your opinion? You think what I'm saying to Red Campbell is right?

—Maybe, said Sonny, I don't know. You'd never know what the likes of Campbell would be thinking …

Red Campbell looked ashen.

—There's only one way, isn't there, that we can find out properly.

He went back to Campbell and dramatically presented him with the Wüsthof.

–OK, then. You go ahead and do it. Do it in memory of Mr Monroe and the good times. Go on, then – go ahead.

Red Campbell laughed out loud – foolishly.

A response not at all appreciated.

–Please don't try my patience, warned Begley, pressing the weapon into his hand.

–We weren't supposed to be involved. Because nobody ever wanted Wilson Gillis to die. It was never meant to happen that way, announced Red Campbell.

As, to their amazement, they watched as Tony Begley turned around and walked away, staring out at the wavering willow.

–Trees, he murmured softly, did you know they can sometimes scream in pain, even communicate underground? The willow is a loner and its seeds fly far away, many miles. Birch will wipe other trees away. Because the birch is a bully. But, all the same, each tree, in its own way, is a special kind of poem – all the time sending little messages underground, kind of like electric signals.

Big Barney Grue gave a tiny, imperceptible quiver of recognition, as though anticipating, at any moment, to be called upon for comment.

But no such request came, from Begley or anyone else.

For the blocky, sweaty man in the oversized suit, he had seemed to, almost completely, drift away – conversing quietly with himself beside the window, tapping out the rhythm of some tune on his thigh, one only known to him.

–He was the only man I ever really loved, they heard him continue, William Walter Monroe – because in a way he saved me, and that's a fact. For things hadn't been going well my way, whenever I first met him. Indeed, on a couple of occasions I had come narrowly close to ending it all. I guess you could say that he showed me a little compassion and understanding.

Yeah, and taught me things. Once upon a time this was nothing more than an old half-forgotten unremarkable little country place, and for sure a long way from the concerns of the city banker and the corporate lawyer and his associates. Who looked down, like they always do, upon our humble abode as representing all that civility deplores. Where there ain't nothing much but folks who are just that little bit too uneducated and who got themselves an exaggerated sense of slight and honour. And who'll talk and smile away with you at the very same moment that they're planning to blow your head off. Because that's the way things play in the outlands. Where all they care about is warring, whoring, hell-raising and hunting. At least that's the way it was before that old WW came around, and he said to me: Tony, my man – we'll play them at their own game. Because the rich, they reckon, is smart and the poor is fool. Well we'll soon see about that, kemo sabe. And goddamnit if he soon weren't running rings around the lot of them, except with this one difference: that never once did he ever get above his raising. Nope.

And, whether it was on account of Tony Begley making those comments, throughout which he'd been remembering that very first night when the doors of Heartland had opened and Monroe had arrived in his bullhorn Caddy, Big Barney Grue was also at that moment overcome with profound regret – finding himself reciting a silent, private prayer in the anticipation of a retribution which he had always known might one day come.

With his lips beating frantically, hearing the steady low drone of an aircraft in the distance.

And saw himself waiting for it to approach and come in to land.

With the lovely Mercedes smiling as she waved at him through the fogged-up window.

–I'm approaching the green hills of Ireland, he heard her say, smiling romantically over her fan.

But knowing, as he always did, in his heart, that she never would.

As he saw himself standing there, remaining impassive in the silence, looking out across the huge blue world, as brushwood blew along the black wet surface of the empty runway, and the sound of the aircraft began to recede.

Leaving him alone to join battle with them, as usual, those pictures that arrived unbidden into his mind – a party of black-clad mourners receiving a tiny painted white coffin, approximately two and a half feet in length, from the hold – and, in dead silence, shouldering it towards the terminal building, with calico roses blowing idly across a patch of glass-strewn waste ground, blooms once intended for both Mercedes Starrs and Bridie Cullen. Those two beautiful women who, for Big Barney Grue, had ultimately become one and the same. Yes, the Bright Jewel of Old Virginia and his own sweet Bridie, from St Martin De Porres Terrace, Glasson – quite indivisible.

As the nerves that continued with their subterranean current pulsing within him, in that instant, becoming almost physically visible as they travelled in regiments through thin air, high above the shimmering night-city of his soul.

Where street lights flickered and gas lines hissed – and somewhere far away, rabbits skedaddled in the endless, dew-covered fields.

Maybe, he prayed, in search of some Paradise where the jukebox Rock-Ola would somehow, miraculously, light up and begin to send out its surging tunes anew – electrically, certainly, but with a lovely warm glow that brought no hint at all of glum foreboding.

♡

Although, evidently not in the equally private world of Sonny Hackett, whose long grey countenance – even for him – now seemed uniquely dour.

Rapt in thought, as he considered the possibility of maybe one day going out to visit the Indian in his caravan and having a chat with him about the whole sorry situation, perhaps when all of this was over.

–Because there must be some way that we can find to work it out, he reassured himself.

As he saw the two of them talking away. Yes, nodding reasonably as they shared a companionable cup of tea.

–Do you think there's a possibility that, one day somehow, a chance like that might actually come? Sonny Hackett heard himself asking the Indian, somewhat guardedly.

–Maybe, he heard his counterpart reply accomodatingly, nodding in that kind of peaceful way he did.

It really was the most wonderful feeling.

–Fantastic! cried Sonny, unthinkingly running his steel comb through his oily hair, wondering would she, maybe, think that he looked like Elvis?

Because she had once, you know.

Long ago, in the days before the Indian.

But that didn't matter, he found himself laughing, not now.

As he slid the comb back into his pocket, and cheered.

–*Whee-hoo*! he heard himself holler, triumphantly punching the back of a chair.

And then, as before, lapsing into a profoundly sullen silence, realising that this had all taken place in his imagination.

Now he didn't know where to look.

For his part, Red Campbell was thinking about holidaying in Spain.

With his partner the Kid, all decked out in a sombrero, glistening with suntan oil, turning brown as a nut, in the days

when he used to promise her the earth and the damn moon –
just as soon as he could get his hands on 'em, with two strands
o' bobwire around them, and whitewashed.

And it would be just like that again – yep, just like before,
in 1977, when they used to be able to laugh about things like
that.

Ah yes, he thought, in old España where they'd been the
talk of the resort – in that old cool cabana where even the
people from Dublin had stood back in admiration of their
breathtaking dancing skills. Because disco had been all the
rage there too, of course, in Alicante.

Boy, when you're young, thought Red, as he flipped her
over and she landed – *Hola!* –perfectly balanced, in her big
sombrero on the floor in front of him.

He shoved his head between his thighs and moaned,
realising that he too was back in the bar.

Coincidentally, Wee Hughie, also, was thinking about
sombreros.

With the big difference being, however, that in his mind
he wasn't in Spain.

Because Wee Hughie Munley happened to be right
up there onstage, at the front of the Heartland ballroom
itself, with that many-mirrored glitterball revolving high
above him, and the crowd going crazy for all his yarns and
wisecracks.

Before declaring, unanimously, that he had to be, by far,
the best comedian, ever, to come out of Glasson County.

Or anywhere else.

–Hey there, you! shouts the sheriff. Just where in the hell
do you think you're going with that goddarn dustbin strapped
to your back?

–*Tiddadump tiddadump tiddadump*, says your man, ha ha!

It really had been the greatest night ever – there could be
no doubt about that.

So what in the heck if their mother washed their clothes in the river and his sister Mary pleasured one or two gentlemen?

After all, you got to eat.

–So who is the joke on now, Hughie laughed.

On the verge of launching into another of his side-splitting routines when he found himself diverted by the sound of suppressed sobbing, and looked across to see Tony Begley, looking up at the oil painting of the little boy.

–Do you think, he was asking Hughie. I mean – that if there does in the end turn out to be an afterlife, that she'll forgive me?

He meant his mother. Hughie Munley knew that.

But, no matter how he tried, he couldn't think of anything to say.

–OK then, I see. I get it, replied Begley, seeming bitterly disappointed, I'm sorry, Hughie, for putting you in that position.

He flipped the blade.

–OK, then – let's get to work and finish this fucking thing. Because, if you want to know, I'm sick to the back fucking teeth of it.

As, behind the counter, Mervyn Walker winced imperceptibly as his mind went drifting back to a little stone bridge where he saw his companion of so many years standing, Wilson Gillis, leaning across the moss-covered limestone parapet, shading his eyes to ascertain whether or not there might be rain.

–Low Anglican, he recalled his friend divulging, that'd be me, Mervyn, and most of our kin. With our sort elaboration tends to rest uneasily. Sometimes, you know, I'll come out here alone and just stand here in silence, for hours, catch or not. Most of the birds I know and can name – waxwing, moorhen, yellowtail. That fellow there'd be a sparrowhawk. Aye.

Mervyn paused and his eyes misted over.

−Time means nothing, Wilson observed, what is it anyway, this thing we lead our lives by? Some say it moves sideways − others that it goes forward. Some attest that it does both at the very same time. What century it is, I don't know. Not out here. All that matters is bream and trout.

Trout and bream.

And bream and trout.

The fishing reel spun rapidly in the failing light, and then, abruptly, locked.

−I'm no different to my father, Mervyn, Wilson continued, and his, God knows, before him. What I do is my earthly duty. I feed the cattle. Turn the land. And see my role as being that of looking to my neighbour, to learn and to labour and to get mine own living. My father used to read that passage every night: it's taken from the Book of Common Prayer. Be true and just in all of your dealing. The integrity of the upright shall guide them. But the perverseness of transgressors shall destroy them.

−Yes, nodded Mervyn, yes I understand. I understand, old friend.

As that grey-haired, seventy-year-old barman, still at his post behind the weathered brown wooden counter, in that calm and practised, almost ritualistic manner, spread his hands across the painted brown surface before crossing himself and reaching down to locate his merchandise.

Seeming dreamy-drowsy, loping rangily now across the floor.

−You sure are busy here tonight, ain't you Merv? laughed Tony Begley, wiping the blade in preparation with his sleeve.

Mervyn Walker smiled and nodded in agreement.

−You got it there, the old barman beamed, I sure got to admit that what you're saying there is absolutely and one hundred per cent true, Mr Begley.

−Tony, please, if you don't mind, Mervyn. Call me Tony, I'd really appreciate it.

—Yes, Tony, that sure ain't no problem at all. I was only just saying that you are absolutely one hundred per cent correct in what you been saying just now ... and that I agree with you, all the way. All the way, Tony – sure as swallows fly.

—I'm mighty glad that you feel that way. Thanks, good old Mervyn. But, here – what's that you're carrying there in your hand? At first when I saw it, I thought it might have been a fishing rod. Because you've done your share of that, in your time, ain't you Mervyn?

—Yes, Tony, indeed I have, replied the barman, whistling a low, little tune as he began meticulously unloosing the ties and unwrapping the jute covering.

—But it's not, he explained, not, in fact, a fishing rod like you say. It's just a little something I got from that old Long John McNulty, way back.

—Oh yeah? said Begley. Back in the good times?

—Yes Tony, Mervyn nodded, Long John McNulty, who I'm sure is someone probably well known to you. But here, would you like to take a closer look?

—Sure, agreed Begley, temporarily pocketing Sweety, get on over here and let's have a look at exactly what you got.

—It's a DP-12, and as you can see here, Tony, it has two seven-round tubes and two barrels. That's right – a double-barrelled pump gun. Two rounds are chambered with each pump. The trigger is then pulled two times, the first to fire the right barrel, the second to fire the left barrel. Pump, and you've got two more rounds. Overall, it's built like a tank, this here gun.

—She sure is some machine, said Begley, but then Long John McNulty – he's the man.

—Yes, Long John, in his time, didn't take no prisoners. Of course, you'd have known him well, wouldn't you – from guess where?

—Guess where, Mervyn? Where's that?

—Heartland, said Mervyn, lifting the weapon as half of Tony Begley's head came off.

—*Kuklok!* was the sound it made as the barman loosed both barrels into the pit of Red Campbell's stomach.

Red Campbell, who was now in the process of contemplating his ravaged torso in what might best be described as an attitude of puzzled detachment.

As Mervyn, unblinkingly, once more raised the gun.

—This is bad, wept Sonny Hackett, this is really so so bad.

—I can see him again, said the Runt McHale, he's over there. He's over there, smiling – standing in the corner.

—Goodbye, groaned his brother.

—I'm sorry, Merv, said Sonny Hackett.

—I know, agreed Mervyn, it's a pity. It really is.

Sinking to his knees as he prayed over Red.

—Let us acknowledge, began Mervyn, that Thou hast for all a divine plan. Thou hast made the rattlesnake as well as the songbird and that we must, at all times, acknowledge Thy presence and wisdom in the healing shower. And that in the weird mystery of nightfall, in the aftermath of deeds of dark and damning atrocity, your wrath will sometimes bear a whirlwind …

—I really did love her, Big Barney was sobbing. I'm sorry, Mervyn, for what we did.

But Mervyn Walker wasn't listening – retrieving the Wüsthof from Tony Begley's twitching fingers.

—Your nightmare's over, he told Jody Kane.

Except that, unfortunately, there was still more to come.

—Here's a towel, Mervyn called out, tossing it to Jody, who was still quivering all over.

As well at that, he was raving – but who could blame him?

—We were supposed to be in New York by now, I heard him screech hysterically, I would have paid the money back. That was my plan – to try and earn some moolah of my own and send it over, every cent, to WW. But Ray let me down again, same as always. Same as fucking always, Ringo.

Jody kept weeping as he dazedly rubbed himself down, searching frustratedly for words which might be of some assistance. And which he eventually succeeded in finding, disdainfully chucking away the saturated towel.

−Hero Kane was the flower of the flock, wasn't he Mr Walker? That's true, ain't it? Even in the orphanage I always used to hear it. That there wasn't one alive who could hope to match him in the ring. And that that's where I got it from − because he, the one and only Hero Chester, it was him who sired me and made me what I am. Even though the roof of our home was the sky, the Kanes came from a noble line, and there ain't no one on this Godforsaken planet − no, not a soul in Glasson County, here tonight or any other time − who hand on heart can say any different. And, for sure, not any of these liquor-blinded sonsofbitches as corralled me and hauled me like a beast. But hard though it might be, I am going to try and forgive them for what they done − because, like my father told me in a dream, Mr Walker, Jody he said no matter what troubles you face or wherever your wanderings take you in in this world, remember that I am always gonna be there by your side and if you feel that any man is low-rating you, just remember that I will be there to provide you with the strength you need and to help you remember − always − your pride! So long, little partner. Vaya con dios, until we meet again …

Then, squinting unflinchingly, Mervyn waved both barrels in the direction of the doorway.

−Go, he warned Jody, and don't even think about looking back.

−Mr Walker, appealed Jody.

—Go, I told you – are you fucking deaf?! shouted Mervyn. And that was the last I ever seen of Jody Kane.

For a while, it almost seemed as if Mervyn had completely lost interest, just standing there cradling the shotgun in his arms.

With his eyes glazing over as he let out a little sigh. Before eventually addressing no one in particular:

—I don't know if I told you, boys, if I ever happened to mention it or not. But sometimes when I'm here alone in the bar, you can't imagine just how tedious it can get. Especially on a Monday or Tuesday afternoon, with the way things are gone in this business. Well, whenever that happens, what I do is I sometimes just drop a little handful o' coins into the chute of that old jukebox and get to dreaming the way that some of you been doing. Thinking about the wind, and the way that it can blow through the grass, in Kansas or some of them other places out there ...

He lifted the twelve-gauge and smiled, a little faintly.

—But you know, I heard him continue, you know what's the one that I play over and over? Do you know, Wee Hughie? Or perhaps you, Sonny?

He shoved the barrels hard in between Sonny's ribs.

—That's OK, he said, because I hadn't, in all honesty, figured that you would. Well then, I'll tell you. It's the one that reminds me of those Sunday mornings when me and ol' Wilson, the two of us would walk with our fishing rods out to Lake Wynter and just stand there together with our backs against the sun, spin-casting our lines from the parapet of that old stone bridge, hoping it'll rain so the fish will maybe rise to the surface. So there you are – do you reckon you might know what it's called, the tune that I'm talking about? That I'll sometimes play, on my own here, on the juke?

–What about you, Mr Grue – you know maybe?

Barney groaned as Mervyn sighed impatiently.

–Hughie? he said. Or maybe Sonny?

–Because there's no point in asking Red – he's gone.

–So it'll have to be you, I guess, Sonny.

As he lifted the pump and looked at him mournfully.

–'The Old Rustic Bridge' is what it's called. 'The Old Rustic Bridge by the Mill', he told Sonny. That's the one that I nearly always play.

–Yes, said Sonny, I think I might know that one, Mervyn, with his head lurching back as one bullet grazed the side of his face, and another blew a ragged rupture through his chest, ripping a hole out his back and he fell across the jukebox with a crash.

–Estar viendo que en el otro de la luna, whispered Mervyn, closing one eye as he elevated the gun, I'll see you on the other side of the moon …

Before aiming the weapon in the direction of Wee Hughie.

–You got any ideas, Mr Munley? You think you might know that song, do you Hughie?

–Big Tom? croaked Hughie.

–That's right, said Mervyn, he used to play it a lot.

He turned to face the big man.

–Guess where, Barney?

–Heartland, stammered Barney, he always used to play it in Heartland, Mervyn.

–That's right, said the barman, wiping his mouth with the back of his hand and pulling the trigger as both barrels blazed, right into the middle of Barney Grue's landslide girth.

–In the Heartland ballroom – that's where he always played, the famous second home of the Killing Floor Hombres.

Then he turned to Hughie, and said:

–I'm sorry it had to be this way, Hughie.

–I understand, said the other man, as he made the sign of the cross.

Then, as soon as he'd told the twins to go, I heard the sound of his bootheels crossing the floor.

–OK, Wade. You can start maybe thinking about coming down now …

His shadow was far-reaching as he stood in front of me, staring.

–Copper for a copperhead, fell the words from his lips as he touched my face with the still-warm metal, motioning for me to open my mouth.

–There's a good feller, he said, and to this very day I can still taste that hideous acrid tang.

–I know, I heard him continue, that it might be appropriate for me to dispense some sentiments of incantatory fervour at this point, figuring like I'm some kind of dark retributive angel, if you get my meaning. If you comprehend my meaning, Copperhead Raymond Wade – and I think, just to look at you shaking, that you do. Eat that metal, go ahead there soldier, and look right into these eyes as you're doing it. Yes, chew on that hot steel and ask yourself, snake, ask yourself why something like that, it ain't gonna happen. Why no talk of great quakes or sixth seals, or suns black as sackcloth, and moons the colour of blood?

He sighed regretfully and gave a weak smile, staring down at the floor as he murmured in a monotone:

–Since his passing that night, I have been as nothing – bereft. A diseased bundle of nerves standing between time and eternity like a withered leaf.

Then, with eyes that were blank and a body that seemed exhausted, he shouted suddenly into my face:

–*Run, and don't stop running,* adroitly swinging both barrels around before pulling the trigger as his shoulders and upper body exploded, drenching the ceiling and the wall behind him in matter and gore.

Yes, *run*, Mervyn Walker had ordered that night, *and don't stop running* – something which I've been doing ever since, trying my best never to think of him – or, indeed, anything about that night or the events leading up to it.

But with it always following the same predictable pattern – that just when you think that you've left it behind, somehow managed to get on top of it once and for all, what happens then is it returns with a fearsome vengeance. And you realise that all it's been doing in the meantime is just sitting there waiting, biding its time, lurking in the shadows.

And then it all starts up again, only now with a clarity that's even more disturbing.

When you find yourself waking in the night-time and look up to see the door slowly opening, with Mervyn standing in the frame, clutching the twelve-gauge.

Throwing back his head and releasing a contemptuous peal of laughter, silently indicating the figure of Jody who has just arrived, bruised and bloodied. Before reaching into his mouth and, almost demurely, detaching a tiny piece of tongue, leaning in as he whispers into my fevered ear:

–Here, liar – this is specially for you. As you can see, it isn't forked.

Opening his hand to offer me the soft pink sliver of moist yielding flesh.

–With luck, he said, continuing, you might one day find it of some practical use, if you ever decide to have a change of heart. Not that I'll be holding my breath, you deceitful, no-good copperhead fuck.

That's pretty much the way things seemed to be set, and how they panned out over the years ever since that night.

With my shredded nerves, ultimately, getting so bad that sleep, more or less, became a thing of the past, with nothing being of much use apart from the hooch.

And you know the way that's destined to go.

I suppose the first time it really began to dawn on me that I might have a problem was on the morning I was standing on the bridge overlooking Lake Wynter. And heard Mervyn's voice coming through the mist, loud and clear as a bell. Until it was almost as if he was standing right there beside me, smiling as he shook his head, with his long arms folded and his ponytail tied up.

−I'm never going to leave you, Raymond, I heard him say, because that's the way it's got to be.

To make a long story short, they found me standing in the supermarket one day, laughing my head off and putting on the voice of Johnny Redlegs, as I slapped the floor and kept on shouting:

−I am the Rider in the Rain, motherfuckers − and my illusions, at last, they are all finally fucking bankrupt. So I am more than ready to meet my maker, being in possession of nothing only my wound. You listening to what I'm saying here, critters? Whoop!

But with there being no sign of Johnny Redlegs when I looked again, just an awkward young assistant looking terrified, to be honest − holding me by the elbow and doing his best to reach someone on his mobile.

Chapter 35

Welcome to My World

'The Glasson County Songbook' is how Fr Conway likes to describe these, now at last finally complete, few pages.

It was he who, like I think I said, first coined the phrase 'spiritual pilgrimage'.

He just has this way of somehow finding the perfect words.

He knew I'd be embarrassed about showing it to him initially – but, as is always the case, in the end he somehow managed to put me at my ease. He's aware of my inadequacies.

–Education means nothing, Ray, you got to understand that, he vehemently reassured me, I mean, did you ever, for example, see Hank Williams' diary? His handwriting is as simple and honest as a child's, as unguarded and sincere as any unblemished child of God.

That was all he had to say, he said.

As off I went – armed with that single note of encouragement, having resolved, once and for all, to allow the truth come *pouring* out.

And just how glad I am, I really can't impress enough upon you – because now I've arrived at what can only be described as what my old friend and me used to call the 'Promised Land'.

A country without guile or manipulation of any kind, where selfishness and lies they simply do not exist. And where, at long last, you find you possess the courage to, once and for all, look yourself in the eye. And accept that, in the end, the only person who can heal you is *you*.

Period.

Because, like that good old pastor – and, indeed, my doctor – says, there couldn't be any doubt but that I had been traumatised at the very deepest level by the events which took place in Mervyn's Mountain Bar that night.

But not just those alone.

Why, only the other night – at first I couldn't believe it – but, once I came to terms with it, sure enough there it was.

She was standing outside the window, waving as she pushed back her long-billed, airman-style cap, as if no time had passed at all.

−You're the only one, Ray, and you always will be. I heard her voice come drifting, and then she was gone.

With my first inclination being – I'm not going to lie about it – to go on the hunt for a bottle – of *anything*, to tell the truth.

Thankfully, however, I didn't.

In AA, they always tell you to try and live for the moment.

But it's not always easy, not when you find yourself confronted by something like that.

I guess I've just accepted that's just the way it's going to be.

And that I ought to be grateful for what it is I have, how things have turned out for me after all my pointless wandering in all those years rambling the length and breadth of Ireland, living the life of a hobo, more or less, sleeping in haggards, outhouses and ditches.

Before, out of the blue one day, Long John McNulty pulled up alongside me on the road and took me in.

—I've got this sprawling old barn of a place, he said, with a cockloft upstairs. It's not much but you'd be welcome to use it.

He's been running a service station here in Midford this past few years – it's been doing real good, and I help out in whatever way I can.

Mervyn's Bar has, long since, become a derelict ruin – and the Heartland ballroom now is a run-down carpet warehouse.

Although, if you've a mind to look close enough, you can still see a chunk of one of the marble pillars – like the remains of some magnificent temple, lying there half-buried in the clay.

Most of the people I grew up with are either dead or have moved away.

Where all the participants of the unfortunate drama are lying, hopefully at peace, on a hill overlooking the town.

That old Merv, Wee Hughie, Barney, and the others.

Thankfully, however, not Jody Kane.

Who, like I say, has heroically – not that it should come as any surprise – succeeded in forging a whole new life for himself in America, with the support and assistance of his beautiful, high-toned Christian wife.

Even if the padre refuses, like one or two other pieces he's had problems with, to believe that particular part of the story.

And which, of course, is his prerogative. All I can say is, I wish it were the case.

Because then I'd never have gotten it into my head, not long after the nightmare had concluded, just to get the fuck right on out of Glasson County, and away from everything got to do with it – and head off to Georgia, like I'd been promising for so long.

I can see how rash and dumb and foolhardy it was, but at the time I'd been hitting the booze so hard, that you couldn't have talked me out of it if you tried.

All I can say, looking back on that period now, is that it was only by the grace of God and maybe the prayers of Jody and his lady that I didn't kill the woman and child in Athlone when, just at the very last second, I somehow managed to brake in time.

Such a screech of metal – to very this day, I can still hear it.

I really was a bad case, at that time.

But, like they always tell you at the meetings – the one most important thing you can do, no matter how hard it might be, is to forgive yourself. No matter how detestable your past transgressions may have been.

And, in my case, boy were they bad – and I won't pretend otherwise.

No wonder I had to endure those punishments.

With the worst, I think, being the night when I heard what I took to be the sound of Mervyn's boots on the stairs, eventually coming to a halt on the landing outside the loft.

As the door handle slowly, as before, began slanting downward and I flung back the covers, looking up to see – nothing.

Working myself into a frenzy the following day, to such an extent that poor old McNulty he had to plead with me to slow down and take it easy.

–For God's sake, Ray! he said, shaking his head and scratching it.

Not being aware, of course, of what it was that was bothering me as I dismissed him completely – continuing to sweep more leaves, haul bags of fuel, do anything at all I could turn my hand to.

Figuring that what was troubling me deep inside would, very soon, hopefully, have completely passed.

And that, within a day or so, I'd succeed in grabbing me a good night's sleep.

It wasn't, however, I'm afraid, to be.

With the next night being even worse.

When I found myself awaking to the sound of those steady, ascending bootheels and the handle of the door turning downward, as before.

Only this time looking into the penetrating eyes of Johnny Redlegs, shadowed underneath his slouch hat brim.

As, from various corners of the dimly lit room, others began joining him – lining up on either side, many of them bearing the faces of the long-since dead.

Before – I can't begin to describe the shock – I recognised the cold, detached tones of our old housemaster from Whiterock Orphanage, also now many years departed this earth.

It haunts me yet, the clinical, resolute stillness of those tones.

As I heard him begin:

–This is a recording of the execution of Raymond Wade, only son of Martin and Teresa Wade, tragically killed in a car accident in the vicinity of the One Tree Crossroads, Glasson County, 5th September 1960 – now defined as vagrant and casual labourer. Pray proceed.

–The witnesses are now entering the witness room. The warden has also entered the witness room at this time.

–Very well.

–One of the execution team members is now in the process of securing the back strap of Old Sparky. The other members are in the process of securing the arm straps and leg straps. The accused has decided to make a last statement. He insists that if he is granted one last opportunity to make amends that he will do everything in his power to expiate his many sins of omission.

–The wires have been attached and secured to the headset and the leg band. The perspiration has been wiped again from the condemned's forehead. Placement of the hood is being witheld until such time as the condemned's partner arrives.

–There are no stays.

–Then you can proceed and carry out the official order of the court.

–His fists are clenched and there appears to be little movement from the condemned, sir.

–We can now confirm the arrival of the condemned's sole living associate – name Joseph Michael Kane, now American citizen and permanent resident of Sweetwater, Georgia.

I had to hide my eyes.

–Stand by for the warden's last telephone check …

I watched Jody's hand slowly reaching down to pick up the phone.

Before he frowned and hesitated.

–Please be advised to place the hood on the condemned and let the execution proper commence. At the count of three, press your buttons.

One.

Two.

Three …

I watched Jody raise the receiver to his ear.

–You are well aware that I never went near America – never so much as set foot in the place. Not that it makes a great deal of difference. Because, whether in Sweetwater, Georgia, Paragoul, Dundalk or Tuscaloosa – I never, for whatever number of years are allotted to me on this earth, ever want to set eyes on you or the likes of you again.

313

So that was how that episode concluded, I am sorry to have to say, with no great appetite on my part for a repeat performance, as I'm sure you can imagine.

And which I genuinely don't think is going to happen – because I reckon, in its way, it has somehow *purged* me, if that's the right word.

At least that's how it seems – especially after what happened this morning.

I could hardly believe it myself as I stood there looking out across Lake Wynter, like I often do whenever I haven't been able to get to sleep.

With this extraordinary sensation coming right out of nowhere – what Big Barney might have described as a 'bunch of electrisms', tingling – almost pleasurably at first – and then extending to my face and neck.

However, growing in intensity – and, I have to say, discomfort – with the result that, in the end, I had no choice but to support myself against the base of the tree, as the prickly current continued shooting down along the length of my arm.

And if a couple of tears came into my eyes as I lay there, clutching my chest, then believe you me there was no need to worry, for they were evidence of nothing but the most delirious, unalloyed joy.

Because, have you ever really listened – and I mean *actually* listened – to a song thrush when it's piping at full register?

At first, to be honest, the truth is I couldn't believe it – which is why I leaned in closer, just to be sure.

With there being, this time, definitely no mistake.

–You're the only one, Ray.

Of course, I entertained doubts – I mean, for heaven's sake, who wouldn't?

And which is the reason I made it my business to clamber all the way right up to the top of the bank, until I found myself eye-level with the overhanging bough.

Before hearing it again, with that wrenching but bewilderingly *comforting* wrinkle of ache:

—If we make it through December, everything's gonna be alright I know ...

And which armed me with the resolve I needed, as I skidded down the bank, not pausing for breath until I made it into the service station.

Where I found the door wide open – with her waiting quietly and patiently inside, unanticipatedly pale underneath the lace of a long black veil.

–Ray, she said, at long last you've come.

As she delicately parted the slight head-covering and I looked up to see that familiar smile.

–We have so much to talk about, Mr Bonny whispered.

Welcome to my world.